# A MATE FOR KAI

THE PROGRAM BOOK SIX

CHARLENE HARTNADY

Copyright ©July 2014, Charlene Hartnady
Cover Art by Melody Simmons
Copy Edited by Kimberly Reichmann
Produced in South Africa


Published by Charlene Hartnady
PO BOX 456, Melrose Arch,
Johannesburg, South Africa, 2176
charlene.hartnady@gmail.com


*A MATE FOR KAI* is a work of fiction and characters, events and dialogue found within are of the author's imagination and are not to be construed as real. Any resemblance to actual events or persons, either living or deceased, is purely coincidental.

With the exception of quotes used in reviews no part of this book may be reproduced or shared in any form or by any means, electronic or mechanical, including but not limited to digital copying, file sharing, audio recording, email and printing without prior consent in writing from the author.


First Paperback Edition, 2016

# A MATE FOR KAI

THE PROGRAM BOOK SIX

──────)○(──────

CHARLENE HARTNADY

# ONE

Ruby stood tall, she smoothed down her dress in one easy motion. Then made herself drop her hands to her sides. Then forced them to unclench and her shoulders to release their tension. She pushed out a breath she hadn't even realized she had been holding.

*Relax.*

*Breathe.*

*Whatever you do, don't kill him.*

Her brother could be a horse's ass. "You are a princess and you are fertile…" He smiled. "That makes you worth your weight in gold." His green eyes narrowed. "You need to do this for your people."

"What about my feelings in this? Please, Blaze…be reasonable." She put her hand to her chest and fingered the amulet that normally rested between her breasts. The one her grandmother had given her. *Oh gram.* If only the old lady were still here. She was one of the few royals able to talk any sense into these idiot males. Their leaders of the future. They were all quite possibly doomed.

Her brother leaned back against his large ornate desk. The one that had belonged to her father when he was still alive. "*You* need to be reasonable. We would be infinitely stronger if the two tribes were to unite. We need this union. It is tradition. Do you care nothing for the old ways?" His cotton shirt clung to his muscled torso. The heavy jeweled ring on his finger blinked in the light streaming in through the vast windows. She kept her back to the view. To look upon the beautiful valleys and peaks of their great kingdom might just sway her. The last thing she wanted was to be swayed.

Ruby felt her eyes fill with tears. "I don't love him. He doesn't love me. It's not right."

"At least you have a potential mate!" he boomed. "The Air tribe is succeeded by princes, there is not one female amongst the royal ranks. Not even one. It is the same with both Water and Wind."

Why did he insist on telling her facts she already knew? "Why not take a human?" Her voice came out in a whisper.

His frown deepened and anger flared in his eyes. "It is not how it is done. We need heirs. To dilute our blood is not an option. I will always put the future of our people ahead of my own needs. Always. The question is, will you? Our tribes need an heir. You are the last of the royal females. You are our last hope. All four kingdoms are relying on you." His eyes bore into hers.

"I don't love him." She choked out, feeling the tears run down her cheeks.

"What is love?" he snarled. "It is nothing. It doesn't exist. You would throw away our future for something so trivial? So intangible?" His eyes burned with emotion. The muscles on his forearms roped as he swiped his hand across his desk. A vase hurtled across the room. Petals, leaves and shards of broken glass crashed to the floor. Water soaked into the thick woolen carpet.

She took a step towards him. "It's real, Blaze. I know it is. I know it enough for both of us. Thunder doesn't love me. He never will. We're not even friends."

His throat worked. "One of the other kings then. Although I would prefer an Air royal, I am willing to meet you half way on this."

"No." It came out more harshly than she intended. "I don't even know them." She twisted her hands into the soft material of her gown, trying hard to calm her nerves. To talk some reason into him. Blaze, and the rest of her brothers, also deserved happiness. They all did.

"Know them." He spat. "That has nothing to do with it. "It's biological. You rut…you produce heirs. If you weren't my sister I'd claim you myself."

She gasped into her hand. "Please don't say things like that. It's despicable and wrong. For me to take a male to my bed that I have no feelings—"

"Feelings are unimportant. Why do I have to keep repeating myself? You've rutted with males before…" He pointed a finger at her like she was a child. "I know you have, so don't even begin to deny it. Where were your feelings then? I don't see you begging to mate with any of the lesser males who have shared your bed. You just seem to have a problem with the royals."

"Do you blame me? You're all a bunch of arrogant idiots. Every last one of you. But I'm just expected to to roll over and become impregnated anyway. Year after year like some choice mare to stallion. In the hopes of producing a daughter who will be passed off to one of the kings on the day she comes of age." Hot tears coursed down her cheeks. "No! I refuse. I won't do it." She felt so strongly about it she actually stomped her foot.

To have a mate that didn't love her, that didn't look at her with love and respect. To have a mate that still went on the stag runs twice a year. That brought the scent of another female back to their bed. A male that only rutted her to get her with child or for his own selfish pleasure.

No!

What if she did have a female child? What then? Her blood ran cold at the thought. Icy cold. She knew only too well. To have her raised to the same fate. She was lucky her dear father had indulged her and that her gram had been so fierce. Her gram had always stood up for what she believed in. She only cried harder at the memory. If it weren't for her gram, she would've been mated off a long time ago.

Her mother had been mated to her father at a young age. She had died young as well. Birthing her younger brother. It was the fate of most females of their species. At least it had been when there were still females left. There were exactly three left in their tribe including herself. About that number in each of the tribes. She was the last royal though. The last golden female.

Their last hope.

No.

There were other options. The royals were just too pig headed to entertain them.

"For the love of scales. Please stop crying. Stop all this talk of love." Her brother's voice softened. "You are my sister. He touched her back, ran his hand down her spine for a beat before pulling away. "Thunder is a good male. He would take good care of you. He has assured me you would be honored and treasured. You would come to care for him and he for you."

Ruby wiped her eyes and sniffed softly. "I don't want Thunder or any of the others. I've met the kings, a handful of times and—"

"Don't speak to me of love." His eyes hardened up. As did his whole stance. "I can scent your heat is close."

She shook her head, a denial on the tip of her tongue but she sucked it back because it was useless.

His nostrils flared. "Yes, you are…Thunder will be here in the morning. You will take the vows forged in fire. I am done arguing about this."

"No…please." Her voice was raw, her mind in turmoil.

His fists clenched and his chest heaved. "You will do this for the continuation of our species and I'll hear nothing more about it."

"I don't want this. It would be nothing short of rape."

"It would be consensual and we both know it," Blaze growled. His dark eyes grew ever darker. "Thunder has given me his word that he will take care of you."

She shook her hair. The thick black curtain swept across her lower back as she did. "No, Blaze…you would do this to me? Your own sister?"

"I have no choice." His voice broke, belying his emotions. So there was more to him than met the eye. More than the ruthless leader and pillar of muscle that he portrayed. Much more hidden in those dark, haunted eyes. Her brother was in there somewhere…she only hoped he could forgive her.

Guilt and shame rose up in her. It billowed and raged. Please god, just let him forgive her.

---

"Thank you for assisting with this detail." The big male nodded once, his boots crunching on the asphalt in the parking area to the left of the castle. He held out a set of keys to Kai.

He gave Titan a smile. "Sure thing." Kai could see that the male was nervous, from the tightness in his jaw. Tension radiated off of the normally cool and collected leader.

All of the males assigned to this detail were feeling the same. It was risky. Escorting human females from vampire territory was not for the feint of heart. There had been incidences in the past. Seventeen human females would need to be safely returned to Sweetwater.

He shook his head, feeling the pressure. If anything happened to any of them, it would spell disaster. Not to mention the females were counting on them in a big way.

This was the last operation Titan would oversee before leaving for Sweetwater indefinitely. Kai was glad Titan and his hand selected team were going after the bastards who were causing all of this shit. Hopefully, now they could face the problem head on. If nothing else, this would show the fascist groups they meant business. That they were done taking things lying down.

The president was on their side. An FBI task force had been assigned to find the ringleaders and to put a stop to this once and for all.

Kai still felt a small pang at having to turn down Titan's request that he join the small group of vampires assigned to the task. If he agreed, he would have to shelve his plans of finding a human mate and would have to do so indefinitely. He couldn't do that. After seeing the females in the last round, after being close to them. No. This wasn't something that could wait. He wanted a mate. Moreover, he wanted a human mate.

As it was, he would have to be patient for the next few weeks while this heat finished up which was bad enough. He hated waiting.

It was a pity about that female, Amber. Talk about being disappointed. She was exactly what he was looking for in a female. Sweet, kind, with a smile about a mile wide. She was also highly sensual, with a body so lush he sometimes lost his ability to think when he was around her. It wasn't meant to be. Kai was okay with that.

There was no way he was going head to head with Lance for a chance at being with her. Brynn was one thing, but Lance. Not a fuck. There was also something about the way the male had looked at the human. Watching Lance and the female's reactions to each other had helped to dissuaded him from taking his interests any further. The look the other male had given Amber was downright possessive. Kai got the distinct impression there was more to this than a passing interest.

"Have your team ready to roll in ten." Titan looked at his watch. "The Sweetwater police escort is already waiting outside our main gate." The idea was that if the locals were involved, nothing would happen. Thus far, the ploy had been to kidnap a female before she returned to Sweetwater, murder her and blame the vampires for her death. If humans were involved from the start, this type of run and frame action would be hard to prove because there would be human eyewitnesses from start to finish. The brief they received for their current mission was to get the humans back to their loved ones unharmed and he, for one, would ensure the females under his care got there safe and sound...or so help him.

Kai nodded. "No problem." He watched as Titan moved away to go and talk with the next team leader. Kai pulled his two-way radio free from his vest. He pressed the button on the side. "Jupiter one, come in, Jupiter one."

He watched the male in the next vehicle pull his own radio out and turn in Kai's direction. "This is Jupiter one, go ahead." Even though they were close enough to be able to talk normally, he followed the necessary procedure anyway.

"Be ready to move out in eight."

After a static crackle. "No problem. Thank fuck we didn't get Uranus."

Kai chuckled. "No one got Uranus."

There was a chuckle on the other side. Jenson's smile took up half his face. Kai shook his head and smiled back. He went through the same process with his other team member as they prepared to move out. Comms were working just fine. Both Jenson and Stuart were decent warriors.

Piece of fucking cake. If anyone got in the way, they were dead. Simple.

There would be two human females per vehicle, with a human, police escort between each vampire SUV. There were a total of nine SUVs and eighteen police vehicles. It would be slow going. In some ways, doing it this way would make them a bigger, easier target. They had tried keeping the procession small in the past. Sneaking a female out in the middle of the night. It hadn't worked. In keeping with the agreement with local authorities, the chief had been informed of every movement. That meant one thing, there was a mole. Someone in the department, maybe even the police chief himself, was an informant. If anyone could get to the bottom of this, it was Titan. Kai felt sorry for the people responsible even though they deserved everything coming their way.

The fascist group had access to short-range missiles and rockets and could easily shoot a chopper from the sky. That was the main reason for the decision not to use an airborne method of transport. The presence of the human police force would be a major deterrent on the ground.

Kai planned on being on his guard. On taking down any fuckers that tried to get in the way.

The females filed out of the human accommodations. They were escorted by guards, one to every two females. Kai had to bite back a laugh. The males were heavily weighed down by a ton of bags. Why did the humans need so many things? It was nuts.

He moved forward and helped the frowning guard by relieving him of some of the luggage. He nodded to the females who giggled and looked at him under fluttering eyelashes. "I am Kai. I will be escorting you home today." He said, even though he had met the females during the first heat of *The Program*.

One smiled and twirled her hair between her fingers. The other one giggled some more. It was going to be a long trip.

# TWO

The male's eyes were wide and bright. "Let's go for a beer." Jenson pointed to a building. The sign on the establishment said Beer Hut in big red letters. It looked classy and upmarket. As in, not so much.

He started to shake his head. "We're not permitted—"

"What are you, a pussy?" Stuart slapped him on the back. "One beer and then we're out of here."

"What would be the point?" Kai could feel himself frowning. "Alcohol does not affect us. The females would be out of bounds."

"It would be fun." Jenson's eyes lit up. "Something different. Besides…" he smirked. "I doubt we would be interested in any type of female in a place like this. A quick beer and then we can head back. Humans interest me, and I plan on making it into *The Program* one of these years…" He chuckled. "A little research on them will only make it easier to make a connection when the time comes. Come on, the castle gets boring."

It was probably the high emotions from the day. All seventeen humans were home safe. The drop-off had been a great success. Of any of the faction groups, there was no sign. The adrenaline had been pumping hard for hours. This was probably just a way for them to blow off steam. A crazy, stupid way but he understood the reasoning behind it. They only had one bar at the castle and it was boring going to the same place all the time.

"No fucking with the locals," Kai growled. "We observe only."

"Does that mean you're game?" Jenson looked excited.

Kai hesitated for a few seconds before nodding. Both of his team members chuckled. Stuart gave him another goodhearted slap on the shoulder.

The first thing that hit them as they went into the bar was the scent of stale beer and cigarettes. Then the pungent smell of oily food and vomit. A fucking fantastic combination. He grimaced. Maybe this wasn't such a good idea. He was about to voice his opinion when the scent of something entirely different caught him deep in the nose.

It was a scent so sweet it overrode all the others. Even though the bad ones were far more pungent. It was a scent so fucking divine that he felt his dick lurch. His leathers suddenly felt far too tight.

There was a group of males playing a game on a table with sticks and small balls. There was a female with them but the scent wasn't coming off of her. There were a couple of more at some of the spread out tables. No hits! An older human female was eyeballing them something fierce. A lit cigarette hung loosely from her wrinkled lips.

The scent.

It couldn't be her.

Not a fuck.

The bartender frowned. He wiped the surface of the gleaming wood even though it was already spotless. Strangely, it was the only clean thing in the place. Kai scanned to the left, and he spotted her. It had to be her. There was just no other way. *Motherfuck.* His cock vibrated and buzzed inside his pants.

Then again, it had been a while since he had been with a female. Days to be precise. No wonder he was feeling so wired. Her scent wouldn't leave him. It was like it had run its silky tendrils inside of him and taken root.

On the forefront, jasmine in full bloom but there was also something more. Something he couldn't quite put his finger on, it had a smoky edge. The combination was unlike anything he had ever encountered.

"Now that's more like it," Jenson growled as he also caught sight of the female.

"So fucking lush. You're so lucky to be in *The Program*. To be an elite. At least you get to actually take a shot at being with one of them in the next round. I will keep working at it." Stuart shook his head.

Kai made a humming noise. He was lucky he had made it. Where he lacked skill, he made up for it in sheer strength and stamina. He could outfight anyone, anytime, anywhere. Okay, maybe not anyone but most.

"Let's get a drink." Jenson elbowed Stuart.

"Yeah," the other male growled under his breath.

"Are you coming?" Jenson did the same elbow thing with him.

"Give me whatever you're having." He folded his arms, his eyes on the female. Try as he might, he couldn't tear his gaze away from her.

Her scent was killing him. Absolutely fucking killing him. The female was standing with two other human males. They both looked to be much older than her. One of the males had his hands on her. He ran them down the sides of her arms and onto her hips. They rested there for all of a split second before he squeezed her ass and pulled her against him. "I bought you a drink, honey. The least you can do is say thank you." They were almost directly opposite him, but on the other side of the room. Although music was playing in the background and the other patrons were noisy, they were still close enough that he could make out everything they were saying. Super enhanced senses came in handy at times.

"Thank you," she stammered. Her eyes darted around the far side of the room, only, not in his direction. The big human kept his hands on her ass. She didn't try and pull away but at the same time, he could see the tension running through her body. The subtle way she curved her spine away from the male. The way her hands stayed at her sides instead of moving to circle his neck or to touch his arm.

"Um..." She licked her lips. "What did you say your name was?"

"I'm more interested in you." He narrowed his eyes, trying to flirt with her. "What's your name, sugar?"

She shrugged. "I can live with Sugar. I'd rather not give you my real name. It's not important."

"Sugar it is then, and my aren't you a sweet one." His leery gaze dropped to her breasts. "How much little lady?"

The female wore cowboy boots and a summer dress that looked to be about a size too big. It was floral, in shades of orange. It didn't disguise the curve of her breast or the flare of her hips. Her hair was long and thick. Blacker than the sky on a new moon night. He had yet to see the color of her eyes.

Her voice was soft. "I'm not sure what you mean," a mere whisper.

"Money. How much for a fuck? We both know that a girl like you wouldn't give a guy like me the time of day. I saw you looking at this earlier." The son of a bitch finally removed his hands from her ass and she huffed out a breath and took a small step back. The male put his hands in front of her face and gave the golden band on his finger a tug.

"That is a symbol of your union." She said in monosyllables.

The big male looked over at his friend and the two of them laughed. He might not be able to tell her eye color but he could see she was frowning.

"You could say that." He laughed some more. "How much? I'm in, excuse the pun." Another hard chuckle that had the hair rising on his skin and the blood igniting in his veins. What a prick. He had to agree with him on one thing though, what was she doing with them? Humans could be strange. It made no sense. "Can we get a two for one deal?" He pointed at his friend. "I'm first though." He glared at the other male.

"Money?" Her voice sounded timid and unsure. "You want me to pay you? I don't have any money."

"Did I just fucking die and go to fucking heaven?" The bastard rolled his eyes and groaned. He took what she had said as permission to put his hands on her again. This time he squeezed her flesh.

"I think maybe this was a mistake." She raised her voice and tried to pull away.

"No mistake." The human male groaned as he ground himself against her. "I'm going to give you exactly what you came here for. This *is* what you came here for isn't it?" He ground himself against her again and Kai could visibly see everything in her withdraw. Her head whipped to the side as she tried to move away.

Her hands went up when he didn't let up. "Let go of me." Her voice was hard. "I told you I made a mistake. Should never have come here. *Get. Off.*" She ground out the last two words. There was a commanding tone to her voice that made even him want to her obey her. Even though he wasn't the one touching her. Weird as fuck.

The human sucked in a hard breath, he let go of her so quickly he almost fell over in his attempt to move back. Almost as fast as his hands fell away, they snaked back around her waist. "Come on, baby… I can give it to you real good."

"I don't want to hurt you," she stammered.

The males laughed.

Her breathing was ragged. "I know kung-fu." Her voice shook with rage. "I mean it. I don't want to hurt you."

Ruby felt fire coursing through her veins. Her whole body vibrated. If this unsavory creature didn't unhand her and soon, blood would flow. She would tear him limb from limb and would only be able to stop when he was reduced to chunks of meat, in a pool of blood, at the floor at her feet.

"Unhand me," she snarled. Yet again, the male removed his filthy fingers only to put them back on her. He seemed to have a strange fascination with her backside. He couldn't stop touching it and squeezing it. It wasn't normal. His breath smelled of onions and other things she did not care to think about. His hard member was a joke. Yet for some strange reason, he kept insisting on rubbing it against her. Like feeling it's tiny proportions would somehow entice her to want to rut with him.

It made her want to kill him.

Slowly.

"You heard the female." It was a voice so deep, so gruff her insides did a flip flop. That her breath became frozen in her lungs.

"Who the fuck…" Onion breath began to say, as his head turned towards… Lord up above, he was tall, as tall as the males of her species. He was built, just as built as the males of her species as well. His hair was thick and dark, as was the stubble on his chin. Those lips, those full sensual lips should not be on a male, yet they made him all the more appealing, all the more masculine. There was something about him. Something... Something...

"Holy crap." This time when the disgusting, human creature unhanded her, he finally kept his hands to himself. "I didn't mean anything by it," he stammered. "It was a complete misunderstanding."

"Next time a female tells you not to touch her. You listen. Am I clear?" The male moved closer. His dark eyes were narrowed. His predatory stare caused a shiver to run up her spine.

"You bet ya..." Onion breath nodded. It was like his neck had suddenly become spring-loaded. He nodded and then nodded some more.

"I'm sorry, little lady. No harm done." It wasn't lost on her how he slowly stepped backwards. When he was a few strides away, he turned and scrambled from the room. Of his friend, there was no sign.

A solid, very warm hand gripped her elbow. It was only then she realized how close he was to her. "Are you okay?" Deep and gravelly. Another shiver ran through her.

His eyes met hers and for a few long seconds she was rendered speechless. His jaw tightened and something flared within their dark depths. It was enough to startle her back to reality. This male affected her. She didn't like it.

It was her heat. It had to be. She was closer than she had thought.

Some of the tension left her with the realization. It wasn't specifically this male. It was just her situation. Ruby nodded. "Thank you for helping me."

The male nodded once. His scent was all around her. Woodsy and earthy, yet fresh and vibrant. There were rusty undertones she couldn't quite decipher. He smelled good. There was a predatory edge, a feeling of immense power that radiated off of him. It was something she hadn't felt or sensed before on any humans. Not that she'd been around many humans in her life. Maybe that was it.

He would do.

The male would suit her purpose perfectly.

Unfortunately, he turned and took a step away. Panic rose up in her. She'd seen the look of interest in his eyes. Maybe she had been wrong. Just as quickly as he turned away, he swung back around. "It's cold out." His eyes drifted to the flimsy dress she was wearing. He couldn't know cold wouldn't affect her like it would a human.

She felt her cheeks heat. She purposefully picked the garment in the hopes of enticing a human male. "I'll be fine." More than fine. She couldn't explain it to him though.

He pursed his lips like her answer wasn't the one he was looking for. For a second it looked like he wanted to say something. Even sucked in a little breath, put his hand up. Then he shook his head. "I need to go."

"Can I buy you a drink?" She'd studied human mating rituals. Although studied was maybe too strong a word. She did know this was one of the more common ways of initiating interest in the opposite sex. At least, she thought so. Maybe she had been wrong.

Another large male slapped the good-looking stranger on the back and handed him a beer. "I'll leave you to it." He grinned widely. Even chuckled as he walked away. The male in front of her rolled his eyes.

Then they narrowed as they landed back on her and he frowned. "I thought you said you didn't have any money. Anyway, I'm good." He tipped his drink in her direction. His frown deepened. "It would probably be best if you left before you attract any more unwanted attention. It is none of my business what you are doing here but maybe you shouldn't be."

It was her turn to frown. "I came in the hopes of attracting attention. This is as good a place as any." When the males went on the stag run, they often frequented such establishments. She was in exactly the right place.

"Why would you want to attract attention?" He probably didn't realize it but he took a step towards her.

"I came for sex," she blurted. Honesty was the best policy. Her gram had taught her that from a young age. The male had just put the head of the bottle to his mouth.

He choked, putting the back of his hands to his lips and squeezing his eyes shut.

Why would her answer shock him? Isn't that why members of the opposite sex came to such revolting places? It wasn't for the food or the drink. It wasn't for the shoddy interior. They came to strut around and fluff their feathers in the hopes of attracting attention.

She needed a male and she needed one soon. Time was running out.

# THREE

*Amethyst.*

Her eyes were the color of jewels in the morning light. They were large, round and framed by the thickest lashes he'd ever seen. In short, they were devastating.

For just a second there, when he looked into them for the first time, he couldn't breathe. Kai was quite sure his heart even stopped beating. Time may just have frozen. A little dramatic, but true.

This female was trouble. She smelled incredible, looked even better, but there was something off about her. Something he couldn't quite put his finger on.

Kai finished coughing and sputtering. *Sex.* This pretty little female was here to rut? He couldn't help but look her over. His dick was still painfully hard. Thank fuck his leathers were tight and his vest, low.

Scuffed cowboy boots. Sexy as hell. At least, on her they were. Right now, he could picture them on either side of his face as he fucked her hard. The dress was loose fitting. It didn't matter, this female would be spectacular wearing a hessian sack. Or nothing at all. He held back a groan.

There were buttons all along the front of the garment. Small black buttons against the miniature, orange flowers that adorned the white material. Although the fabric was thin cotton with a conservative neckline, falling to just above the knee. It too, was sexy as fuck. At least on her. Her breasts were plump. Her scent was killing him.

Slaughtering him, one inhalation at a time.

Kai swallowed thickly. "Good luck with that. Although, I suspect you won't need much in the way of luck." Not looking like she did.

She pulled in both her lips before popping them back out. Full and lush like the rest of her. Those jewel-like eyes burning into him. He could see that a million thoughts raced through her mind.

"Maybe try and steer clear of the mated ones." He knew he sounded like a pussy but didn't give two fucks. It angered him that she would go there. He didn't know why it irritated him. He shouldn't care either way. "There is something sacred about a bond between two people. Even if they don't know it themselves."

Her eyes widened and her mouth fell open slightly. "You're right," a heartfelt whisper. Her eyes filled with shame. "I don't know what I was thinking. I guess, I wasn't thinking." She looked down. "I was wrong. Stupid." She muttered to herself. The female didn't give any further explanation or justification.

Although he could sense an immense strength in her, he also picked up on fear and a deep vulnerability. For reasons unknown, it made him want to protect her. "Go home. Don't do this..." He wasn't sure exactly what she was looking for but she wouldn't find it under some male. He held back a snort. Since when did he give a fuck? So what if she wanted to rut? Vampires did...all the time. She didn't strike him as the type. She was so out of her depth it was scary.

"I can't." He could hear the emotion in her choked out words. *Shit!*

"Why not? Just turn around and walk out that door."

"I can't because..." Her eyes were brimming with unshed tears. So damned beautiful. So sad. Who was she? Why was she really here? Why...? His nose twitched as he caught another layer to her scent. A layer so rich and velvety. Just smelling it felt like a hand had wrapped itself around his cock and given a light tug. Make that a hard tug. He clenched his teeth.

Arousal.

She was as turned on as fuck.

A low rumble erupted from somewhere deep in his throat. His instincts rode him hard. He was tempted to take her right there. To pick her up, place her on the nearest barstool, give her exactly what she needed. Crazy thing was, he didn't think she'd put up too much of an argument. He didn't think any of the lowlifes here would mind too much either.

Her scent grew thicker, stronger with each passing second. What the hell was this? He knew humans could be receptive but this was just crazy. He knew that if he put his hand to her core, it would come away dripping wet.

"Fuck," he growled. "I have to go." He absently rubbed the back of his neck.

"Don't. Please." She grabbed his wrist. Her grip was firmer than he would have expected from such a puny human. Then again, the top of her head was just below his chin which was unusual for a human female. They mostly didn't make it past midway on his chest.

He looked down at where they touched.

"I have a room across the road. I don't normally do things like this. I hope you believe that." Her amethyst eyes were wide and pleading.

"I believe you." It was true. He did believe her. Although he couldn't say why. He really shouldn't, she was in another male's arms just moments ago. Maybe because of the slight shake of her hand. The tremble of her lips. The fear in her eyes. "I don't even know you." It was a stupid reason to give. It wasn't something that would normally matter. He'd rutted females before without ever knowing their name. Probably would again. It wasn't a big deal.

Her eyes flitted over his shoulder for a few beats before coming to rest on his. She smiled.

*Fuck.*

Such beauty. Such innocence. Such sex appeal. How were they all possible and all at once? He wanted and he wanted badly. It was so unfortunate she was human or he might have taken her up on her offer.

"Corona." She pulled her shoulders back just a tad.

Kai cleared his throat. "Sorry…what?" He could feel that he was frowning.

"My name…it's Corona."

"Oh." He nodded. "I can't go with you. I want to…" His voice was thick. "Really fucking badly. You have no idea." He made a soft groaning noise. It was a true reflection of the frustration he felt inside. "I can't though."

"You can." She stepped forward. A mere inch separated them now. If she came any closer she would feel just how badly he wanted her. How close he was to…

"Go." Jenson said, the word came from somewhere right behind him, slightly to the right. When had the male snuck up on him?

"We're leaving and right fucking now." He couldn't take his eyes off of her as he spoke. Disappointment flared in those beautiful amethyst orbs. "I'm sorry," he whispered. "Go home." He added, using a gruff tone. "It's not safe for you to be in a place like this." It was in the bad part of town. Filled with lowlifes. She couldn't look more out of place if she tried.

Her brows came together in a deep frown. "I can take care of myself." The bright purple turned a more sinister shade as she bristled with anger.

"Kung fu." He couldn't help but to smile as he remembered how she'd warned the asshole human about her abilities. "You're going to need every move in the book." Fuck she was hot. Even though human males would not be able to scent her arousal. Not really. They would still be able to pick up on her need, on an instinctual level. It really wasn't safe. "Go home." He tried one last time. He didn't know this female. As much as he wanted to, he would never know her.

It took everything in him to turn and walk away. He dropped his beer on the bar with an un-ceremonial clunk and turned to face his amused subordinates. "We're leaving."

"I'm not done yet." Stuart smirked. He waved a half full beer. "Neither are you…by the look of that female. I'm not sure I would be able to just walk away."

"Yes, you would. I would kick your ass otherwise. I'm done and so are you." Kai tried to keep the growl from his voice and failed. He didn't have huge amounts of will power. What male would? Christ. The female was a vision.

Stuart held up his hands. "Okay, okay…no need to get testy. We wouldn't tell. I would take it to my grave."

"Don't be an idiot," Kai growled. "It's not happening. End of fucking story. They would scent her on me. I won't give up my place." He turned around and strode from the building. Moving as quickly as what humans would deem an acceptable pace. He tried hard not to notice that the female was still in the same spot where he had left her. That her arms were folded across her chest. Kai tried even harder not to notice that she was worrying her bottom lip between her teeth. That she watched his every move.

Somehow, and for some odd reason, he felt like she needed rescuing. Like he should find himself a white horse and some silver fucking armor. That he should save her. Maybe if she lived on a castle on a hill somewhere, maybe if she was a fucking princess he would but she wasn't. She was a regular run-of-the-mill human with problems about a mile wide. They weren't his problems though and neither was she. Once Jenson and Stuart climbed into their own vehicles, he climbed into his. He signaled for each of them to ride out first.

Kai checked for oncoming traffic and then pulled in behind Stuart. He flicked on the lights in his vehicle and ran a hand through his hair. Then he sighed loudly. One thing was for sure, he would never look at cowboy boots the same again. Kai sighed once more, the sound was heavy.

"Jupiter one to Jupiter base." His two-way flared to life. He could hear that Jenson was smiling.

"What?" He growled as he depressed the button on his own radio. Kai didn't feel like their shit. Not right now.

"You should shower when we get back." There was a crackle of static.

Kai wasn't biting. He pursed his lips and gripped the steering wheel tighter.

"This is Jupiter two." *Fucking Stuart.* Kai could hear that he was smiling as well. "With all due respect, you smell like a bull in musk." The male sniggered.

Kai couldn't help but grin. "Fuck you!" He growled. "I'm hoping you don't actually know how an aroused elephant male would smell." He took his foot off of the accelerator, ever so slightly.

"I would imagine that one would smell, just like you." Jenson chuckled. These little pricks were loving every minute of this.

Kai depressed the button. "Enough bullshit. This is a secure line. I want radio silence until we get back to base." His eyes were firmly on the two red lights on the road up ahead. The other vehicles pulled ahead and turned a corner, disappearing from sight.. The two vehicles pulled ahead of him.

"Yes, sir," Jenson said.

"Over and out," Stuart added.

Kai dropped the two-way radio on the seat next to him. Although his foot was still on the accelerator, the SUV came to a sudden and startling halt. The seatbelt bit into his chest just as his forehead hit the steering wheel. White hot pain flared.

He felt something hot on his face. His eyes rolled to the back of his skull. He felt himself float as darkness descended.

# FOUR

*What if he was really hurt?*

There had been a fair amount of blood on his face. His lip was cut, his nose bloody. There was more blood smeared across his forehead. He looked okay now though. In fact, his lip didn't look busted up anymore. Maybe she had just imagined it because of all the blood. It was probably just from his nose. All superficial. What if it wasn't just superficial though?

Maybe he had internal injuries?

Humans were weak. This male may look strong but he wasn't. Not at all. It made her feel stupid for tying him to the bed.

He still felt warm. Very warm. She allowed her fingers to trail along his arm. His heart was strong and steady. His breathing was slow and rhythmic.

The male moaned.

Yes. Maybe he was okay after all? The last thing she had wanted was to hurt him. She'd been as careful as possible.

The ropes had to go. The male would panic if he woke up to find himself bound to the bed. He was no match for her. If anything, she would need to go easy on him. Take things slow. The last thing she wanted was to accidentally kill him. She began to untie the knots. To strip away at the bindings. He would need all of his strength and all of his faculties. He would need to call on every reserve to survive the next few days. She prayed he would. He was a good male. At least, he seemed like he was.

She moaned. It felt like her womb clenched. It was crying out for seed. Her thighs were damp with her need. Her clit throbbed. One touch was all it would take. He needed to wake up. Right now. She only prayed he would be able to handle her. Even males of her own kind struggled to handle a female in heat. Ruby would never forgive herself if she hurt him.

He scrunched up his eyes and made another groaning noise. Then his eyes flashed open.

"Shhh." She whispered, placing her hands on his chest. "Are you okay?" He needed to stay calm.

"What the..." He made a groaning noise and scrunched his eyes shut. "Oh...it's you. What happened? What...where am I?" He looked around the room. His brow was furrowed. His eyes narrowed. There was very little to see.

Dust, rock and this bed. Ruby had lit a few candles. The large cave was bathed in their glow. It was cozy. It was a lot better than the room in Sweetwater would have been. More private.

"What…?" His gaze moved back to her, to her eyes, her face, her neck, her breasts. "Why are you naked? Shit…you look better than I imagined." He groaned again. This time it was drawn out, his voice had that deep husky edge. This wasn't pain…it was something else entirely. Something raw.

Her nipples tightened. Tingles ran down her spine. "You were in an accident." Her voice had a husky edge. She smoothed the hair from his brow.

"No…that can't be right." He seemed to remember something. "Jenson…Stuart." They must be his friends. The other two males from the bar.

"They are fine. I assure you." She clenched her teeth but a moan still escaped. Her need was beginning to cause her pain. Especially with a male so close by. It only made it worse.

"Fuck," he snarled. "I'm…this is…" He scrubbed a hand over his face. She'd washed him up already so it came away clean. Then he groaned again and his hand ran over his engorged shaft that pushed up against his pants.

"What the hell is wrong with me?" Even though he was human, he was still affected by her heat.

Good.

It would hopefully help him through it.

"Are you feeling ill? Does your head hurt? Are you injured in any way?" She knew she was rambling on like a mad woman but couldn't seem to stop. She needed to be sure he was okay.

He swallowed thickly, his throat working. "I have the overwhelming urge to fuck you." His nostrils flared. "I don't know what's wrong with me. I don't understand what the hell is going on."

"Your friends are fine. You were hurt, I'm going to take care of you." She straddled his lap, moving to the clasp on his pants. She wasn't playing fair. No male could resist a dragon shifter in heat. It wasn't possible. The heat only happened once a year, with plenty of warning.

These caves were littered across the four kingdoms. A small number of them were used by the few remaining females of the species. Sheer torture. Three days of agony. Only this time it would be different. This time she would have a male to slake her needs. Her brother would never think to look for her on Air territory, smack bang in the middle of Thunder's territory. At least, she hoped not. She hoped not for the sake of this male.

Fuck!

Hell!

Christ!

He couldn't think. Sweat poured off of him. His dick was so hard. It throbbed. His balls ached. The little bastards were sitting somewhere in his throat.

Why was he here again?

What the hell had happened?

Had he left the bar with this female?

Shit! The female. She straddled him. *Oh God, at last.* His dick sprang free as she pulled on his zipper. He groaned.

He watched as she positioned herself over him, taking his cock in one of her hands. This was wrong, although he couldn't say why. He wanted to tell her to stop but he couldn't bring himself to say the word.

Her beautiful eyes swept to his. "I'm sorry." She whispered, as she impaled herself on him. Her mouth fell open and her eyes filled with rapture.

He growled, gritting his teeth. Tight as fuck. Thankfully, she was wet. The evidence of her arousal coated her inner thighs, caused her pussy lips to glisten with her need. It was crazy but the only thing he could think right now was how good she felt and how good his dick looked inside of her. She was stretched around his thick girth. She took him, all of him. That was some fucking feat. It was the one thing that had worried him about a human female since some of the vampires had trouble.

"Sorry." She whispered to him a second time.

What?

No.

He ground his teeth. What the hell did she have to be sorry about? This was nothing to be sorry about. Not by a long fucking shot.

She arched her back. Her lush tits bounced, she thrust herself back onto him. That was it for him. Tickets. He roared as he poured himself into her like a fucking teenager. Scratch that, he'd never come this quickly. Not fucking ever. Even when he took a female for the first time.

In her defense, the female, Corona continued to ride him. She mewled with each and every thrust of her hips. Her pussy fluttered around him. She was close.

"Sorry." He growled, as he turned her onto her back. He may have finished first but he would ensure she came too. Or so fucking help him. Her eyes widened in confusion. "Should've kept the boots, sweetness." He growled as he pushed into her. Three thrusts later and she cried out. Her nails bit into him. Her legs closed around him.

This female had strength he didn't think possible. He kept moving while she squeezed the shit out of him. Her pussy felt like heaven. Velvety, soft, heaven.

"Oh god." She released her hold. "Sorry. Are you okay?" She smoothed her hands down his back. Unclenched her thighs. Her hips still bucked underneath him, although not with as much urgency.

Which was great since he couldn't seem to stop thrusting into her. "Better than fucking okay." His dick was still as hard as nails. "I can't stop."

"Don't then." She all out growled. It was so damned sexy he almost came again. Not happening. No fucking way.

He grabbed her thighs and pulled them up so that her knees were at her ears. Flexible as hell, as well. It made him fuck her harder. What he couldn't understand was why had he turned her down? Wait a minute…why was he here if he had turned her down?

"Oh god." She groaned as her pussy clamped down hard. As her hands closed around his ass.

No way. No. He may have come quickly the first time but he sure as hell planned on having some staying power this time round. It looked like his dick had other ideas though. His balls definitely had other ideas.

Her teeth clamped down, her eyes rolled back and her face turned red. A deep guttural cry was forced from her lips. He was fucked if it wasn't the sexiest thing he had ever seen. Her sheath damn near strangled him from the inside out.

"Fuck!" he groaned as he came again. His fangs throbbed. Her scent. Her sweet, sweet scent. It consumed him. He kissed her neck and licked at it. Nipped at her.

Corona mewled.

She didn't have a clue who he was. *What he was*. Kai didn't fuck around with the humans. He couldn't remember why that was. *Didn't want to*. There was a reason why he couldn't have her blood. He couldn't remember why that was either. Surely one little sip.

Then his fangs were inside her. Her blood flooded his mouth.

Devine.

Utter rapture.

His eyes rolled back and he made greedy suckling noises. Then the all consuming pain hit. Like he was being seared from the inside out. Like fire ran through his veins. Every hair on his body stood on end. Every nerve ending sprang to life. It was agony. His sacs clenched hard as another orgasm took him. It was vicious. It was cruel. He came so fucking hard it felt like he was being ripped apart.

Ruby paced. Her eyes felt wide and her breath came in rapid pants. She was having a nervous breakdown, or a panic attack…or something. Of all the males in Sweetwater to choose she went and found herself a vampire.

A vampire.

Right now, he was unconscious. A gorgeous heap of hard muscle, slumped across the rumpled sheets. A vampire. For scale's sake. What were the odds? How could she not have known? Now that she knew, it seemed stupid she hadn't picked up on it. The size of the male. The strength. That predatory, deadly vibe she picked up off of him. Then again, she was used to being around the type and she had, had very little interaction with humans and no interactions with any of the other species. Still, she knew something was different about him. She should have put two and two together. She should have, at the very least, known that he was not human. Her gram had spoken to her of the other species. All of the elders spoke of other non-human creatures like wolf shifters, vampires and elves.

That rusty tang to his scent. A blood drinker. A vampire. *Oh lord! Oh no!* A human as a father to her child was one thing but a vampire? There was no way around it, she would have to confess to Blaze. He would he mad. Fire breathing mad. Tear down the walls mad. At least a human would have been neutral. Her child would have been born a dragon shifter. There had been males that had taken human mates. It was rare but it had happened. The human females bred easily and always had dragon shifters. Always males, but always with shifter traits.

A vampire.

By fire. A vampire was another story entirely. It was too late. It was already done. Even if she had the willpower to walk away now, it wouldn't matter. She was in heat. Full blown heat. His seed was already inside her. Her hand moved to her belly. She gazed down at the sleeping male. She didn't have the willpower to leave. In a half a minute he would awaken and in all his aroused glory and she would be unable to take even a single step in the opposite direction. She was just as much his prisoner as he was hers.

Her brother was going to kill her. She wouldn't blame him if he tore her head off himself.

By becoming pregnant she was, hopefully, forcing his hand. He would thank her in the end. They all would. Her people would hate her and she would probably end up an outcast but by doing what she was doing, she was saving her people. The dragon shifters would rise from the ashes and be strong again. Her heritage would live on through change. There was no other way. A single tear tracked down her cheek. She would love this child despite his heritage. This child would be everything to her.

The male on the bed groaned and her clit throbbed in response. Ruby wiped her face. This was no time for crying. She inhaled deeply. It had been a long time since she had lain with a male. Her channel stung a bit from the rough rutting and yet she wanted more. Needed more.

He groaned and sat upright. His muscles rippled beneath his skin. The male might be a vampire but he was a fine specimen.

"What the hell was that?" He roared. As soon as his dark eyes landed on her they heated. "I…what…?" He shook his head as if such an action would clear it. "Who are you?"

"C-Corona…I already told you." She took a step towards him, quickly closing the distance. His sex jutted from between his thighs. Already fully engorged and in under ten seconds. This was a strong male in his prime, that was for sure.

His eyes narrowed and his hand closed around her throat. Not hard enough to close off air but enough to hold her in place. "Bullshit." His nostrils flared and his gaze dropped to her breasts. He licked his lips. His finger traced her areola and her flesh tightened almost to the point of pain. "What is this?" The same fingers traced her markings.

"Fucking beautiful," he whispered. He probably didn't realize he was doing it, but he gently guided her to the bed. All the while his fingers skimmed her markings, the tops of his hands brushing against the undersides of her breasts. "Golden. Exquisite. What the fuck?" He groaned as his eyes widened. His shaft was positioned at her opening. Her legs were wrapped around his hips. "What am I doing?"

His gaze flashed to hers and he groaned. The sound so agonized she felt sorry for him. She burned too. Just as fiercely. She wanted to tell him but his grip tightened ever so slightly making talking impossible.

"Who. Are. You?" He ground out as he thrust into her. The male released her throat, curling his fingers around her neck. They both gasped at the instant relief. It didn't last. He drove back into her using hard strokes. Hard but not rushed. His eyes drifted closed and he made a small grunting noise. "Who are you? Please." He bowed his head back. "I can't think straight. Can't stop. I need more of you even though I'm already inside you." His eyes opened, looking panicked yet his hips kept thrusting. "Tell me. Your blood it…" He let the sentence die grunting as he pushed back into her. "It…it's not…" He frowned, planting a hand on her hip as he drove back into her again. His chest rubbed against her nipples which were as hard as pebbles. Her orgasm was building. That familiar tightening had begun inside her.

Ruby had to tell him something. He already knew she wasn't human. What was it gram always used to say? Maybe she couldn't tell him everything but she could definitely confess some of it. "I'm not human." She moaned as the tightening grew more intense. Her toes curled and her breath came in heavy pants.

There was sweat on his brow and his eyes were so dark, so intense. "No shit." He gasped. His mouth was what dreams were made of. His lower lip just a tad plumper than the top. He was a beautiful specimen. A vampire. A brute. A savage. A blood drinker.

She fought for air and then cried out as her body spasmed around him. Although it had been building inside her, the intensity of her orgasm took her by surprise. Her eyes dropped to where their bodies were so tightly joined, to where his cock plowed into her…over and over. He stiffened and groaned, his hand clutched at her thigh. The other ripped at the covers. His eyes were wide. Laden with pleasure. His beautiful mouth tight. His breath rushed through his nostrils. The muscles on either side of his neck corded. His thick biceps roped. "Motherfucker." He groaned, his body falling onto hers. Her chest heaved against his. Her own perspiration slick against his. The male's weight was crushing but it felt good. It wasn't going to last long, but right now, she felt sated.

"I'm a dragon shifter," she whispered, between ragged pants.

He tensed. His breaths grew silent for a second before picking up again. He pulled himself up onto his elbows. His shaft was still inside her. He was still hard. "What?" He frowned. "Fuck!" His eyes widened. He was panicking just as she had been earlier. "But you don't exist. You don't. Your scent"—he scrubbed a hand over his face, the stubble catching—"your blood. Fuck! Your name. It's not Corona is it?"

She shook her head. "No. I read that off the label of one of the drinks."

"Corona, as in the beer?" He gave her the ghost of a smile before turning serious. "What is it then? Why are we…why is this?" He looked down between them. His cock throbbed inside her. "No," he growled. "Not again. What is wrong with me?"

"I'm not sure." She said, glancing away from him. Ruby was not a liar. Not normally. "I was told that the reason we stay away from the other species is because of the severe attraction that can develop. This type of thing can sometimes happen. It's rare."

"Rare. We're attracted to each other and it's making us aroused to the point where we can't think straight. As in…we're stuck here for the foreseeable future? Doing this?" He rocked into her and they both groaned.

Ruby nodded. "Yes…we won't be able to get enough of each other but it will pass. We just need to ride it out."

"Ride it out." He frowned. "As in literally?" He moved again.

Ruby bit down on her lower lip. She was feeling a bit tender, but it was also good. Her nipples tightened underneath his touch. His skin was warm against hers. His breath hot.

"I can't be here." He groaned, his hips continued to move. His shaft wasn't as deep inside her as it had been earlier. She ached for more. "I can't seem to make myself leave though."

"We're stuck here…together." Her voice radiated tension and frustration. *More*. She needed more.

"Why did you apologize earlier?"

She looked down at his chest. A wide expanse of hard muscle. "I took you. I'm sorry." There was so much more to it but she couldn't tell him that he was more than likely going to be a father. It was something he would never know. Guilt flooded her. It was wrong but it was how it had to be.

He drove in deeper and they both groaned. "My dick actually hurts but I can't stop."

"I'm also a bit…tender."

"I'll try to be gentle but I can't stop just yet." He kept moving. "For some strange reason, I want you on your back. I hope that's okay?"

Ruby nodded. He was being governed by his instincts right now. The need to rut, to dominate, to impregnate. Only, he didn't seem to realize it. He appeared to buy her story. The male thrust deeper and her breaths became a little unsteady.

"What…did you mean…by…" He swallowed hard. His voice was thick with arousal. His hair clung to his forehead. Sweat dripped off of him. He was beautiful. "You took me?" He groaned as he thrust a little deeper. Pleasure with the slight edge of pain. She could feel it too. Both sensations intertwined.

"I took you away." She was panting hard. "I shifted." She struggled to get the words out. The sensations too much to focus on anything else right now.

He frowned, his lower lip firmly between his teeth. And there they were, his fangs.

"Beautiful," she moaned. Who knew vampires were beautiful? They had been described as vile creatures. As monsters. Blood drinkers. "You're beautiful," she repeated.

He gave her a tight smile as he continued to move inside her. "Thanks…I think." She'd hoped the slower pace would stave off her orgasm for a bit longer but that was not to be. Everything was tightening…yet again…her muscles hurt. Her thighs burned. Her throat felt raw.

"Took me. How did you do that?" His pupils were dilated. His voice was so rough, like his throat had been worked over with nails.

"I shifted into my dragon form." She struggled to catch her breath. Another hard moan broke free. "I picked up your vehicle..."

"My SUV?" There was an edge of doubt.

"Yes," a drawn out cry. "Ohhhh yes." Then she was reaching. Her throat closing. Her muscles tightening up to the point of pain. Her back bowed. This orgasm was even stronger than the last. Her body shook from head to toe. It hurt. It was exquisite. She hoped they would be able to rest now. *Please*.

"Christ," the male growled. His body also tensed. "So tight." He groaned, his face was in the crook of her neck. His body jerked against hers. "Fuuuuuck." He groaned as his body continued to jerk against hers. Her spasms began to die down. Pleasure still coursed through her. Her lungs ached. Everything ached.

He growled loudly as he pulled free from her. Ruby moaned. She hated the feeling of emptiness. The loss. At the same time there was relief. Things were very tender between her legs.

His eyes flashed red and his lip curled away from his gleaming fangs. So beautiful in his anger. "I still want you." He punched at the pillow next to her. "How the hell can I still want you? This is insane. I need to leave. You had no right to take me. My people will be looking for me. I will be missed."

One of his hands was still on her hip, his thumb drew circles on her skin. He didn't seem to know he was doing it. His touch was soft and tender. This would be her last time with a male. The thought saddened her. She was such a romantic at heart. It was something her brother had always teased her about. "I am sorry," she whispered. "More sorry than you will ever know." It came out choked. *Don't cry. Don't.*

His gaze softened ever so slightly.

"I didn't want to…" She swallowed hard. Her mouth was dry. Her tongue felt like it was stuck to the roof of her mouth. She licked her lips. "I didn't have a choice. It was already too late." Not a total lie.

His demeanor softened some more. "You were already too aroused?"

She nodded. "My need was…is still…intense. I couldn't help it. I saw your car and…picked you up." She stopped there.

He snorted. "You picked up the whole SUV?"

She nodded. "You hit your head. Sorry."

He clenched his jaw and sucked in a breath. "I can't believe you actually picked up an entire vehicle."

She nodded. "It's true. I took you here. Your car is safe."

He sucked in a breath. "I'm going to be thrown in the dungeon for this. My kings will have my balls." He moved back on top of her and slipped between her legs, as he spoke. They both winced as his shaft made contact with her slit.

"Tell them I took you. That you didn't have a choice." She rubbed herself up against him. Ruby didn't care about the pain. The rawness. She needed more. She needed this male.

He tipped his head back and laughed. His eyes twinkled and a dimple appeared in one cheek. She had the ridiculous urge to kiss it. To kiss him. This wasn't about intimate actions. This was about saving her people. Forcing Blaze's hand. It was two people rutting. Nothing more.

Her heart felt heavy as he looked back down at her. A smile still graced his lips. "No…" He shook his head. "I can't tell them that you took me. I doubt they would believe me even if I did. A dragon shifter? A female, abduct an elite male?" He paused. "No way. I would be the laughing stock. I'd rather be lashed. Rather be locked away in the deepest cell. We're here now…I'm going to have my fill of you." He gently eased himself into her. "Even if it hurts." His expression turned pained. "You should tell me to stop."

She shook her head. "I can't. Take me…please."

He cupped her chin in his huge hand. "What is your name? I'm—"

"No!" She practically yelled. "No names. No details. We'll rut, we'll sleep, we'll eat and then we'll do it all again. In a few hours, days…whatever…we'll part ways and never look back. Never speak of this again."

He kept his gaze locked with hers. For a frozen moment, he contemplated her words. Ruby almost hoped he would refuse her. Then he nodded once. "I hope we survive this…this attraction…this craziness. I can't believe something like this could happen. Has it happened to you before?"

She squirmed beneath him, loving the feeling of being filled but she needed him to start moving. "No. Never." *The truth*. Well sort of. It had never been like this though. She'd only ever endured alone.

Then he growled and pulled out of her. His eyes glowed and his jaw was tightly clenched. He sniffed loudly. "Are you in heat?" His shaft pushed up against her opening. He didn't move away. He couldn't. The drive to rut her was too great.

Ruby tried not to react in any way. "No. We very rarely go into heat. I would know if I was…in heat. It's happened to me before." Using every reserve she had, she forced herself to feel anger. "Do you think I would actually purposely seek out a vampire to rut, with the intent of becoming pregnant? That's crazy." She meant the last. It was crazy.

He huffed out a breath and pushed back into her. She cried out, her head falling back. The feeling of relief was immense. "Rut me, please. I don't want to talk any more. I want you to move…now."

"You are showing all the signs of being in heat." He rocked into her as he spoke. "Every single one. You smell good. Really good. Different to what a vampire or human would scent if they were in heat but the signs are there. You're driving me crazy." He grit his teeth as he drove into her.

"I'm not. This is what happens when another non-human is attracted to one of our kind. I should never have left our territory."

"Why did you?" A rough growl.

Her back pushed down into the mattress with each thrust. Slow and deep. He was good. Really good. He did this often, unlike their males. Ruby could tell. He worked her without having to think about it. Knew exactly how to touch her. Not that she needed too much coaxing right now.

Ruby groaned. So darned good. "It was an act of defiance. Against my…" She chewed on her lip. "No details…remember? It was stupid of me."

"Yeah…fuck…" His face contorted, his eyes squeezed shut for a second. When he opened them they were glowing. He was about to lose it. His eyes glowed a beautiful golden color at that moment. "Oh god! I need you to come for me." His jaw was tense. His fingers sought her bundle of nerves and she cried out, bucking against him. Her fingers...make that her nails...dug into his back.

He sucked in a ragged breath and gave a strangled growl. The spurts that erupted from him were less this time. It seemed she had milked him dry. The male groaned loudly and continued to rock into her. The spasms that racked them both slowly eased. The big male collapsed on top of her. By the sound of his breathing, she could tell that he was asleep. She tried to get out from under him and failed.

This was his instinctual way of protecting her while he slept. Keeping her trapped under him. Still impaled on him so that no other could have her. Although Ruby could hardly breathe, she still fell asleep as well. She was more exhausted than she'd ever been in her life. They wouldn't rest for long. Desire would soon overtake them...again...and again.

Two nights and two days. They barely stopped, they barely talked. It was one rut session after another. They bathed in a nearby pool...rutted in the nearby pool. They ate, they slept in short snatches but mostly they rutted. Ruby had never been more thankful for their enhanced healing ability. They couldn't seem to get enough of one another. Desperate was a word she would use. Another was insatiable. The nameless vampire took her to places she had never been, would never go again. He never once kissed her or tried to take her any other way besides on her back. One thing was for certain, she had to be pregnant after this. Had to be. The knowledge gave her untold joy, at the same time, her heart broke into a million pieces.

# FIVE

Gleaming scales. Greens and blues in every hue under the sun. The beast's breast was so bright, he almost had to look away. Pure, liquid gold. The same amethyst eyes as her human form, only slitted. Her wings were wide. They seemed delicate, paper-thin. Yet, he could see that they were powerful. Could feel the air they displaced with each hard flap. Her tail was forked and long. It swept gracefully from side to side behind her muscular body. She might be a female but she would be a force to reckon with. Her teeth were long and sharp. Her talons looked deadly. Deep groves marred the earth at her feet, where she had landed moments earlier.

Within three seconds, she was the female he had come to know. She shifted easily. If he hadn't seen the change with his own eyes, he would never have believed it. Dragon shifters were real. Not just a thing of legends but living and breathing.

They hadn't talked much so he couldn't say he really knew her. Her body. Now that he knew, inside and out. His groin tightened at the thought of their time together. The way she felt beneath him. Her legs around him. Her cries of ecstasy. The way her eyes widened as he thrust into her. How her lips parted as she was about to come.

"You are fucking beautiful…do you know that?" He couldn't help the words as they tumbled from him.

"Really?" Her amethyst eyes crinkled at the corners as she smiled. "You think my dragon pretty? Or were you referring to me in this form?" She glanced down at herself.

He shook his head. "Not just pretty…beautiful. So are you…now I mean. You're beautiful in both forms." His eyes moved to her plump breasts, to the exquisite designs that adorned the area below them. Golden tattoos. Much like the one that wound its way around his own arm. His was black. It folded itself around his right bicep and down the back of his forearm in curves and sharp edges. He was an elite. One of the ten. The ink was a symbol of his achievements. At least he hoped he was still part of the ten. That this whole thing with the dragon shifter hadn't messed things up for him.

It was time to face the music. Time to find out.

It had been worth it. Every second with this female was worth it. "I'll miss you." He blurted. It was true so he didn't regret admitting it.

By the tightening of her jaw, he could see she didn't like that he had said it. "You don't even know me." She smiled. There was a sadness there. Was she also apprehensive about leaving? About their agreement? Did she also regret having made it?

"I know we agreed not to contact each other after, but I..." He was still attracted to her. He still wanted her. Not in the same way as before. Their initial attraction had made him more than a little crazy. This was different. More real. Kai still wanted this female. It made him want to change her mind. It wasn't rational. His kings would never allow...

"No!" A harsh growl. Her eyes flashed with fear. "We are too different. My brother... It would never be permitted. I enjoyed my time with you but it has come to an end. I'm sorry about the scratches on your car. And about your back." She blushed. It was the cutest thing he had ever seen.

"My back is long healed. The car..." He shrugged. "It's just a car. It will be repaired." The SUV was pretty banged up. There were deep grooves on the hood. The door on the passenger side was dented. She had picked it up with her sharp claws...twice. Once to take them up the mountain and again to bring them down. No wonder it was a bit worse for wear. "No worries."

"Will you tell them what happened? Your kings?" She licked her lips.

He shook his head. *Not a fuck.* "No. I haven't changed my mind about that. Even if they were to believe me, it might cause shit for you…for your kind." It wouldn't be right.

She smiled. "You would do that for me? For my people? Even after I adducted you?"

Kai nodded. "I guess so." He had to grin. "You did take me so that you could have your wicked way with me. It was intense…it's never been like that for me before. Not with anyone else."

Her eyes moved away from him. They darkened. She crossed her arms, almost in an attempt to cover herself which was crazy since they had been naked the entire time they were together. He knew her body inside and out. She looked nervous and…guilty. She still felt bad for taking him. "Don't." He gripped her elbow, pulling her to him so he could hook an arm around her shoulders. She softened against him but not completely.

This female felt good in his arms. Too fucking good. "Don't do that. I will admit that I was pissed, but I understand…I felt it too. I've never felt that way before, it was special. What we have…make that, what we had…" He swallowed thickly. He didn't want this to end.

"It was special. I don't know your name." He cupped her chin and tilted her face up. "I don't need to know your name or anything about you to know that it was different…I will never forget you."

Her eyes were wide. "I won't forget you either." They welled with tears.

*What the fuck?*

Then she blinked them away and pulled in a breath through her nose before continuing. "What will you tell them?" She blurted, clearly trying to change the subject. "You've been missing for days and they'll scent me…on you."

"I'm hoping that they won't know what a dragon shifter smells like. I didn't know what you were and neither did my subordinates." He shrugged. "Vampires are hugely attracted to human females, it won't be too much of a stretch for them to buy my story." He had to chuckle. "Although it seems that our attraction for dragon shifters is far more pronounced. Who knew? Maybe we should organize a meet and greet between our species?" He meant it as a joke.

Her expression changed from relaxed to horrified. She shook her head. "No way. It wouldn't work. There are so few females of our species." Then she squeezed her eyes shut, like telling him was a bad thing. What difference did it make to the vampires? It's not like their species interacted.

He tried to lighten the moment. "Then I guess I'm one lucky male to have spent some time with you. I'm sure you are highly sought after." She stiffened against him.

The female tried to pull away from him but he tightened his grip on her. "Shhh." He ran his hand up her back. Slow and easy. "I'm sorry. I didn't mean to upset you." Kai thread his fingers into the hair at the nape of her neck. He leaned forward and tried to kiss her but she turned her head to the side at the last moment and he caught just the edge of her mouth.

"I need to go now," she stammered.

"One kiss." Kai didn't like the idea of her walking away. Of this being over. He realized, realistically, that it needed to happen. The female was right; they couldn't be together.

She shook her head, her eyes refused to meet his. The female didn't explain further. Who was he to push her? Instead, he forced himself to release her. To step away.

Their time was at an end.

"I wish you well." Kai touched the side of her arm. "I hope you have a good life and that all of your hopes and dreams come true. You are a sweet female. You're going to make some male very happy one day."

Her beautiful eyes turned stormy. "If only that were true. Thank you and I'm so very sorry." She gave him a teary smile. Her lip quivered.

Before he could reply, the female moved away from him, simultaneously there was a cracking noise and her body stretched out. Scales appeared on her skin. Her jaw elongated. Her teeth erupted. Seconds later, a dragon stood before him staring at him with those sad, amethyst eyes. She lowered her head and leapt into the air, her magnificent wings sprung open. With minimal effort she took to the sky and moments later was gone. Swallowed by the night.

Kai felt more tired than he'd ever been in his whole entire life. Drained. Wrung out. He had meant what he said, he would miss her. He would remember their time together. With the shake of the head, he made his way back to the vehicle and climbed inside. His heart felt heavy. It was worry over what his future would hold. Of the shit storm he was facing back home.

The SUV was pretty banged up. He put the key into the ignition. "Please start. Please." The engine turned over on the first attempt. *Thank fuck.* He didn't relish the thought of a long-ass walk.

Kai found himself driving on autopilot, it was wrong of him but he couldn't face his kings right then. Instead of going straight back to vampire territory, he pulled in at the only hotel in town and got himself a room for the night. After a quick shower, he fell into bed and was asleep instantly. He dreamed of a beautiful female with amethyst eyes. If only he knew her name.

---

The office interior was spacious. No expense spared. Then again, that's how Brant rolled. Deep mahogany wood, gleaming wooden floors, Persian carpets. Formal, intimate, professional. His king sprang to his feet the moment he was ushered in. His eyes blazed. "Where the fuck have you been?" Brant snarled, he bashed his fist against his desk.

"I—" The door behind him flew open, it banged against the wall. A chip of plaster crumbled to the floor.

"Firstly, are you okay?" Zane's voice was relatively calm considering his entry to the room.

The male's eyes were dark. They gave nothing away. His face was passive. His forehead glistened with perspiration.

"I am fine." Kai assured him.

Zane narrowed his eyes, his nostrils flared. "You were with a female," he snarled. His nostrils flared again. "That scent, it's familiar to me." His brows drew together in confusion. "I can't quite place it."

"Maybe you know the female Kai spent the last few days with," Brant spat. "Why is a human female's scent familiar to you?"

"I don't know. It doesn't make any sense," Zane growled. He paused for a few beats. *Why would the scent of a dragon shifter be familiar to Zane?*

Before he could think on it, his king continued with a slight shake of the head. His dark eyes settled on Kai once again. "What would possess you to give up your place in *The Program*? Maybe you should explain that to me." He folded his arms across his chest. By the tension in his jaw. Make that the tension in his whole body, Kai could see that he was pissed. Beyond pissed.

"I met a female in a bar." It sounded weak. He normally had a solid willpower. Kai clasped his hands behind his back. "There was an instant attraction. Although I left with Jenson and Stuart, I couldn't stay away. I couldn't just leave her. It was unsafe in that environment for a female such as her."

"You didn't think to inform anyone that you were going back to help her?" Zane ground his teeth for a second.

"It should've been quick. Go back, get the female and drop her off at a place of safety. It should've taken no more than 15 or 20 minutes. It was stupid of me to go alone, especially considering my attraction to her." He huffed out a breath. The excuse was thin. Yet, it was what it was.

"Very fucking stupid." Brant sat back down on his chair and even leaned back into it. It looked like his rage from earlier had passed.

"You picked her up and dropped her off but what then, decided to stay? Hang out with the female for a bit? Surely you realized we would have scented her? Why didn't you contact us after you decided to stay with her?" Brant played with the cufflinks on his shirt.

*No cellphone reception. You see, I was actually abducted by her. The female was no human, she was a dragon shifter. A huge one at that and strong too. The female picked up my SUV. She kept me a prisoner in a cave in the middle of the mountain somewhere. I was a sex slave for the last few days. A willing sex slave I might add.* There was no fucking way he could say that, besides, he had promised the female he would keep her existence a secret. That he wouldn't reveal her people. He still didn't know why he had done that. Maybe he was feeling possessive in the heat of the moment. That had to be it. Whatever the reason, he was a male of honor. They would never believe him anyway. Not a chance in hell.

"What the fuck happened?" Zane snarled. "I'm losing my patience. Do you have any idea how many teams were out scouring for you? We informed the president of the United States that you had been abducted by a fascist group. The FBI sent reinforcements. Titan is heading up a team whose sole purpose has been to find your sorry ass instead of doing his assigned task. It's a fucking embarrassment. You had better have a good explanation. It had better not involve your dick inside some human female. Although, by your scent, I'm pretty sure that's exactly what it means."

Shit.

This was bad.

Worse than he thought.

Kai raked a hand through his hair. He made a noise of frustration. "I'm sorry." He looked Zane straight in the eye. "I don't have any good explanation except that she drove me crazy. I couldn't turn her down. Couldn't leave if my life depended on it. It was a crazy two days…I should have called." Lame. Stupid. Downright irresponsible.

Zane cursed a whole string of hard words. His reaction was to be expected.

Brant chuckled. "I told you." He growled, his gaze on Zane. "You owe me money."

Nice. It looked like his kings had been placing bets during his disappearance.

"You've been so dependable in the past. One of my best. You're young but I've always been able to rely you. Fucking hell, Kai." There was such disappointment in Zane's voice. "I was convinced you had been taken, that you would never actually choose to take a path like this. I can smell you didn't use protection." Yeah, two days of rutting with condoms would've made him smell like a rubber factory. He shook his head, looking solemn.

"She wasn't in heat." He ground out between his teeth.

"Was she at least on birth control?" Brant asked, looking bored.

Kai could recall how the female had said that her species very rarely went into heat. That they always knew when it was going to happen. "Yes," he finally mumbled. It wasn't like he could offer more than that.

"If we get slapped with a lawsuit so help me…it could turn nasty…" Brant stood up from the chair, a finger pointed in Kai's direction. "What if she accuses you of rape? Did you think about that? Maybe she's connected to one of these groups trying to taint our name. We have to always be on our guard and assume the worst."

Kai shook his head. "She won't do that. She is a good female. There is nothing to worry about. There won't be any repercussions."

"What the fuck happened to the SUV? Also, you said two days yet you were gone for three." Zane crossed his arms over his chest. His voice was deadly calm.

Fuck! How did he explain this one? "I was involved in an accident." Try and stick to the truth as much as possible. "I was exhausted after our…two-day session and I wasn't paying attention, so I had a run in with a street pole."

Zane frowned. "Those deep scratches were not from any street pole I've ever seen." His brow was raised. His bullshit detector clearly on high alert.

"There was a tree next to the pole and a couple of bushes." So thin it was laughable.

Zane sighed. The sound loaded with frustration. "I wish you would just tell us what fucking happened."

Brant snorted, he was looking at Zane. "He met a human, fucked her from here until next Sunday and then wrapped his vehicle around a pole." He shrugged. "I believe it. Fucking idiot." As he said the last, his eyes turned to Kai. "I must say, I'm interested as to your whereabouts on the third night."

"I checked into the local hotel so I could recover." He didn't elaborate, they could check.

"Were you hurt?" Zane was looking at the far wall.

Kai shook his head. "No, just exhausted."

"You could've called." Zane's voice was barely audible. "Well…" He seemed to have calmed down. His arms were relaxed at his sides. The tension had eased out of him. "I hope it was worth it. You are off *The Program*. There will be no human mate for you."

It was strange. He had been so thrilled to be a part of *The Program*. Beyond excited. Yet, the thought of being out didn't bug him as much as he thought it would. He bowed his head slightly in a show of respect and acknowledgement. "I'm—" He had been about to apologize but Brant assumed it was to argue.

"Shut the fuck up," his king snarled. "We need males that can follow directions. Human females are too fragile."

"I *can* follow directions," Kai said on reaction. Feeling like an idiot as soon as the words were out. His actions had shown otherwise. He chewed the inside of his cheek to keep himself from saying anything more.

"No, you can't." Zane shook his head. "You're out. I can't have you on my team either."

"You're kicking me out?" He knew for a fact that others had messed up. York had rutted a human. Gideon had done the same. He shook his head. "No… Please. It's not fair…"

"I know what you're thinking," Brant chimed in. "You're not the only male that has taken a human without permission, am I right?"

Kai nodded. "Yes." Why him? He wouldn't name names but they both knew who he was referring to.

"You're the only male to have disappeared for days on end. We look like a bunch of idiots. As soon as we are done here I have to call the president of the United States, to inform him that one of my males couldn't keep his cock inside his pants. We'll look like a bunch of idiots. There are repercussions to this. Big fucking repercussions. Not just to you but to our whole damned species." Brant's eyes blazed.

Zane took a step forward. "You will receive 15 lashes and will spend the rest of the week in the dungeon."

"I understand about *The Program*." There was still no feeling of disappointment. For whatever reason, a human female didn't seem as important anymore. "Whip me, humiliate me. Lock me away. I don't care, but please, I worked so hard to make it onto your team. Please don't strip me of that." His hand shook. His throat felt thick. "Anything but that."

Zane looked him deep in the eye. "You should've thought of that before. I'm not saying that you can never be an elite again but right now, no fucking way. You have a lot to prove to me and have a lot to make up for." He shook his head. "I had big hopes for you and in many ways this has stung more because of that." Then he walked away.

Kai took a step towards his retreating back but he knew instinctively there was nothing he could do or say.

Brant cleared his throat and Kai turned back around. "Do I need to call a couple of guards, or can you make your own way to the dungeon?"

Kai felt like he was ten years old. "I can do it myself." He tried to keep the growl from his voice and failed.

"Zane was worried. He will get over himself. Take your lashes, do your time, work harder than you've ever worked and I'm sure he'll take you back given time." Brant fingered the end of his tie. "You're lucky it's not me...I would write you the fuck off."

Kai nodded. "I hope you are right...about Zane."

"I know the male." Brant rolled his eyes. "I know him better than I ever thought fucking possible. Don't ever repeat this, but he is soft on the inside. You disappointed him greatly. He took your actions personally, like you were slighting him."

"That's not the case." Kai felt more frustrated than he'd ever felt before. He wished he could explain things. It was better this way, he'd given his word. He would stick it out. If he'd made the team once, he could do it again.

He walked out and headed down the stairs. Kai walked through the lobby. He ignored those around him. He'd never felt so unsettled. Then he opened a door that lead to another set of stairs. This time, they would take him to the bowels of the castle. The dungeon. Frustration ate at him. Just a few short days ago, his future had been before him, clearly mapped. Right now, he didn't know where he was headed. He wasn't even sure what he wanted.

Fuck.

Kai clasped the back of his neck. Maybe a few days of solitude was exactly what he needed. There was a driving force inside of him. He felt full to the brim of energy, only, he didn't know what to do with it. Or what to make of it. Fuck! Why was this happening to him? Why had he met this female with amethyst eyes? Why was he so damned cut up over losing her? She wasn't even his to begin with. She never would be.

In a moment of frustration and anger, he punched the wall. In the past, something like that had always hurt. He'd cracked a bone or two and had torn open his skin on the knuckles. The release had always felt good but he'd also felt stupid because he didn't actually achieve anything. It was one of those heat of the moment things. Something to laugh at later.

This time, the wall exploded. They were underground alright because well, with a piece of the wall missing - it was reduced to rubble at his feet – he could see earth and lots of it. What the hell? Kai looked down at his fist. There was no sign of bruising or bleeding. The wall must have been old. He would need to request that the foundations of the castle be checked. He shook his head and continued down the stairs.

# SIX

Blaze paced to her four post bed. He gripped one of the dark wood columns for a beat or two before pacing back. "I cannot even begin to believe you did this." Her brother was so angry he struggled to talk. His hand shook. His whole body vibrated with his rage. "You care nothing for your people. You think nothing of me."

"I'm sorry." She tried to stand tall, to hold her head up high.

"Don't lie to me. You're not sorry." He walked away from her and went to go and stand at the window. Although he looked like he was staring out at the view, she knew better. He was lost somewhere deep in his thoughts. She had known that he would be torn up but she hadn't expected it to be this bad. Blaze was a plan B kind of guy. If things didn't follow the chosen path he was quick to change course and forge ahead. She relied on his doing just that.

She took in a large breath, held it for a moment or two before slowly releasing it. "No, I'm not. I'm not sorry at all." She shook her head and tried to touch his arm but he yanked it away. With a barely audible snarl, he spun and paced to the other side of the room.

"I'm pretty sure Thunder will already be receiving news of this. It's a travesty." His hands curled into fists which he used against the wall, in sharp punches. Their lair was built into the side of a mountain. The wall onto which Blaze beat, was hundreds of feet thick. Layer upon layer of volcanic rock. He may as well try and move the entire mountain. Still, Blaze raged on. Only once his hands were bloody and his breathing labored, did he stop. Males.

His beautiful emerald eyes were laced with red, they were narrow slits, showing his dragon was just below the surface. "I made promises. You were supposed to carry the future heir." His voice broke and he sank to his knees before her. This is not what she had expected. The rage yes. This level of pain…definitely not. She grit her teeth to keep from crying.

"He will not be pure." Her brother looked up at her, his green eyes were overly bright. He said it like it was the most despicable thing imaginable. An abomination instead of a child. Her child. Even though the little one would carry his blood as well. "He won't be a true royal."

"No, he won't be pure but the baby will be mine...*our* family." Ruby grit her teeth and squeezed her eyes shut for a second. When she opened them, his jaw had tightened.

Lord help her. "The male was not human." She blurted before she could lose her nerve.

"What did you say?" He was on his feet in an instant. "Who then? A lesser? Some male that you deemed to love? Who is he? Why did I not know of this? You don't scent of a dragon." He frowned heavily. Once again Blaze took to pacing. Convinced that she'd rutted one of the lesser dragon shifters despite her scent. "It's unacceptable. What the hell were you thinking? No, don't answer that. You weren't thinking were you? You and your dreams of love, of finding that special someone. How could you do this?"

"I didn't rut with a lesser." She swallowed thickly, trying hard to find the words.

"If not a lesser then who? One of the other kings? A prince perhaps?" Blaze narrowed his eyes. "I told you that you could pick one of the royals. Thunder was the preferred male but you could've pick any of them. Why would you go behind my back?" He looked excited at the prospect of the child having been sired by a dragon royal.

"It wasn't one of the royals." She cringed as she admitted it.

Blaze spun on his heel and was on her in an instant. His hands closed over her elbows, he gave her a yank. She jerked forward. It was the first time he'd ever put his hands on her in such a way. Although rough, he didn't hurt her. His actions scared her a little though.

Blaze huffed out a deep breath and let go of her. "You need to talk and you need to do so now." His nostrils flared. "Not a human, not a dragon shifter." They flared again. "Fuck." He spoke the words so softly. Under his breath. The males had picked up such human slang during their stag runs. "Please… I hope I don't scent what I think I scent." He was breathing deeply. His nostrils flared and red bled back into his irises.

"It was a vampire." She stood tall.

Blaze roared. All hell broke loose as he shifted. Right there. In her bedroom. Deep beneath the ground. His claws scraped against the floor. His wings beat against the walls and ceiling. Furniture crashed. She smelled smoke, could feel heat. Blaze roared a second time, the sound of his fury radiated throughout the castle. Ruby crouched as far away from him as she could get, her hand on her belly.

# SEVEN

*Two months later...*

The hallway stretched out ahead of them. There was a *T* junction at the end. Left to go back to his room and right to go to the bar.

The last thing he felt like doing was hooking up with anyone. The thing he needed the most, was to hook up with someone. Kai sighed. He was damned either way. "I think I'll pass. Maybe next time." The thought of a warm body. A random someone, did not appeal to him. It almost made him laugh out loud. That's what she had been. The female. The one who had fucked him up.

"Stop being such a pussy and come with us." Jenson rolled his eyes. "You're still not over that human female, admit it."

"It's not that." *It so was that.* Those amethyst eyes. That shy smile. If she had been human he would've sought her out a long time ago. Her long black hair, her cherry lips. It killed him that he didn't even know her name. He didn't know a single thing about her except that he wanted to know everything about her.

"It's not healthy. It's been too fucking long." Jenson shook his head.

"Don't you think I know that?" He snapped, a little more harshly than he intended. Kai locked his jaw for a few beats. "Fine." He sighed. "One drink," he growled.

Jenson gave him a hard slap to the back. "That's more fucking like it. We will talk with a couple of the females. Have a few dances and then you're getting laid."

"Don't get ahead of yourself." Kai stuffed his hands into his pockets. He knew that Jenson, and some of the others, were only trying to help him but it was beginning to wear on his nerves. It was none of their business. Full fucking stop.

The only person who cut him any slack was Jordy. Thank fuck for his best friend.

"I need to get this out." Jenson stopped walking. *What now?* The male took a deep breath, keeping his eyes tracked on the wall just ahead. "This needs to stop. It's not healthy. Someone needs to get tough with you. To lay it on the line and it looks like that someone is me."

"You already said that. I'm sick of hearing the same thing over and over again." Kai tried to keep the growl from his voice and failed.

Jenson turned to face him. The male was frowning. "It's only because we care. I'm not sure who this female was or what exactly it was that she did to you." He shook his head. "It's not right. You've been taking blood from your best friend. Your best fucking friend."

Thankfully Kai's hands were in his pockets just then or he would've beat on the other male. Punched the fuck out of his face. Thing was, Jenson was only trying to help him. It came from a good place. He couldn't hurt the male for that. As much as he wanted to, he couldn't.

Kai clenched his teeth so hard that he was sure he heard a tooth crack. His breath sounded harsh to his own ears. His mouth pursed tight, his nose flared with each inhalation. "It's not just the female. It's everything." It wasn't much of an explanation but it was all he was giving.

"You made a mistake. A mother of a mistake! Big fucking deal." Jenson paused. "You keep saying how upset you are to be off the Elite Team, yet you do nothing but sabotage yourself. Instead of fighting for your place back. How do you ever expect to get in by denying yourself? Blood and sex. They are basic vampire requirements. Get your head out of your ass. Look at yourself…" His gaze flashed down to Kai's feet and back up again. "You've lost your edge."

"I get plenty of blood. More than enough." His voice shook with both anger and frustration. Everything Jenson said was correct. Spot fucking on. The problem was, Kai wasn't ready to act on it yet. He wasn't ready to banish the dragon shifter from his mind. To purge himself of her memories and the time they had together. He wasn't ready to move on. It was that simple. The only problem was, he didn't know what he needed to do. There was no finding her. No future for them even if he did. For now, he was in limbo. He hated every minute of it yet couldn't seem to move forward.

"More than enough blood," Jenson mumbled. "From your fucking friend."

"Blood is blood." Kai said, his voice sounded flat and emotionless. He didn't feel like fighting.

"You need to rut. You are acting like a male that lost his mate. I know it is possible for us vampires to fall that quickly." The male raised his brows. "Did you bond with her? Is she the one?"

Kai shook his head. "No." He growled but not as a denial, rather as a way to shut the male up. Kai doubted the dragon shifter was his mate. Yet, he couldn't help but feel that maybe she was. It was impossible to tell. Their attraction was so raw and so intense. He longed to see her again, to spend time with her so that he could explore whether or not there was something more there. Their coming together had been special. At least to him. By the look in her eye, and the sorrow that surrounded her, he was sure she had felt the same.

If only they could be given a chance to find out. *His mate*. It was a possibility.

"If you think there might even be the smallest of chances, then you need to go after her. You need to fight for her or you will never forgive yourself. I might be young, I've never been in love, but I'm still not an idiot. I know enough to be able to give you this advice." Jenson ran a hand through his hair. "And if the female meant nothing, you need to stop this path of self-destruction. You need a new start."

A new start. It did have a nice ring to it. Kai needed to try and forget her. He'd lost sight of his goals. The elite team. *The Program*. They were right there. He could have them back. Kai waited for the rush of excitement. It didn't come.

He nodded. What Jenson said made sense. It was logical, only it didn't fit.

"Drinking from your best friend. It's not right. Even if Jordy is seriously fine. I can't believe you haven't…"

"Don't," Kai growled. "Jordan and I grew up together."

Jenson groaned. "I would so go there. Those long legs wrapped around my—"

"Stop!" Kai choked out a laugh. "That's one visual I don't need. I said I'll go with you already. You need to make a move on Jordan instead of talking about it. Maybe you are the pussy, not me."

He widened his eyes. "One of these days I'm going to pluck up the courage. Just you wait." Jenson chuckled, he gave Kai a shoulder knock. "One drink at the bar. Baby fucking steps, bro."

Kai nodded and they picked up their pace, turning right at the end of the hallway.

The bar was busy. It was busy every night. It was a place for vampires to unwind and to hook up. Kai tried not to notice how, at least, a few heads turned in his direction. Even as an ex-elite, he still held appeal. Then again, he was a big, strong motherfucker. Where some of the human females had seemed a little weary of him, vampire females were greatly attracted to him.

Jenson ordered for them both and slid a tumbler his way. It was cold, the ice chinked as he picked it up.

"Whiskey," Jenson announced unnecessarily. Kai could scent the alcohol masked behind the sweet, coppery blood. A vampire's mixer of choice.

Kai nodded and took a deep drink. The whiskey burned in the back of his throat. He grimaced.

Three females approached. Kai swallowed thickly, taking another deep drink of his whiskey. He could do this. Jenson was right. He needed to move on.

"Finally decided to come out and play?" The tallest of the three females touched the side of his arm. She drew her full bottom lip in-between her teeth.

"Carmen," Kai said.

She smiled seductively. "Long time no see."

He nodded, finishing his drink.

"Too long." She moved in a little closer. They had rutted in the past. They were compatible. After such a long dry spell, he should've been vibrating with need, yet there was nothing.

*Sweet fuck all.*

*Damnit!*

"Drink?" He tilted his glass in her direction.

The other two females laughed at something Jenson was saying but he kept his eyes on hers. Bright blue. They were beautiful, as was her waist length hair. She hadn't so much as given him the time of day before he became an elite warrior. She was a prize and much sought after. Any minute now, his dick was going to take notice. It was going to happen, he just had to try harder. Kai allowed his gaze to travel across her body. Tall, with acres of soft skin, her breasts were like juicy plums. Sweet and ripe. *Nothing.* He felt like groaning in frustration.

She licked her full lips. "I would much rather get out of here, but if you insist."

"Vodka or champagne?"

"You remembered." She giggled and twirled a strand of hair around her finger. "Vodka, please."

Kai turned to the bar and placed the order. A vodka for the female and another whiskey for him. Hers came in a tall glass.

"So, how have you been?" She smiled. The castle was huge. Four wings and five floors, as well as three levels of basement. Their territory spanned thousands of miles with numerous villages. It wasn't nearly big enough. Especially the stone walls of the structure he was standing in. Everybody knew everybody's business, almost as soon as they knew it themselves. Even if they didn't have all the facts, rumors and half truths were the order of the day.

"I'm good." His voice came out quiet, yet rough.

She sucked in a small breath. "I like you, Kai. I don't normally spend time with a male unless he is an elite or at the very least, he needs to be a leader. But for old time's sake, I'm willing to go to your room with you."

She liked him. Like fuck. Carmen liked the fact that she would be seen as the female to break his dry spell. The female he couldn't resist. He didn't give a fuck about her motivation. He just wasn't interested. Not at all.

Kai was just getting ready to tell her what she could go and do with herself when another female slipped between them. She hooked her arm around Kai. "There you are. I was wondering when you were going to show up." Jordy threw him a *sugar couldn't melt in my mouth* smile.

Kai couldn't help but to chuckle.

"We're dancing." She narrowed her eyes on him. "Right now."

He glanced back at Carmen, catching the ass-end of an eye roll.

Even though a fast, house track was playing, Jordy threw her arms around his neck, moving slowly to the upbeat tempo.

He mouthed thank you and grinned at her. Kai wasn't sure what he would have done without this female. When his life had pretty much come crashing down around him, she'd been there for him every step of the way.

"Don't mention it." Jordan pulled him tighter. "I never liked her much anyway." She whispered in his ear. She released him, ever so slightly, her hips still swaying to the beat. Her eyes closed for a few seconds, seeming to enjoy the music.

Kai had to laugh. Others might misinterpret this banter as jealousy on Jordy's part. It couldn't be further from the truth. They had been friends forever. It wasn't like that between them. Not at all. Not that Jordy was unattractive or anything. Far fucking from it. He just didn't see her in that way and she didn't see him like that either. Their friendship worked. They were best buddies and it was as simple as that.

Jordy's arms tightened around him once again. "I think we should rut," she blurted. Her voice a mere whisper.

Kai froze. "Come again. I swear I'm going deaf."

"You heard me." Her dark chocolate eyes locked with his. Her face serious. "You can't go on like this. Let me help you."

He shook his head. "No fucking way." Kai looked around them, not liking it that so many others could listen in on their conversation. "Let's get out of here."

Jordy nodded. He kept her hand linked in his. For once, it felt weird. He often held her hand like this in busy places or put his arm around her. The gesture suddenly felt intimate.

They didn't talk, the whole way back to her room. He swallowed thickly as he crossed the threshold into her private space, closing the door behind them. Jordy turned to face him, she folded her arms. "Why won't you tell me what happened? You need to speak about this. I don't even know the first thing about those two days, but whatever it was, it's eating you up inside. You've always told me everything." A look of hurt crossed her face.

"I was with a female. Other than that, there's nothing much to tell." Kai took a step into her bedroom. "There really isn't." His answer was both the truth and a lie. It wasn't like much had happened, yet it left him changed. It left him stuck. Limbo was not a fun place to be. How did he even begin to explain it? There were things about his time with the dragon shifter that he didn't want anyone to know. He just wished for the hundredth time that he could move on.

Jordy shook her head. He could see that she was worried. "I overheard those things Jenson said to you earlier. He's right. I'll help you get over her." She pulled her dress over her head. Standing before him in just a tiny thong. So this was where this whole thing had come from. It wasn't just a coincidence. Jordy had overheard them earlier. As his best friend, she was worried about him. "Let me help you," she repeated, softer this time.

"Jordy, no," he growled.

"Listen to me." She took a step towards him, and like the pussy he was he took a step back.

Kai shook his head. "No damned way."

"Yes. You need to get over this female. You won't talk about it. You haven't had sex since you were last with her. Let me help you." She took another step towards him, her hands curled around his biceps. "We're best friends. You've been taking my blood. You've already seen me naked on plenty of occasions. What's sex between friends? It's one more little step. Most vampires rut. It's no big deal."

Kai had to smile. It was true. They had gone skinny dipping plenty of times. He'd walked in on her a couple of times while she was…busy and she'd done the same to him. "It might mess things up between us." It would fuck up what they had. No damned way would he allow that to happen.

She rolled her eyes. "Our friendship runs too deep for that to ever happen. We've known each other since we were kids. Who better than me to help you with this?"

His gaze dropped to her breasts. Perky with pink tipped nipples. He was ashamed to admit that, on occasion, he had thought about rutting his best friend. He was a male after all. He'd thought about what she would feel like. What she would taste like. It had been a very long time since he'd harbored such thoughts though. He didn't see Jordy like that. Not at all.

She made a noise of frustration. "Don't second-guess this. You need to rut. Don't be an idiot about it." She narrowed her eyes on him and then stepped out of the scrap of lace that covered her sex. He could scent her arousal.

"What the fuck is that?" He growled, sniffing the air.

She laughed. A rich throaty noise. Her laugh had always been catching. Only, he didn't feel like laughing right now. "We're best friends but I'm still a female and you're still a male. I get turned on every time you drink from me but it doesn't mean anything either. Let me touch you."

"Fuck," he growled. It had been too long. Way too long. They were friends. The best of friends. Both Jenson and Jordy were right. He did need to get over her. The dragon shifter. He grit his teeth for a half a second. Thank fuck his body didn't react. His cock could have its own damn mind at times. At least for once, they were on the same page. The only time the bastard seemed to get hard anymore was when he thought of a ravishing creature with an amethyst stare.

Jordy smiled at him. "We would go back to being straight up friends afterwards." She let her thong fall from her grip. "I swear."

"I don't know about this." He shook his head. It was all kinds of fucked up.

"Well it's a good thing that I am sure enough for the both of us." She undid his belt buckle.

---

The living room which was large and welcoming, it was also a gilded cage complete with a stunning view. Stars twinkled in the night sky. Mountains loomed in the backdrop, just as beautiful by night as what they were by day. "You can't make me stay." Her voice shook but she fought to control it. Her emotions were running high. It was the hormones. Her very rampant hormones.

Coal ran a hand over the dark buzz on his scalp. It was shorter than what was considered fashionable. Gave him a dangerous look. It suited him straight down the line. "Our brother tasked me with ensuring your safety. That means you are staying right here where I can see you." His eyes were black. Pitch black. Their mother had named him well. He was the second born and therefore second in line to the throne. He was even more arrogant than Blaze and that was saying something.

He took a long, elegant stride towards her, putting a hand on the back of one of the couches. "Blaze has made up his mind. You, attending the meeting won't change anything." Coal pulled himself upright and took another step towards her. His eyes locked with hers. "He's worried about you. We all are." He glanced down at her belly.

Ruby allowed her hand to trace its curve. Her eyes fell shut as she said a silent prayer. Everything would be okay. She had to believe that. To believe anything else was not an option. Her stomach churned with worry. Bile burned in her throat so she swallowed it down. What would her vampire say?

She squeezed her eyes even tighter. Not hers. He was the father of this baby and that's where it ended. Blaze was crazy. Her brother was on a mission but there was no way he could succeed. Or could he? Hope unfurled inside her. No! It would cause her more heartache to even allow herself to think it. Her place was here with her own kind.

"I have to go. Please, Coal." She grabbed ahold of his hand, feeling the hard metal of the ring against her own finger. Golden with an emerald, encrusted in diamonds.

Coal allowed her touch for a few seconds before pulling away. "Stop this." His voice had become rough like sandpaper. "You're acting like a child. This behavior has got to stop."

"No! I'm acting like an adult. Just because I refuse to have my life dictated to me does not make me a child." She had to work to keep her voice even. "Blaze has gone to discuss me. This baby…" Frustration ate at her. "It's my life and my future. I should be there."

"You continue to refuse to obey your king. If it were me, I would've punished you."

"Just because I refuse to allow myself to be handed to the highest bidder." She made a noise of frustration. "To spend my life like a battery hen."

Coal frowned. "Speak plainly. What the hell is a battery hen?"

Ruby had researched humans any opportunity she could find. She knew mating with humans was their species' only hope. She'd always imagined herself mated to one. Funny how life had a way of changing direction when you least expected it. She knew nothing about vampires. "Some humans keep chickens in confined spaces. Tiny cages that are not much bigger than the hens themselves. They are expected to lay eggs, day after day. They have no life. No future. No other task in life save but to lay eggs. They live a terrible, lonely, sad—"

"Always so damned over dramatic." Coal shook his head. He ran a hand over the light dusting of black hair on his scalp. His dark eyes seemed to darken further. Behind him, the crescent moon hung low in the sky. "You would be nothing like one of those"—he waved his hand about— "hens. You are a royal princess and could've been a queen. Mother to the future of our people. Now you are nothing. So selfish and irresponsible."

"I sacrificed for the good of our people. None of you would listen. Our kind is a dying breed. There is no way I could've saved us. I'm one female. Don't you see that?"

He shook his head, looking disappointed. "You did what you wanted without thinking of anyone else."

She ignored his jibe. "I can only hope Blaze does the right thing. That he takes a human female. That he allows all of you to take human females as mates. It is the only way."

"No! It would be despicable to dilute our royal blood with that of the humans. It would be wrong to allow any of our dragons to lower themselves. Humans…pah!" He said the word like it disgusted him. Coal was the only male that had never been on a stag run. He refused. "Our king will take one of the lesser dragon females." He looked smug. "As will I."

"No," she gasped. This was not something she had thought would happen. There were only two fertile females besides herself. Both were members of the Earth tribe. Tensions had always run high between the Fire and Earth tribes. Blaze and their king, Granite, did not get along. It would be a cold day in hell before the Earth king allowed any of the females in his tribe to mate Blaze. It would further strengthen the Fire tribe and, in so doing, would weaken the standing of the other tribes. There was no way the male would submit. "But that would mean," she whispered.

Coals jaw tightened. "You brought this upon our people. This was your doing yours alone."

"It was never my intention. Why can't he just take a human? It would be so much simpler." She blurted. "It's inevitable that the other tribes will—"

"We would crush them if they tried." Coal made a low gravelly noise from somewhere deep in his throat. "I don't want to hear anymore of it and neither does Blaze. We will request the hand of one of the two lesser Earth females. There is always the small chance that the one he chooses of them will be able to supply Blaze with a royal heir. If Granite refuses we will go to war against them."

What had she done?

Why were they so damned stubborn?

What did Blaze have against the humans? With Coal it was a case of feeling superior to them. Not wanting to lower himself and dilute his royal blood. Such short sighted thinking. Blaze had more sense though. At least, she had thought he did.

Ruby should've known that Blaze would not be swayed so easily. A soft knock at the door brought her out of her reverie.

Coal looked irritated at the intrusion for a few seconds before schooling his expressions. "Enter."

Scarlet dropped in a light curtsy before her brother. The female completely ignored Ruby. The two females of the Fire castle pretended she didn't exist. She was out of favor with the king. Pregnant with a vampire child. No longer a potential queen or a potential anything. Not worth their time or effort. Most of the males were still respectful if not kind towards her. It was like they understood what she was trying to achieve. No one had ever openly declared their wishes to take human mates but she knew this was a secret hope amongst the males.

It was a lonely, sad existence. To only feel the warmth of another twice a year and then only in the physical sense. It wasn't right. Most of the males would never be fathers. Not if they carried on along the current path.

"I'm glad you came." Coal said, rubbing a finger along her jaw.

Scarlet giggled. She looked up at Coal from under her lashes. The female would like nothing more than to sink her claws into her brother. Ruby turned away from the pair, not wanting to hear the flirtatious remarks bouncing between the two of them. The dragon shifter, lesser females were spoiled rotten. They were treated like gold and could have their pick of the males. As a result, they weren't very nice, which was putting it rather mildly.

She needed to go. Ruby desperately needed to see…the vampire…the father of her child. She needed to speak with him. To explain. There was a good chance he would hate her for what she had done to him. Ruby couldn't blame him but she still needed to try. She wasn't foolish enough to envision a future where the two of them were together. She didn't even know the male.

Maybe he wasn't even as handsome as what she had imagined him to be or as sweet or as kind or gentle. Maybe he wasn't such a deft lover, with incredible hands and an even more incredible…Ruby felt heat climb up her neck and spillover onto her cheeks. She needed to stop this train of thought. Needed to stop imagining what his lips had felt like on hers. The male would hate her when he found out. Of that there was no doubt in her mind. She only hoped that she could somehow make him understand why. Maybe there could at least be a future where her child got to know his father. Maybe that wasn't too much to hope.

Ruby wasn't foolish enough to believe that any of the vampire healers would be able to help her. She pushed it from her mind. Stay positive. Breathe. Even if it only ended up being the two of them, her and the baby, they would be just fine.

Scarlet giggled again. "Come with me," she murmured.

"I'm busy right now. Babysitting duties. I thought you might like to keep us company. To keep me company." She felt sorry for Coal. Having to settle for a female like Scarlet. She'd only met a few humans at the bar that day and would not be so naïve as to judge them based on that single interaction. The males loved the stag run. They spoke fondly of human females. It wasn't just about rutting. There was a general affection for the species. If only Blaze would listen.

Ruby checked the balcony door. To her surprise, the key was in the lock. If she had been on babysitting duties, the first thing she would have done would have been to remove all exit routes.

Blaze was in vampire territory. He was about to drop a serious bomb. She needed to be there for the aftermath. It was not a particularly long journey, nor a particularly difficult one. There were risks attached but this was something she needed to do. Maybe a little exercise was just what she needed to enable the release. Two weeks overdue. No one had ever been two weeks overdue but then again, a dragon shifter had never been pregnant with a vampire child before either.

Ruby snuck a look at the couple. Scarlet kept her hand clasped around one of Coal's biceps while the other roved his broad chest. They were deep in conversation. Ruby shook her head. *Thank you Scarlet,* who would've ever thought the female would've helped her out. Scarlet was tall with fiery red head of hair. Right now she was telling Coal in minute detail what she planned on doing to him later. Her brother was lapping it up.

Keeping her chin up and her back straight, she walked to the balcony door. Not moving too quickly, she kept her movements casual. She winced at the light clicking noise the lock made as she unlocked it. Thankfully there was not a breath of wind. The door opened noiselessly. Without turning back, Ruby pulled herself onto the ledge of the balcony and fell into the dark chasm. There was the familiar popping and cracking as her body morphed into that of a strong and powerful dragon. Her clothing ripped and fell from her quickly expanding body. She was smaller and leaner than Coal. That made her infinitely faster. *Catch me if you can, brother.*

If she'd still been in a human form, she would've had a smile a mile wide. She felt light and free. Her little one tucked safely, deep down in her large belly, behind hard, impenetrable scales.

Her wings beat furiously as she quickly ate up the distance between the high peak that was her home and her destination, the vampire territory.

# EIGHT

It was only when she lowered his zipper that it really dawned on him that Jordy meant to rut with him. Like, climb onto his cock and ride him. There was nothing unusual about friends rutting with one another. In fact, they were the odd ones out for not having done it sooner. It didn't feel right though. Make that, it felt distinctly wrong. Their relationship wasn't like that. Besides, he didn't want a random fuck. Not even with his best friend. He wanted the dragon shifter. *Her.*

Nuts.

Crazy.

Not going to happen.

"Stop, Jords." He held his pants together, preventing her from pulling them off of him. She tried to swat his hand away. "I mean it, Jords. You can't do this. I value our friendship."

"So do I and that's why you need to shut the hell up." She continued to tug on his pants, trying to get them down. "You won't regret this. I promise."

"We haven't done anything yet and I already regret it, Jordan." He growled her name.

"Look." She huffed. "Suit yourself. You know where to find me if—"

Just then there was a loud knock at the door. The person didn't wait but walked right on in like they owned the fucking place.

The male's eyes widened. "Oh shit." It was one of the royal guards. Kai couldn't remember his name just then. If it had been any other male he would have punched them. A royal guard? What the hell? The male spent the next few beats eyeballing Jordan's naked body. By the look on his face, Kai could see that he liked what he saw. Little prick!

"What do you want?" Kai growled as he pulled his zipper back up.

"Um...shit." The male finally had the good grace to tear his gaze away from Jordan so that he could lock eyes with Kai.

Jordan didn't seem too fazed by the whole thing. She casually picked up her dress and then pulled it over her head.

How dare the little fuck just walk in like that? It had to be something important. "Why are you here?" He worked to keep the growl from his voice and failed.

The guard cleared his throat. "Your presence is requested in the Royal Suite. Right fucking now." It was like the male had suddenly remembered why he was there.

*What the fuck!*

"What's wrong?" He could hear the worry in his own voice. "What's going on?" He couldn't think of a single reason why he would be summoned to the royal chamber...

It couldn't be good though. He'd never been summoned there before.

Shit!

The guard smirked. "It's that female you messed around with in Sweetwater. The one…"

Shit!

Kai couldn't help it, he closed the distance between himself and the male and gripped him by his vest. The leather didn't offer much purchase. "What about her?" He all out growled.

The male's expression hardened. His jaw clenched. "I'm not at liberty to say." He grit out. "Come with me and you'll find out soon enough."

"What did you do?" Jordy gripped him by the arm. "What happened with that female? What are you hiding?"

Trying to keep his expression passive, Kai turned to her. "It's going to be okay." He could only hope. If this was about the dragon shifter, he was in a world of trouble. Maybe it was some human female claiming to be pregnant by a vampire. It would be normal to assume that he was the culprit. It might not be her at all. Yet, he couldn't help but to wish that it was about her because if that were true, then maybe he would get to see her again.

He was fucked in the head.

Kai followed the Royal guard. Remaining close on the male's heel. They moved quickly through the castle.

"All I can say"—the guard glanced back at him from over his shoulder— "is that I'm glad I'm not you. You poor fucking bastard." Kai could make out his chuckle as he leapt up the stairs four at a time.

Taken aback, he sucked in a deep breath and followed the guard. He was oddly disappointed when they stepped into the Royal chamber. Of the female with the amethyst eyes, there was no sign.

Brant looked pissed though.

Oh fuck! By the tic in Zane's jaw he could see the male was pissed as well. Beyond fucking pissed. He'd never seen Zane so rattled.

"Why the fuck didn't you tell us?" Brant growled. An all out, spine tingling, sweat inducing growl. It wasn't the animalistic noise that had his blood running cold but the scent that came off of the other two males in the room.

Both strangers. Both scented of smoke. It was a subtle edge. One he had scented before. On her. The dragon shifter.

Both males looked at him like he was a piece of filth. The nearest male's lip curled away from his teeth in a silent snarl directed at him. "A lesser. She didn't even have the good grace to pick a royal vampire. What possessed her?" They spoke funny, like they weren't from this century.

"Hold your damned tongue," the taller of the two said. The male next to him bit back what he was about to say.

"Did you know the female you spent time with was a dragon shifter?" Zane asked. His king sounded altogether too calm for his liking, especially considering the male was anything but.

Kai nodded. "Yes." He'd barely gotten the word out when a fist connected with his jaw. Kai heard a crack. Pain blossomed as his head was whipped back. He had to take a step back to stay on his feet.

Zane moved back into place. His eyes stayed on Kai. They were filled with that same disappointment as before. Only this time, there was a good dose of anger reflected in their depths as well. Kai massaged his fractured jaw. Although he could feel it swelling, he could also feel it healing.

Brant folded his arms across his chest. His white dress shirt pulled tight. His tie was still on, although loose around his neck. The sleeves rolled up to his elbows. "I guess you didn't think it was important to mention the female you messed with was a dragon shifter."

Kai didn't say anything. The tension in the air was thick. Although there were plenty of seats, everyone remained on their feet. Of the queen and the royal heir, there was no sign.

"Why didn't you tell us?" Zane asked, his voice barely audible. It came out sounding deadly anyway.

Kai forced himself to remain still. To hold his king's intense gaze. "I didn't think anyone would believe me." His jaw throbbed but he tried to ignore the pain. "I…wanted to…protect her…I guess." He didn't really understand his reasoning himself.

"How noble." The closest of the shifters sneered. "For a lesser…"

"I wouldn't expect you to understand." Kai narrowed his eyes at the male who growled deep in his throat. It was a soft, menacing sound.

"These two males are her brothers. The male over there…" Brant casually flicked a finger in the direction of the taller of the two males. He wore loose fitting, cotton pants and nothing else. No shoes. Bare-chested. "Is the king of his tribe. You know how to fucking pick them. Don't you?"

The male's hair was shaggy and dark. Same color as his sister. *As her.* It was an unruly mess. His eyes were a vivid green. Unlike anything he'd ever seen before. Just like with the female dragon shifter, they reminded him of sparkling jewels.

That's when Kai realized what Brant had said. *The king.* He was also her brother which made her...a princess. He'd fucked around with a dragon shifter princess. Wait a minute. If she was a princess, why him? Why had a female such as her picked and seduced him?

"Does this male have nothing to say for himself?" The other dragon shifter bit out between clenched teeth. "He defiled Ruby and slighted our kind. At the very least, we deserve an apology. This male needs to get on his knees."

Ruby.

Her name was Ruby.

Brant cleared his throat, his stare directed at the smaller of the two shifters. "Thank you..." His eyes widened for a second. "Inferno. Did I pronounce that correctly?"

The male gave a quick jerk of the head as confirmation. His hair was just as big of an unruly mess as his brother's but his eyes were that same brilliant amethyst color as Ruby's. Although, they didn't hold the same warmth, the same passion as the female he remembered. On this male, Inferno...what a fucking pussy name...the brilliant purple looked cold and deadly. Then again, he couldn't really blame the male. Spending time, as he had done, with a dragon shifter female was obviously frowned upon. Too fucking bad. It had happened. He wasn't going to apologize for it.

"Good." Brant nodded his head. "It has been brought to our attention that—"

"I can speak for myself." The dragon shifter king stepped forward. "I'm Blaze." His eyes were firmly on Kai. He said his name because he felt Kai should know it, not as a cordial introduction. The male pursed his lips for a moment as if trying to calm himself. "I'm not sure exactly what went down. How you ended up with my sister but I'm pretty sure she blindsided you."

What the fuck? Why would he say a thing like that?

"You wouldn't have had too much choice in the matter. Although I would love nothing better than to make you kneel before me and to take your life."

*Nice guy.*

Zane growled low in his throat. The tendons around his neck bulged. "Touch him and you will regret it."

"He would deserve everything he got." Brant narrowed his eyes at Kai. "Every single fucking thing. I'm not starting a war over this lying son of a bitch. You would be welcome to kill him." The male glanced at Blaze. Another pussy name.

"Touch him and you die," Zane growled. "We will talk about this later." He added, glancing at Brant.

Blaze, held up both his hands. "No one is killing anyone and there will be no war. At least, not if my one condition is met."

Zane ground his teeth so loudly they could be heard gnashing together. "I could not command such a thing. It would be up to Kai to decide." The shifter had obviously already divulged what the condition was. Zane didn't like it. Kai had a feeling he wasn't going to like it much either.

"Bullshit," Brant snarled. "I will command it then. He fucked around and needs to pay the price. I think the dragon shifters are not being unreasonable."

"You'll command no such thing," Zane snarled right back. Although the suite was large and airy with a living area, a separate dining area as well as an open plan kitchen, it was starting to feel cramped and stifling.

"The choice would be simple." The dragon shifter king's eyes shone with determination. "I know that you will have had very little choice in the matter. Ruby can be…persuasive, at the best of times. Also, a vampire is no match for a dragon shifter. I have taken this into consideration."

Kai could see how Brant bristled but Zane put a hand to the other male's chest, silencing whatever it was he planned on saying.

Kai felt irritation rise up in him. He didn't like the way this male talked about his own sister. The things he was insinuating. He found he didn't give a fuck what the dickhead shifter thought about him but it was just plain wrong to talk about Ruby like that. "I'm a strong male in my prime. A warrior. I didn't need to be coerced, persuaded or physically bettered in any way. Ruby is a beautiful female, I wanted to be with her." She may have kidnapped him but it was true.

"That's settled then. You were an active participant. You therefore need to accept your fate with honor." The shifter king smiled. There was not an ounce of humor in the gesture. "My ultimatum is that you mate her or I will kill you by my own hand."

*What the fuck!*

Mate her? This was a whole other story. Sure, Kai was excited as fuck about the prospect of seeing her again. Spending some time with her. Maybe just maybe there would be something there…but to outright mate the female. No fucking way. Then he pictured the female. Their explosive coming together. Like an orgasmic whirlwind. Maybe mating the female would not be such a bad thing after all. That type of compatibility didn't happen often. If she was the sweet, soft female he believed her to be…maybe. They would need time. It wouldn't need to be very long.

"You will," the male snarled. It was then that he realized he was shaking his head.

"It is something we can discuss," Zane said. His demeanor was calm and casual, like he wasn't talking about Kai's whole life. His future.

Mother fucker.

What the hell.

He was surprised the Dragon shifters didn't have shotguns slung across their backs. Make that double barrels, aimed at his ass. If the situation wasn't so fucked up he would've laughed at the visual.

"There is nothing to discuss." Blaze cocked his head, his gaze on Kai. "You will mate my sister and that is the end of it."

"There is one term I wish—" Whatever Zane was about to say was cut short by a loud commotion outside. There was yelling, snarling, followed by more shouting.

"What the fuck?" Brant's sentiments matched his own.

By the time Zane was at the window looking out. The noises had dulled and by the way Zane released the blind, there was nothing to see.

The dragon shifter king cursed under his breath.

"That isn't what I think it is." Inferno growled, his eyes on his brother. He too cursed. "Is it?"

Blaze shook his head, running a hand through his hair in what looked like frustration. "Why couldn't she leave it alone? I wish she would listen to me...just for once."

The commotion from earlier reared up again. Only, this time, the noises came from the stairs that led to the Royal Suite.

Blaze paced to the other side of the room and then back again.

Kai's heart felt like it was about to beat out of his chest.

"Unhand me." It was her. Ruby. The dragon shifter. *Her.* "I can walk. I'm not some invalid. You don't need to touch me," she snarled.

There was a loud sounding crack. "Oww!" A male growled. "Female, you need to stop hitting me." His voice held a pleading edge that made Kai want to smile. Ruby was one hell of a female.

"Don't touch me again." She said, just as she walked through the double doors leading to the chamber. Her eyes shone with defiance. Her chin was tilted up. Her shoulders were back. She was naked and magnificent and pregnant.

Fucking pregnant.

Fuck.

"Ruby." The dragon shifter King sounded bored.

"Blaze." Ruby tilted her chin even higher, looking down her nose at her brother, through long lashes.

Brant's eyes widened and he diverted his gaze. Zane did the same. The two royal guards turned their gazes to the ceiling.

Good.

They were right to look away, at least, they were if they valued their eyes.

Where had that come from? She wasn't his female. He felt actual relief when the males kept their gazes elsewhere. Although vampires were far from being prudes, they didn't walk around stark naked. Shifters seemed to hold no such reservations.

Kai could feel his mouth hung open. That his eyes were wide in his skull. Fucking pregnant. Her belly looked tight, it was neat yet well-rounded. His child. His. Fuck.

"No." He growled. "It can't be." Another loud growl was torn from him. It had to be a mistake.

Brant slung his dress shirt over her shoulders, which Ruby accepted with a small nod of the head. She worked her hands through the sleeves, quickly doing up two or three of the buttons, to secure the garment, which fell high on her thighs.

The younger looking shifter gave a haughty laugh. "What, are you such a damned idiot that you can't recognize a female in the middle of her heat?" Inferno scoffed. "Then again, you are a lesser male and a vampire at that. So maybe it's not so surprising. Idiot."

"Fuck you." Kai pointed a finger at the dickhead shifter. "I was told that…never fucking mind." He snarled. For some reason, he still couldn't dump this female in the shit. Blame it all on her. He couldn't. If it made him an idiot. A fool, then so be it. The thing that got him the most was that the shifter male was right.

"Everyone needs to calm the fuck down," Zane said. "You need to calm down." He looked directly at Kai. "We need to be calm and rational about this. What's done is done. It cannot be undone."

"That's for fucking sure," Brant muttered.

Calm down.

Now.

Like fucking hell.

"There is nothing to talk about." Those vivid green eyes locked with his. "You will mate my sister or you will die by my own hand. Choose. Now." The male had similar golden tattoos across his chest. They seemed to shimmer and brighten. Maybe it was just his imagination, but it was as if scales appeared beneath the ink. Maybe they were melded together with the ink. It was hard to tell. It wasn't his imagination though when the male's teeth elongated. When tendrils of white smoke drifted from his flared nostrils.

"Stop this," Ruby said. For the first time since arriving this evening, her voice was timid and unsure. "I resigned myself to doing this alone. You know that. I have no need of a male in my life."

Kai hated hearing her say that. If it were up to this female he would never have known about this. She didn't need or want him. The knowledge burned him.

"You should've thought of that before." Blaze snarled, taking a step towards his sister.

Call it instinct. Call it more of the same stupidity. Kai snarled right back at the shifter king, taking a step towards the male. King or not, his show of aggression towards Ruby, towards his unborn child, was unacceptable.

Ruby might not be his but the child she carried inside her belly most definitely was. Everything in him bristled. Every nerve ending, every muscle, every goddamned tendon. Everything readied itself to protect what was his. So this is what an angry dragon shifter looked like. Bring it on!

Zane instantly stepped between them. The male's hand felt heavy against his chest. "Everybody needs to calm down. Kai was not aware that the female was in heat. This has come as a shock to him. A shock to us all, I assure you. We need some time to digest this." He took a deep breath. "Kai is struggling to think clearly right now."

*Like fuck.*

He chewed on the inside of his cheek until he tasted blood. Zane went on. "They need to be granted an opportunity to discuss this. We need to be given some time to come to terms with this. We can discuss it further in the morning."

Blaze frowned. "We're not staying. This isn't some game. It's not a discussion. It's fucking simple. Either he mates with my sister or he dies." The male raised his brows.

"There is no way I will mate a female that lied to me." Kai shook his head. There were so many things on the tip of his tongue. Things he wanted to say to hurt her. She deserved to be hurt. Yet, he couldn't help but remember the sadness that had been in her eyes. It was still fucking there. The unshed tears that threatened to fall. The way she apologized to him with such sincerity. At the time, he believed it was because she had abducted him, but now he knew there was more to it. So much more.

"I'm sorry," she whispered. Those purple orbs focused solely on him. Once again they were filled with tears. For just a second it felt like they were the only people in the room. She pulled her bottom lip between her teeth. Kai wasn't falling for her vulnerable act. Not again.

He shook his head. "It's not good enough. You lied to me." He worked his jaw. Mistake. The throbbing started up again. Kai ignored it. "You lied about something so important. You stole from me." Then he turned and walked out. He didn't give two fucks. The Dragon shifters could come after him. They could fucking kill him for all he cared.

"Please give me a chance to explain." Her voice followed him as he fled down the stairs. No way. No fucking way.

# NINE

*The next morning...*

Ruby watched as Blaze paced. Up and down...and up and down. His feet sank into the woolen rug with every step. Dawn had long since come. Dragons were early risers. It seemed that vampires were not.

They were in one of the towers. It had numerous bedrooms, a living area, dining area and a station for preparing food. Although she wasn't sure why since meals had been brought to them.

"You should never have come. I can't believe you risked...yourself like that." He looked angry. His eyes shone. His muscles bulged and his jaw worked. Tension radiated off of him. This was the first time he had addressed her since last night.

"I'm fine. The young one is safer when I'm in dragon form. I was hoping to spur on my release."

His only answer was to growl before continuing with his pacing.

What looked like anger clouded his featured but Ruby knew better. It wasn't rage. It was worry. *Over her.* He treated her unborn child like he was nothing. Less than nothing. Making a face of disgust every time he spoke of his nephew, yet, she knew his fear was not just over her. It was also for the child. Her brother was greatly afraid. Though he would never admit it. Not even to himself.

That's what this was all about. This sudden urge to find the male responsible. To make him do the honorable thing. It was borne of his fear.

Two weeks late. No one had ever been so late before.

She touched a hand to her stomach and sucked in a deep breath, willing her racing heart to slow and her breathing to normalize. Everything was going to be fine. It had to be.

"Please stop this craziness. Let's go back to the kingdom of Fire." Her voice hitched from the emotion that coursed through her. Seeing him again. The big vampire male. So beautiful, kind and trusting. So sweet and yet fierce. He was a good male.

She hated the anguish and the pain that had rolled off of him. The anger that burned in his eyes. What she really wanted was a chance to explain.

"No." Blaze was resolute in his response. His stature stiff and unyielding. "He will do the honorable thing or he will die."

"He didn't even know I was in heat. I tricked him. I abducted him and held him against his will. It was all my doing and yet you're going to make him pay."

Blaze laughed. "Against his will." He made a noise of irritation. "Yes. The male must pay." A rough snarl. "He lay with you. Any male that lies with a female must understand the potential consequence and be ready to face up to his responsibilities. I can only hope that the vampire healers have some sort of explanation for your condition."

And there it was. The truth. The real reason why they were here. "I can speak to the healers." She held her breath a few beats, trying to rein in her emotion. "I'm sure they will be just as much in the dark as our own healers though. This is the first vampire/dragon pregnancy. Try and think logically about this. Let's just say that he agrees to becoming my mate, where would we live? I would not be happy or comfortable living amongst the vampires and I'm sure he would feel just as out of place on top of a mountain peak in the middle of nowhere. He would be surrounded by dragons. A lamb amongst the wolves."

"Then you would need to remain here."

"What?" A shudder raced through her. "And raise my dragon son amongst vampires?"

"We still don't know exactly what it is you carry. A bloodsucker? A fire breather? Neither? The child...if there even is a child...might not be strong enough to hold his own amongst our young." She heard his voice catch for the briefest split second. Most would've missed the subtle sign. Her health and that of the child affected him. *It did*.

"There will be a child and he will be strong." Ruby clutched her belly with both her hands.

"We don't know if..." Blaze didn't finish his sentence at the sound of others approaching. "We'll talk about this later. You need to know that I haven't changed my mind."

Arghh! He could be infuriating. There was no time to think on it because there was a knock at the door.

"Enter," Blaze said.

The door opened and the vampire kings filed in along with several of their guard. Of her vampire male there was no sign.

"Good morning." It was the taller of the kings. He dressed strangely. In many different layers that looked stifling. There was a string knotted around his neck. Gold trinkets glinted on the edges of his sleeves. A bizarre ensemble. It didn't seem to serve any function that she knew of. The other king was dressed in leathers from head to toe. She could see how this might afford some protection. Both forms of dress still struck her as peculiar. Then again, the vampires didn't have to worry about undressing quickly or wearing garments that broke easily if one was unable to undress before shifting. For a shifter, the leathers might prove to be a tad…uncomfortable. The two species were so different.

"Morning." It was the more built of the two males. His head was closely shaven, reminding her of Coal. Her brother was going to be mad. Fire breathing mad. He must've been completely captivated by Scarlet because Ruby was long gone before he could have made any attempt to follow her. The male would never have caught her though, even if he had tried.

Blaze had the good grace to nod in response. Inferno just stood there, his hands folded behind his back.

"Where is the male?" Blaze locked his jaw.

The king wearing the leathers stepped forward. "We requested that Kai not attend this meeting."

Kai.

His name.

The father of her child. Kai. Disappointment rushed through her. Ruby had been hoping to see him.

"I told you." Blaze's eyes seemed to glow. His whole frame tensed. "This is not up for discussion. Either he mates Ruby or he dies."

The male in the leathers narrowed his eyes. "I understand your feelings about this."

"You couldn't possibly understand...you couldn't begin to understand." Blaze shook with anger.

"You're right." The vampire king paused. His jaw tight, his fists curled. "Kai still refuses to talk about those two days. Whether out of some misguided respect for the princess or fear of retribution...fuck..." He snarled. "For all I know he's afraid of being singled out as a pussy. It sounded like he didn't have much choice in the matter."

"He didn't but that doesn't change things." Blaze's stance softened somewhat.

"If he didn't have a choice then how can he be held liable for his actions?" The vampire king bristled.

"Easily. The detail is not important. That male impregnated my sister. He must do the honorable thing or I will be forced to take action."

The vampire king sucked in a deep breath through his nose. "You are right." He allowed his gaze to fall to his booted feet before locking once again with Blaze's. "You mentioned that the pregnancy might be in jeopardy."

Ruby couldn't help but to gasp. The males ignored her. Somehow, hearing it said out loud made it worse. More real perhaps. She squeezed her eyes shut for a half a second.

Blaze nodded. "It is not something that I wish to discuss in an open forum. It is part of the reason why we are here. That male needs to mate her and she needs to see your healers."

"There is nothing that can be done." There was a tremble to her voice. It irritated her. "You know that."

"We know nothing," Blaze grit out. "This is not a dragon child."

"He is part dragon." She stood taller, looking Blaze in the eyes.

Her brother cocked his head. "And part vampire." There was a rough edge to his voice that warned her to stay out of it. To remain silent.

"We do not need to discuss the details." The king in leathers spoke up. "You wish for Kai to mate with this female because she is with child. His child, yet, the pregnancy is in jeopardy. You have my word that we will do whatever it takes to ensure Princess Ruby is well looked after. That our best healers assess her condition immediately. When the child is born, safe and healthy, Kai will mate with this female. Not a moment sooner. Can we agree to those terms?"

"Kai doesn't want to be with me." His name rolled off of her tongue. It's was a beautiful name and suited him perfectly. She licked her lips. "It's wrong to force him. To force us." She knew arguing was fruitless but had to try anyway. She'd gotten the vampire into this mess.

"You should've thought about that before you lay with him." Blaze's words cut her because they were true.

"You left me with no other option." Another hard truth. She thought she had been doing the right thing. Not just for herself or for her child but for the good the kingdom. All four kingdoms. Right now, she wasn't so sure. What if she had been wrong?

She felt tears and blinked them away.

Blaze's eyes smoldered. Their heat aimed solely on her. "I gave you several choices."

"None of them were right for me." Her voice came out surprisingly strong.

"You will mate with that male or so help me."

Stress was not good for the baby. She felt tense. Her stomach was tight. Adrenaline surged within her veins. She needed to calm down and right now. For the good of the baby. For the good of her son…or daughter. There was a small chance.

"Please think about it." It was the strangely dressed taller king that spoke. His stare was locked on her brother. "Princess Ruby can remain with us. Free to go at any time of course."

Her younger brother laughed. "As if you could keep her here against her will." Inferno shook his head.

The vampire king with the close cropped hair worked his jaw. "Once the child is safely born, Kai will mate with the princess. I will ensure personally, that he acts with honor. That is, if the princess wishes it. I will not force her to accept him."

How sweet. It seemed vampires weren't the blood drinking monsters they had been made out to be. It was quite possible they were more civilized than the dragon shifters. Certainly more civilized than the royals of her species. Ruby pulled in a deep breath. Kai didn't want her. She'd never even entertained the possibility of them being together and therefore she had never envisioned a future with him in it.

This was not the time to discuss such things, she'd already said too much. At best, this would give her an opportunity to explain things to Kai. At worst, it would buy them some time to try and think of a way out of this mess. That is, if Kai would even talk to her.

Blaze ground his teeth. "Let me think on it."

Unexpected.

Maybe he would concede after all. Probably not.

"Take as long as you wish." The king in the leather outfit nodded once. "You are welcome to stay as long as you like." Then he turned and walked out.

"Yeah." The strangely dressed king picked some lint off of his clothing. "Give it some thought. Let one of the guards know when you are ready to discuss this further. Let us know if you have any further requirements."

"A willing female perhaps." Inferno's brows were raised. He hadn't just said that.

"Ignore him…" Blaze gave their idiot younger brother a dirty look. "We don't need anything." He said the last in such a way that sounded like a dismissal.

She couldn't blame Inferno. The dragon males were starved of female company.

# TEN

Kai felt like he was climbing the fucking walls. He hated that his kings were debating his future without him. Possibly the future of his unborn child.

Ruby.

Just thinking of the female angered him and saddened him in equal measure. Why had she done this? What had possessed her? She didn't seem cruel or evil. She didn't come across as selfish. Ruby. With the amethyst eyes and cherry lips. Hair as dark as the night. His cock sat up and paid attention just thinking of her. It irritated the fucking hell out of him that he could still become aroused at the thought of this female, even after all she had done to him.

He clenched his teeth, forcing himself to remain calm. To wait in silence, even though he felt like tearing the paintings from the walls, breaking every bit of furniture in this room. He felt like running away. None of it would do any good, so he allowed himself to fall onto a nearby couch. He raked his fingers through his hair, squeezed the back of his neck, and signed loudly.

The only thing Zane had told him was to stay put and not to talk to anybody about this. His king had also tried to find out more about what had happened during those two days. Had the dragon shifter forced him? Had she lied to him? Zane had said that he needed to know.

For whatever reason, Kai didn't want to tell the male anything. His word was his word and he would stand by it even though the female had lied to him. It didn't sit right with him that her own brothers spoke of her with such disrespect. That she didn't seem to have a voice of her own. Despite all that had happened, he couldn't bring himself to tell Zane that he had been abducted and that this was, technically, none of his fault. The truth was, that it didn't matter. The child she carried was his. What was done was done.

Jordy had been to his room twice. She'd knocked on the door and insisted he let her in. Thank fuck for locks because she'd tried to let herself in on both occasions and had beat the hell out of his door. He couldn't blame her, she was worried about him. This was the first time he had left her in the dark. They normally confided in each other about everything.

With a flick of the wrist, he glanced at his watch for what felt like the hundredth time since Zane had left. Half an hour had passed. May as well have been an eternity.

When the knock at the door sounded, he leapt to his feet. The knock was different to that of Jordy's. Two soft taps verses her much harder ones. He stood rooted to the spot, his eyes glued to the door.

Fuck.

Kai didn't want to mate this female. Fuck that! He also didn't want to die over her. Ruby. The mother of his child. Jesus this was one hell of a fucked up situation. One he never thought he would find himself in. How could he have been so stupid, so idiotic. He bought all of the bullshit hook, line and sinker. Those big innocent eyes. The way her lip quivered. The way she felt in his arms. All a lie.

There was another soft tap. It definitely wasn't Jordy, by now she would've knocked harder and called out to him to let her in.

"Who is it?" He knew he sounded like a pussy but he didn't give a fuck. He needed answers and didn't want to have to explain anything to anyone. Besides, Zane had told him to keep his mouth shut. He planned on doing just that.

"It's me." He could recognize that deep throaty voice anywhere. His king. Once he opened that door, his future would be spelled out for him. Kai didn't like it.

He turned the key and opened the door. Shit, Zane looked worried. Agitated was a better description. His eyes flashed from left to right. "Let me in," he growled.

Of course. "Oh, right." Kai stepped to the side, closing and locking the door behind Zane. When his king gave the lock a pointed look, Kai added, "So that we're not disturbed."

Zane gave a tight nod and walked through into the living area. He didn't sit down. "You fucked up."

Way to go for stating the obvious. Kai grit his teeth to prevent himself from saying anything. He gave his king a tight nod.

"I can't believe you fucked around with a dragon shifter." Zane made a noise that belied his irritation.

Once again Kai remained silent, he kept his gaze firmly on his king.

"A princess," he choked out between clenched teeth. "You are lucky they have been reasonable about the whole thing."

"You call that reasonable?" He blurted.

"You're alive so, yeah, I would call that reasonable. I put forward an ultimatum of our own. I'm not sure whether the shifters will accept it or not but it's looking promising."

"What kind of ultimatum?" It came out sounding gruffer than he intended.

Zane narrowed his eyes. "We weren't left with much of a choice. That male plans on killing you if you do not honor his sister and I fully believe he intends on following through with his threats. I know this has come as a huge shock. It is easy to see that you didn't have a clue about her being in heat. You were blindsided and fucked over."

"I didn't know." Kai shook his head, not willing to say anything more on the subject.

Zane nodded his head. "Well…" He sighed. "She was and now she's pregnant. I can understand how that must make you feel and how you must hate the thought of having to mate a female that would lie to you like that but we're left with very little choice."

"Fuck that." He growled. Anger coursed through him. There was nothing she could say to him. Nothing she could do to make this up to him. She'd used him for his seed. If it was up to her, he would never have known about being father. That was just plain wrong.

"Look, I don't know anything about dragon shifter pregnancies. Not a damned thing. We have asked that she remain here while—"

"Not a fuck." Kai scrubbed a hand over his face. This was such a messed up situation. She was pregnant with his child. His baby. "Yeah…" He sighed loudly.

"Maybe that would be for the best. I don't know…fuck! I have no idea what to make of this. I don't want to have to see her day after day yet she is the mother of my baby." He clenched his jaw for a second. "She should stay."

Zane gripped his shoulder and squeezed. "You need to keep it together. We don't know a fucking thing about this species. It's a dangerous situation. We need to tread carefully." He paused. "Her brother mentioned something about there being a problem with her pregnancy. I'm not sure exactly…"

He didn't hear anything else that his king said. There was the sound of blood roaring in his ears as his heart pounded. Sweat trickled from his brow.

Problem.

There was a problem with her pregnancy. Up until recently he didn't even know about this child. The thought of becoming a father was a new concept to him. He was struggling to come to terms with it. To accept it. He felt angry and betrayed. So confused he didn't know if he was coming or fucking going, yet hearing that there were problems with her pregnancy caused panic to well up in him.

"What the fuck is wrong?" He grabbed Zane by the biceps. "What did they tell you? What do you know about it?"

"Calm the fuck down."

Kai released Zane. He walked to the door and glanced back. "I can't. Where is she? I need to see her."

"You can't," Zane growled. "Not right now. Her brother is still deciding on my ultimatum. I don't want you walking in there all gung ho and fucking this up. I don't know exactly what the problem is. He didn't want to give specifics but I could see that he is worried."

Kai cursed loudly. He turned to face Zane, then scrubbed a hand over his face. He was breathing far too quickly. Shit! No wonder she looked so upset, so fucking vulnerable. It's what had drawn him to her in the first place. A female that needed rescuing. He had been so sure that's what she was and yet, he'd also been terribly wrong about her.

"I've asked that she remain here. That our healers see to her. You don't have to mate her unless she births a healthy child. It would be all kinds of fucked up if you were forced to mate with her and the pregnancy…"

Kai snarled. He couldn't bear to hear what his king had to say. "Don't say it. With all due respect my king don't you dare fucking say it." His chest heaved. He tried to look away, to look down, to submit in some way but found he couldn't tear his gaze from Zane's.

His king's eyes darkened up, his jaw tightened. "I'm going to let that slide. Just this fucking once. I bought us some time. If the male refuses…then my hands are fucking tied. Do you understand me? These dragon fucks are strong. We know fuck all about them. We need to stay on good terms with them. That might mean you have to mate this female."

It took everything in him to nod. He understood but that didn't mean he agreed. He didn't know if he had it in him to take the female as a mate. But to die at the hands of the dragon shifter king, to never know his unborn child…he didn't know if he could do that either.

"She might be the mother of my child." His voice was thick with emotion. "But, I'm not sure I can ever mate with her."

"Speak with her. Maybe you could find it within yourself to understand. With dickhead brothers like that, her life can't have been easy." Zane gave him a ghost of a smile.

Ruby had spoken about being with him, being in that shithole bar the first place was an act of rebellion. He couldn't remember her exact words, only that it was something along those lines. It was no excuse for her actions. "I need to see her." He put up a hand when Zane tried to talk. "Please just let me know as soon as it's possible. I need to know exactly what the hell is going on. I don't foresee a future with this female but she is carrying my child." His voice broke. Mother fuck, he hated feeling this confused and out of control. Hated it.

Blaze and Inferno walked ahead of her. They were in a large open area behind the castle. They kept walking until they were a distance away. The vampire guards that had been assigned to watch them, trailed behind. Inferno snarled in their direction. Smoke drifted, almost lazily, from his nose and mouth. His hands were curled, resembling the claws they could so easily become. The vampire males moved away at the outburst. Inferno snarled a second time and they retreated further, giving them privacy.

"Where are you going?" Ruby continued to follow behind Blaze. They kept going until they hit the tree line. It was still day. It was dangerous to travel when the sun was high. Surely they didn't plan on leaving now? Blaze quickly stepped out of his pants.

No.

He turned to face her. Naked as the day he was born. It wasn't his state of undress that rattled her but rather what it signified. He was about to shift. He was leaving. "You've got one month to convince the male to mate you."

Ruby gasped. "What? No! Don't do this." She grabbed his arm. "Please don't...you can't do this."

"I didn't do a god damned thing. You did. You brought this on yourself."

Inferno removed his pants as well. "You managed to seduce him once, I'm sure you can do it again." Her younger brother could be such an arrogant ass. He smirked at her. "You had better, if you want him to live."

"One month." Blaze held up a finger. "I think it is reasonable. If you are unmated when I return, I will be forced to take matters into my own hands. Do you think I want to kill the father of this child?"

Ruby didn't know what to think. Blaze was a lot of things, but he wasn't a ruthless killer. She shook her head.

He sighed. "Try and work things out with this male. Go and see the vampire healers."

"I will," she all but whispered. Kai would never forgive her and she couldn't blame him. She had no right to ask him to. "I don't think that there is anything the vampire healers can do though. It's up to me now. I just need to stay strong and positive. I'm alone in this." Her voice cracked but she managed to somehow keep the tears from falling. Damn these hormones.

Blaze's jaw tightened and his Adam's apple bobbed as he swallowed thickly. He was worried about her. "Take care of yourself."

"I don't belong here," she whispered.

"You are carrying a vampire child. You are exactly where you belong."

"Don't force him to mate with me. I'll stay. I'll raise this child here. I'll do whatever you tell me to do, just don't force him. Please." She'd caused Kai enough trouble.

Blaze looked her in the eye for the longest time. She could feel her heart beating in her chest. "It is you who has forced him." With that, there was a cracking noise as he began to shift. Ruby quickly stepped back. For a second she was tempted to follow but she knew that defying him at this point would have dire consequences. This wasn't just about her anymore. There were other lives at stake. There were things Kai needed to know. She put a hand to her belly.

# ELEVEN

Ruby stared up into the sky, watching as her brothers became specks in the distance. Almost invisible to the naked eye. Invisible to humans. They would avoid any flight paths and stay high to keep from being seen.

The male moved in next to her. "They left," he said. Without having to look, she knew it was the king that wore the strange clothing. Ruby had heard him approach. She could scent him as well.

She nodded her head. "Yes."

"I take it that they have agreed to our terms?" He asked.

"Sort of."

"What does that mean? I'm Brant by the way." He held out his hand to her.

Ruby wasn't sure what to make of it. She'd read a multitude of novels and knew this was the human way of greeting. It seemed strange he would use it on her. Instead of questioning the male, she reached out and took his hand. They shook twice before he released her. "My brother has given me the space I need."

He nodded, looking satisfied. "You are welcome here. I will ensure you are assigned a room. Zane informed me Kai's eager to meet with you, to discuss the child and…" He let the sentence die.

Ruby nodded.

"Although the male is eager to see you, this child comes first, would you like to see the healers now?" Concern shone in his eyes.

Ruby shook her head. She really did believe that the healers couldn't help her. Either a female would make it through the releasing or she wouldn't. Either a child would be born or it wouldn't. Dragon healers had never been much help and she truly believed the same was true of the vampire healers. This child might be part vampire but it was most definitely a dragon shifter. She could feel it inside her. This pregnancy had progressed normally. Everything was as it should be. At least, mostly everything. "I would like to meet with Kai first." Her breath froze in her lungs at the prospect.

She couldn't wait to see him, to talk with him and yet, she was afraid. So much had changed. The way he had looked at her when he found out…Ruby rubbed a hand over her belly. *I'm here for you, baby. It's you and me.*

Brant nodded. "Follow me, I will take you to him." He removed a device from his pocket. It was a phone. The first one she had ever seen. She'd read about these devices. Dragons had no use for them. They did not possess the technology required to operate them. The male pushed a couple of the buttons and put the phone to his ear.

There was a grunted greeting from the other end.

"I am on my way. The princess is with me," Brant said.

"Good." A deep voice on the other side. "Kai is out of his mind with worry."

He was worried. For her. No, he had obviously been told about the possible problems with her pregnancy.

"We'll be there in five." The male beside her pressed a button on the device and pushed the phone back into his pocket.

"Is there anything we should know?" The male frowned down at her as they continued to walk.

"Like what?" Ruby wasn't sure what he meant. She frowned right back at him.

"Like…I don't know. You can obviously still shift. I take it you eat normal food." He was pulling a face. His expression spoke of confusion.

"Three meals a day, although"—she put a hand to her stomach—"a snack or two would be nice. I tend to get a bit hungrier…at the moment." She rubbed her belly.

"Have you felt him move yet?" His whole demeanor softened as he spoke of the child. There was a goofy grin on his face.

*What? Was he being serious?* The male was joking. "Of course not." She laughed. "That's silly. One thing though, dragons like meat. Lots of it. And we prefer it rare. As in still bleeding, if possible. Raw is fine or very lightly seared."

It was hilarious because the vampire male pulled a face and visibly paled. He was a blood drinker but the thought of eating bloody meat disgusted him. How strange.

"No problem. Is there anything you can't eat?"

She shook her head. "I'm not a big fan of eggs and eggplant. I don't eat any form of dairy."

"Egg and eggplant?" The male smiled. "You are a weird one...no offense, princess."

It felt good to be treated normally. Ruby laughed. "None taken." They walked into the castle. Vampires stared at her. All out stared. They stopped what they were doing and stared. Many of them sniffed at her. Their nostrils flared and confusion was written all over their faces. This was going to be fun.

"Um." Brant looked uncomfortable. He pushed a button on the wall next to the steel sliding doors. It looked like an elevator. At least she was sure it was one. The thing dinged and opened. Yup, definitely an elevator.

Brant put a hand to her back. "After you."

She peered into the small boxlike room. "I'm not sure…"

"You've never been in an elevator?" He frowned at her.

Ruby shook her head. So it was an elevator.

"You'll be fine. I promise."

"I can't go in there. What if I need to shift? I'll kill myself. No." She wrapped her arms around herself. "Dragons don't do small confined spaces. We wouldn't die but shifting in a small space is akin to torture. It might be dangerous…for the baby."

"No problem. Good to know." He was looking at her like she was crazy. "We'll take the stairs."

Once they were on the landing on the next floor, he turned to face her. The male rolled his eyes. "I'm can't believe I'm about to say this. Go easy on Kai. You kind of fucked him over with this whole thing. Tell him all of the information he needs to know. Be honest. Once you are done, I'll have the guards take you to our healers. When are you due?"

"Due? I'm not sure what you mean." She shook her head.

"When is the baby supposed to come?"

"The baby? No, not for a while yet." At least, she didn't think he…or she…would make an appearance just yet. She rubbed her belly. It had become a habit.

He seemed to relax. "Okay. This is Kai's room." Two guards stood on either side of the door. "If you need anything, have one of them call me. Zane and I..." The door opened and the other king emerged looking tense. Brant cleared his throat. "As I was saying, Zane and I have your best interests at heart."

"I also have Kai's best interests at heart." The leather clad male said. His voice deep and ominous. "I also need to think of him."

"Yes," she whispered. "Of course."

"This child is important." Brant looked down at her belly, he shifted from one foot to the other. "Relations between our species is important. I will be sure to keep in contact with all parties involved. If you have any concerns, call me."

Zane raised his brows. "What Brant is trying to say is that we don't want a war and I don't want to see Kai come to harm...we also want to see the child safely born, of course."

"Stop..." Kai stepped into the doorway. He filled it with his immense bulk. Even next to these two males. The kings of the species, he was formidable. Right now she found it laughable that she had ever believed him to be human. Even for a second. She had been desperate. Not thinking straight. Maybe she had simply believed what she needed to at the time.

Brant growled. He didn't like that a subordinate was telling him what to do. Typical behavior of an arrogant royal. It seemed that they were the same regardless of species. Zane put a hand to his chest. "Let's get out of here." His deep voice vibrated. "They need to talk."

After what felt like the longest time, Brant nodded.

---

Talk.

Understatement of the fucking century.

They needed to talk big fucking time.

It irritated him how gorgeous she looked. She was wearing leggings and a lose fitting top. Even her pregnant stomach appealed to him. She worried her tongue across her bee-stung lips. He suddenly understood what that adjective meant. Plump as fuck lips, the color of overripe cherries.

"Come inside." He growled, as he yanked the door open.

She flinched. Fuck! He hated that he made her feel that way. Scared of him. He huffed out a pent up breath. Once the door was shut, he put his forehead to the cold wood for a half a second. *Calm the fuck down.* "You're safe with me." He worked to keep his voice calm and neutral.

When he turned around, her lip was between her teeth. Her forehead lined with worry. "I know that." Her voice was calm. Her arms were folded over her chest. It made her bump stand out even more. Small, neat, his baby. He had the sudden urge to drop to his knees and to run his hands over her belly. To talk to the unborn child. *His baby.*

Instead, he stuffed his hands into his pockets. "Sit." He urged. "I need to know what's wrong with…him." His eyes were glued to her stomach. Kai tried to swallow down a lump in his throat. If anything happened to the baby. *His.*

Shit.

He ran a hand through his hair waiting until she was comfortable. If sitting on the edge of a sofa with a straight back, could be deemed as comfortable. Kai stayed standing.

"What do you know about the…problem with my pregnancy?" Just hearing her voice cut him. It bought back memories of their time together and his belly tightened along with other things. *Fucking head in the game.* It was just his body's reaction to a female in his space. It meant fuck all. The fact that he still found her scent so damned appealing meant even less. It was his body remembering the pleasure she had brought him.

"I don't know a damn thing," he said. "Who am I? I'm just the father of this child. The fucking father." *Pull it together.*

Her eyes were wide. She clasped her hands tightly. He was upsetting her and it wasn't good for the child.

"I'm sorry." He managed to choke out. "All I know is that there is something wrong." He spun away and dug his hands into his hair. He took a deep breath into his lungs and turned back. "Tell me. I need to know everything," he growled. "I deserve to know everything."

This time, she kept her eyes on him and squared her shoulder. "I should've released two weeks ago.

He frowned. "Come again."

Her frown deepened. "I'm two weeks overdue."

"So soon? That would mean that, as a dragon shifter, you're only supposed to be pregnant for…" He did the math in his head. "Six weeks? Is that right? That can't be right." He said the last to himself.

She nodded. "Yes. Six weeks. I'm two weeks late. It's never happened before. A female has never carried this long. A female can be a day or two late. Maybe three at the most but a whole two weeks…never."

His eyes moved to the bump. To the way her hand caressed the curve of her underbelly. *His baby.* "What does that mean? How is it bad? Our females carry for much longer."

"Good to know. It is a mixed species baby. A first. There has never been a vampire/dragon child before. I hope it is the main reason for the delay. I am"—she nodded, swallowing hard—"pretty sure it's the reason for the longer wait. How long are your females pregnant?"

"A year."

Her eyes widened and she gasped. A hand flew up to cover her mouth. Her sexy as fuck lips. "What? No! That can't be right." She shook her head. "How long after that before the baby hatches?" She looked horrified. Then again, he was sure that he did too.

What the fuck!

"I'm not sure what you mean." *Please lord, don't let this be what I think it is.* He forced himself to stand his ground. Tempted to grab ahold of her and to shake her until she gave him all of the answers he was looking for.

She shook her head, looking confused. "Hatches as in—"

*Fucking hell!* "Explain your pregnancy to me. One step at a time, including timelines. Start at the beginning." He spoke quickly, sounding panicked. Warriors did not panic.

"Well, a male and a female…"

"You can skip that part," he growled.

"I'm sorry!" She yelled. "You're making me really nervous and I can't think straight when I'm nervous."

He sucked in a deep breath and closed his eyes for a few beats. "I'm sorry. Let's start again, a dragon shifter becomes pregnant and then?"

"An egg develops inside her for six weeks." She spoke so matter-of-factly. Like this was common knowledge. "The female then releases the egg which needs to be left to mature for a further five or six weeks." She paused. "Why are you looking at me like that?"

"Vampires give birth to live young."

"Really?" She gasped. "I know humans do too. I assumed that all non-humans…had eggs…like us…"

He shook his head to signal that she had been wrong in her assumption. Very fucking wrong. What did this mean for their baby? His eyes moved back to the bump. Small, tidy, very rounded and tight. It looked like an egg. Could it be? Kai went and sat down. He lasted all of three seconds before he jumped back up. An egg. An egg!

"Do you think he might be without a shell?" Ruby swallowed thickly. She licked her lips. "I haven't felt even the slightest movement so that can't be it…can it?"

"You might not be far enough along." Kai shrugged. "I don't know too much about pregnancies. You look like the thought of him…shell-less…" It felt weird to talk about his baby being inside an egg. *A fucking egg.* "Worries you."

"It would be dangerous for me. Possibly very dangerous." Ruby looked pale. Her amethyst eyes looked huge.

"In what way?" The feelings of panic returned.

"I'm a dragon, we breathe fire."

Fucking hell! They were oil and water. Ying and fucking yang. Their species didn't belong together. What had possessed this female to leave her kind, to seek out a male for the purpose of becoming pregnant? She had to have known what she was doing. In retaliation? As a *fuck you* to her obviously controlling brother? What was her reasoning? A dozen of such questions swirled around inside of him but none of them were important right now.

"How is fire breathing significant? Wait a minute…do babies of your species breathe fire as well?" He recalled how smoke had wafted from the shifter male's nostrils.

"Even our unborn young, when developed sufficiently within the egg, breathe fire. More and more as they ready themselves for the hatching. There are others of our species who later lose the ability…it is what makes the Fire dragons so strong, but that's not relevant. This child will start to breathe fire soon."

His jaw dropped. "They breathe fire before they're even born?"

She nodded. "Yes. I would regenerate if…" She rubbed her hand over her belly. "It would be excruciatingly painful but I'm sure I'd be okay. I think." She didn't look sure.

He couldn't imagine how being burned from the inside would feel. Kai swallowed thickly. He grabbed the back of his neck. Then rubbed a hand over his mouth. "You might just be carrying a bit longer because of my vampire blood. You could still have an egg inside you."

"There is no way of telling. I guess I didn't think this through. I thought you were a human. I'm so sorry…I was desperate…I…"

"Ruby." He whispered her name and she stopped talking and chewed on her lower lip instead. Gone was the fierce female. The vulnerable one was back and in full force. "There are more important things right now. I can't believe this is happening. Shit…" Kai grit his teeth and moved to his haunches in front of her. "Thing is, it is happening whether we like it or not. We are going to have a serious talk about…why you did what you did. I'm angry." *Understatement of the century.* "I don't like you very much right now." *Fucking understatement of the millennium.* "I doubt anything you say could change that."

Fuck! Her eyes filled with tears. She blinked them away and pulled herself more upright. Her eyes hardened up. She was working hard not to cry.

Kai looked down for a moment or two, feeling himself calm. At least she wasn't using tears to get to him. She seemed so genuine, so…nice. *Why? Why? Why?* Once again he pushed away the questions. "Regardless of how this happened though or how I feel right now, you are carrying my child." He couldn't help it any longer. His hand moved to stroke her belly.

Ruby tensed up. She released a small huff of air as soon as his hand made contact.

"Is this okay?" Emotion made his words thick. He couldn't help himself. Feelings of…he wasn't sure how to label them…just pure, intense emotion…rose up in him. It was like nothing he had ever experienced before.

"It's fine." Her voice shook. "I don't mind."

He brought both of his hands to her stomach and closed them around the very egg-like mound. "I want to be there for him. My feelings for you won't change that. Whatever happens between us will never change that. I'm with you every step of the way. I promise…" He lifted his gaze.

Ruby was crying. Big tears rolled down her cheeks. "I'm sorry." She blurted, wiping them away. She looked embarrassed. "It's just…I thought I was alone in this. I didn't think my child would ever know his father." She fanned her face, looking up at the ceiling. "I'm sorry. I hate crying. I'm so hormonal. I cry for anything right now. Just ignore it…ignore me."

Kai let go of her belly. He wanted to touch it some more. To nuzzle his face against it. Now he understood Lazarus' need to carry his mate around. Especially now that she was so swollen with child. Twins. He couldn't even begin to imagine. York was just as bad. He grunted at anyone who came anywhere near Cassidy. He talked to the baby and hugged and kissed her tummy constantly. Kai had thought it so strange to watch grown-ass males reduced to…that. Now, he could summon up a good dose of understanding.

Kai watched her wipe her eyes. "It's logical for you to feel this way." He said, as he stood upright. Hell, he had almost broken down and drizzed like a pussy since finding out about the baby and he wasn't even pregnant. He had to work hard at remaining civil towards her, which was challenging at the moment.

"I dropped a glass the other day and cried like a baby when it shattered. I'm normally not so fragile, I swear." She shook her head, looking really tired.

"I already called medical. We're meeting with a human doctor and one of our best healers."

Ruby looked away. He couldn't help but catch her look of despair. When she looked back at him, determination shone in her eyes. "I am hoping they can shed some light onto this. I didn't realize our species were so different. I suppose I should have guessed. You need to know that intervention is rarely successful for either mother or child. I am willing to try anything though."

"Good. Let's go, they are waiting."

# TWELVE

They turned down yet another corridor. The space felt cramped. That's because it was cramped. *Don't think about it.* They were under the castle. Her pulse raced and her breathing became more elevated. Her fear only grew worse with each step. *Don't think about it.*

"Are you okay?" Kai frowned as he glanced at her.

Ruby shook her head. "No. Dragon shifters don't like confined spaces. We need to be in areas large enough to accommodate a shift or we..." *Oh god...oh god.* "Lose it. I..." Her eyes darted around the hallway. The narrow, stifling, far too narrow hallway. There were no windows. They were underground. Oh god.

"Shit! You're claustrophobic?" Kai stepped towards her.

"Yeah. We all are but some of us suffer from it worse than others." She could barely breathe or think. It felt like her throat was closing.

"Why didn't you say something sooner?" He put his hands on her hips. "Look at me. You're eyes are glowing." Kai squeezed her flesh. "Damnit." He looked worried. A deep frown marred his forehead. His eyes were so dark, his mouth a thin a white line.

"I thought I could handle it. I didn't know it would be this far underground." She shuddered. "I can't lose it or I'll shift." Oh good lord. Oh no. She could feel the tingling in her bones. The rubbing of her scales beneath her skin. She whimpered.

"Ruby." Rough and demanding, yet with a coaxing edge. She loved the way her name sounded on his lips. What a time to think a thing like that. "You've got this." His voice turned soft and soothing. Not soothing enough.

The rubbing grew worse. "You should move away from me. I might hurt you if I shift."

"You're not going to shift." He ran his hands up and down her arms and she closed her eyes, concentrating on the warmth of his fingers. The softness of his touch. The tingling subsided…at least a little.

"I'm going to pick you up. Don't panic. Just breathe deeply and try to stay calm." He obviously had some kind of death wish or something.

"No. Just move away from me, I'll try and make it back out on my own." There was still a panicked edge to her voice. She really didn't want to hurt him

"Not a fuck." His voice was soft, given the nature of his words. Human curse words. From all the novels she had read, she knew them well.

Kai didn't wait for her to argue further, he picked her up and pulled her against his chest. He made a small noise in the back of his throat that she recognized as strain.

The fear instantly evaporated as she nuzzled into his chest, breathing in his masculine, coppery scent. There were hints of soap and the minty scent of toothpaste on his breath. She could feel it took some effort for him to put one foot in front of the other. Ruby kept her eyes closed. "Are you okay?"

"I'm not sure what it is you had for breakfast but man oh man, you're heavy." He grunted with the effort.

Ruby giggled. She was nervous. Being so close to this male. Feeling his heart beat beneath his skin. Feeling his warmth. "I'm a dragon shifter. You carry me, you carry my dragon."

"I'm carrying your dragon? That huge beast?" He choked out a laugh. "In that case...I'm one mean motherfucker."

"My dragon is not a huge beast. She's lean, sleek and elegant."

"Yeah, whatever." He snorted.

Ruby could hear that he was smiling. She couldn't help but smile too. He made another tiny noise that indicated he was taking strain. She could feel his arms shake with the effort of holding her. Despite the outward signs of fatigue she could feel he had picked up the pace.

"You can put me down. I think I'll manage now."

His arms tightened around her. "No." His voice was low and deep. "Sit tight."

"Why do vampires use human cuss words so much?" Maybe if she took his mind off of his efforts.

"Human cuss words?" He sounded confused. "Oh..." He was smiling again. "You mean words like fuck."

There was a tightening inside her although she couldn't say why. "Yes...words like...fuck."

Kai groaned and staggered a step. He was really struggling with her weight. Kai picked up the pace again within a stride or two. "Um...well..." He paused. Then he chuckled. "The humans stole a lot of choice words from us. They were the ones that decided they were vulgar and bad...not us. It's normal for vampires to talk that way. Humans are timid about a lot of things, take sex..." He swallowed hard. "Never mind."

"What were you going to say?"

"We're here," he growled, sounding angry.

She could hear a door opening and then she was being placed on her feet. He kept a hand on her hip until she found her balance.

Ruby opened her eyes. The ceilings were low but the room was otherwise spacious. It would be cramped if she shifted. Her wings might end up mashed against the ceiling but she wouldn't come to any serious harm. She could breathe.

"Are you okay?" Kai gripped her elbow. "You have that deer in the headlights look again."

"No. I'm fine. I wish there were windows. I'll be okay." Her eyes moved about the room, coming to rest on two females standing in the far corner, next to a bed.

"Hi." The tiny female lifted her hand in greeting. From her scent and stature, she was the human of which Kai had spoken.

"Good morning." The taller female scented of vampire. There were small lines around her mouth and eyes, as well as a few strands of grey that streaked her hair. An elder. The first she had seen since arriving here.

"My name is Becky and this is Eleanor." The human motioned her hand to the vampire elder. "I am a doctor, a human healer. I have birthed a couple of mix…for lack of a better word…babies. Eleanor is the most experienced vampire midwife we have. You are in good hands."

"Before we get into this, you need to know that dragon shifters birth eggs?" Kai blurted.

The human healer opened her mouth before closing it again. The vampire female just stood there, her eyes wide.

Finally the human, Becky, made a squeaking noise. "Interesting… Okay… It's normal there would be differences. I just hadn't been expecting something quite so…majorly different." She pursed her lips for a moment. "Shew. I think that maybe we should sit down and put the kettle on for tea."

"As in, the hot beverage that humans like to drink?" Ruby asked. She'd read about tea and coffee but had tried neither.

"The very one." Becky pointed a finger at Ruby. "Can I make you a cup? Herbal, that is? Then again, caffeine would probably be okay for a nonhuman. No, we'd better make it herbal just in case." She looked flustered.

Kai shifted from one foot to the other.

"Eleanor…can I make you a cuppa?" The human asked.

The elderly female frowned. "Why not."

"What about you?" Becky turned to face Kai.

His jaw tightened, as did his entire body. He was wearing a T-shirt and blue jeans. She noticed that some of the males were wearing jeans at the bar she had frequented when trying to find a father for her baby. Up until then, she'd only read about the attire in books. Well, he looked really good. Mouth wateringly so. In some of the naughty romance novels she'd read, they spoke of how the fabric lovingly hugged the males thighs and ass. There was a whole of hugging going on below that male's waist and boy was it loving. His shirt pulled tight across his chest and arms. The dark ink on his bicep was really quite exquisite.

He flexed his muscles for a beat. "I don't think this is the right time to be drinking tea. You need to examine Ruby. She should've dropped…her egg by now."

"Released." She said, almost under her breath.

"Yes… Released." He gave her a nod and a tight smile.

"It's exactly the right time to drink tea." Becky raised her brows and spoke in a no nonsense way that reminded her of the school mistresses back at home. The female narrowed her eyes at Kai. "Eleanor and I need as much detail as possible before we commence with the examination." She walked over to a small table in the corner and flicked the switch. Then she opened the cupboard below and took out four mugs.

Kai huffed out a breath and put his hand behind his neck where he squeezed. She noticed it was something he did when he was anxious.

"Becky is right." Funnily enough, Eleanor also sounded like a school teacher. "Let's all go and sit down." She pointed to a sitting area. "I'm sure you must be tired after the long walk."

"Exhausted," Kai muttered.

Despite the situation they found themselves in, Ruby had to laugh. "I'm sorry." She mumbled when both healers looked at her like she was crazy.

His whole demeanor remained stiff and tense. For just a moment there, she'd forgotten he was still angry with her and rightly so. Just because she carried his baby or maybe because of it. Just because he had been kind to her, didn't mean anything. He helped her because of their unborn child. There was no other reason. They didn't even know each other. Not really.

She chose a two-seater couch but Kai made his way to the single chair in the corner and sat down, legs splayed. He rested his forearms on his thighs and clasped his hands together.

A lot of the questions the healers asked had already been covered in their earlier conversation. At one point there was a loud clicking noise accompanied by the sound of boiling water. Becky got up to make the tea. She handed one of the cups to Ruby. It was steaming and hot to the touch.

"I didn't give you any milk because it's herbal." Becky said.

"Dragons don't drink milk. It gives us really bad indigestion."

"You're lactose intolerant? That's interesting." She put her own cup down on the coffee table in front of her. "I suppose it does make sense considering you are part reptile."

Ruby nodded and took a sip.

"Oh my word... Isn't that too hot. You'll burn your mouth."

Ruby smiled. "Nah... We're used to much higher temperatures. This is nothing." She held up the mug.

The human female smiled at her. "Okay, so we've established you're overdue, at least you would be if you were carrying a dragon shifter child. We don't know whether you are carrying an egg or live young. I think we need to try and establish which it is." She spoke slowly and carefully. "I have a machine that would allow us to have a look inside your belly. At least, this would be true if you were human. Vampires and humans carrying vampire young have some sort of a protective membrane that does not allow us to see inside of them. I'm pretty sure it's going to be the same with you, but we need to give it a try. What do you think, Eleanor?" Becky looked across at the vampire female who had yet to touch her beverage.

"I don't know anything about your fancy equipment. None of it works but there's no harm in trying." She looked thoughtful for a second. "I would take a look at the womb opening to establish how soon the birthing...releasing might take place."

Becky nodded. "Definitely. You need to understand..." The female looked from Ruby to Kai and back again. "These tests might give us some sort of an indication but they are not conclusive. Mother nature has a way of taking things into her own hands."

Ruby nodded. She licked her lips. "Interventions are rarely successful. The only metal strong enough to breach our skin is silver. It's poisonous to us. Eggs are rendered barren and females have even died after coming into contact with the metal. There is normally nothing that can be done."

"It's the same with vampire females." Eleanor looked grave. "In this, our species are not so different. We will do what we can for you, my child." The older female took her hand and squeezed. The vampires in general may have stared and spoke about her behind their hands, but the ones she had met, had made her feel welcome and for that she was grateful.

"I'm going to give you a gown and ask that you lie down. Um..." The human frowned. "It's a bit of a strange situation. I believe that the two of you had a one-night stand?"

Ruby felt herself frown. "Sorry, a one…" Then it dawned on her what the healer had meant. "Yeah, that would be right," she said.

Kai was frowning.

Becky nodded. "I need to ask, would it be okay if Kai were to remain in the room for your examination?"

They both said yes. Kai growled the word. His jaw worked. The air in the room around them felt loaded with tension. Ruby was sure that if you listened hard enough you would hear it crackle.

He rubbed his hand over his mouth. "Is that okay?" He turned those fathomless, dark eyes on her.

Ruby nodded.

"Are you sure?" Becky asked. "I would need to do an internal exam. You won't be wearing any underwear. You have every right to say no."

The male bristled. His large frame seemed to grow larger. If he was a dragon, smoke would've been coming out of his nose. Possibly even a flicker of fire.

"He is the father of this child. He can stay. Whatever tests we need to do, I don't mind him staying through any of them. I am not modest when it comes to my body." Ruby had no qualms with being naked. Even if she did, she had no right to make him leave. She hadn't planned on ever telling him but things had changed. Something in her eased. He may not like her, he may even hate her for what she had done but he was here for her. He was here for their little one.

Kai gave her a small nod. His expression was still hard and unreadable.

"Okay then. Here's a gown." Becky handed her a soft garment. It was loose fitting. "The tie goes at the back. You need to be bared from the waist down." She added the last unnecessarily.

Ruby nodded, she stood up and began to remove her top.

"No, no..." The female's eyes widened. "You can change behind the screen over there." She pointed to a partition.

"Oh."

Kai was squeezing his neck again. He even stood up and began pacing.

"Sorry," she mumbled.

The vampire elder laughed softly. "An easy mistake, child." The wrinkles around her eyes were more pronounced. Her gaze was filled with warmth. Ruby made her way behind the material partition and quickly changed into the gown.

When she emerged they were all standing by the bed.

"Good." Becky gestured to the mattress. "Lie down over here."

It was fucking killing him.

Destroying him.

How the hell could he be reacting to this female at a time like this? How could he react to her at all after what she had done? It was wrong. Despicable. He didn't know where to look or what to do.

Kai caught sight of her perfect ass as her gown gaped when she pulled herself onto the bed. Tight yet full. He could picture her on all fours, that perfect ass up in the air. *No!* These thoughts were wrong. He made a choking noise and turned his eyes to the ceiling. She was so innocent about her nakedness. Ruby seemed so pure and innocent full-fucking-stop. Good thing he knew better. She was a liar and a fucking thief. Best he not forget.

"Are you okay?" Becky asked, her eyes glinted in humor. Bloody human! She saw right through him, that was for sure.

"Fine." He ground out, sounding anything but.

"Let's lift up your gown." The doctor said, still smiling. This time, it was directed at Ruby.

Fuck no.

Please no.

"Sure." Ruby pulled the fabric up over her belly. Her knees were bent. Her legs slightly parted. From this angle he couldn't see much…thank fuck. His eyes were focused on her belly which seemed bigger now that it was uncovered.

His baby.

His son…or daughter?

"Is…" He cleared his throat. His voice was loud and like a fucking chain saw in this space. "Is there a chance we might have a girl?"

Ruby smiled. A fucking beautiful, radiant smile. It was pure joy. She rubbed her belly. By the way she touched it's curve he could see it was something she did often. Hell, he'd seen her do it so many times already. She loved this child. That much was clear. Something tightened in his chest. She nodded. "There is a possibility…I think…" She frowned. "Do vampires have female children?"

He had to smile. "Yeah, we do."

Her beautiful smile lifted the corners of her edible mouth. Where the fuck had that come from? He stopped the thought in its tracks. "Dragon shifters do too but it's so rare. It practically never happens. I am the last of the royal females." Her gaze turned wistful. He could see that she no longer saw him. That her mind was far away. "For so long I've prayed to the gods that I never have a female dragon." Her hand gave a lazy rub over her belly. "It is strange for me to suddenly be wishing for just that…although…" She looked dismayed. "My biggest wish is for a healthy baby. I don't mind either way."

"Why would you not want a female child?" Kai blurted. It seemed weird considering the lack of female births.

Ruby tensed up. He could tell it was something she didn't want to talk about.

Becky must have picked up on it too because she chose that moment to squeeze a liberal amount of gel onto Ruby's stomach. "Let's, hopefully, have a look at what's going on in there." She grabbed a device that fit snugly in her hand, it was attached by a wire to a large machine with a screen.

Becky spent a few minutes moving the device around on Ruby's stomach. "You're sure you haven't felt any movement?"

Ruby shook her head.

"Not even something that felt like gas?" Becky glanced across at Ruby who shook her head. "I can't see a damn thing." She muttered to herself. "Nothing at all. A fluttery feeling? The feeling of bubbles?"

"No, nothing out of the ordinary. Aside from being two weeks overdue, there doesn't seem to be anything wrong. The biggest worry aside from the child being shell-less…" Ruby pulled her bottom lip between her teeth for a few beats. "Is that the egg might end up hardening inside of me. During the release, the egg is meant to be soft and malleable, allowing for it to pass relatively easily from the female. It is for that reason we need to be very careful during the release. We need to make sure the egg does not drop from any tall distance. You see, if the shell gets damaged in any way…" She looked down at her belly before looking back up at Becky. "At any sign of labor, we try not to shift into dragon form because this can pose a threat to the egg as well."

"You spoke about the egg hardening up." Eleanor took a step towards the bed. "What did you mean by that?"

Ruby shrugged. "I'm trying not to think about it too much. Trying hard to stay positive. There is more risk of this happening if the release is overdue. Once the egg is released, the shell quickly hardens becoming almost unbreakable. It's dangerous for the female if this happens inside of her. She can rip during the release. Be seriously injured or even die."

Ruby chewed on her lip some more. "If the egg completely hardens inside a female, there is no way to free it without intervention. The only thing that works is a silver blade. By then, the female is usually in a weakened state and this almost always results in death." She sucked in a deep breath.

Kai felt his hand shake. *No! Fuck!*

The three females turned to look at him and it was then he realized that he shouted out the words instead of saying them in his mind.

Becky narrowed her eyes on him. "I'm sure that won't be the case with Ruby." She grabbed some paper towels from a nearby table and handed the wad to the dragon shifter.

"How can you be so certain?" The words left him before he could stop them.

The tiny female put her hands on her hips. "You know what, we don't know for sure but Ruby is right, we need to stay positive. There was another birth, of twins, not so long ago that where against all odds, the vampire female gave birth to mixed twins. They are all happy and healthy now. It was Stephany's main saying during the whole pregnancy. Stay positive. Stay calm and keep looking forward." Her eyes bore into him for a few more seconds before she looked back at Ruby. "We're here for you." She gave Ruby's arm a rub. "Both of you." Her gaze softened as it landed on him once again. "Don't hesitate if you're worried about anything. You need to call me…or Eleanor or both of us. Now"—Becky paused as her gaze drifted to Eleanor—"would you like to do the internal?"

Eleanor shook her head. "By all means, you go right ahead." Becky pulled on a rubber glove.

Internal. What the hell?

Ruby handed the used towel to Becky who threw it in the trash before returning to the bed. She positioned herself at the foot of the bed. "You're going to need to open your legs a little wider for me, honey." Hell no! An internal. Becky squirted some of the gel onto her gloved hand and rubbed her fingers together. He couldn't look. He refused to look. Why the fuck had he looked?

God, he was such a prick. Such a fucking asshole. He made a noise that came out sounding pained. Kai looked away. He hated himself right now. She was pregnant and a liar but she was also afraid.

Out of the corner of his eye, he saw Becky move between Ruby's legs. "Are there any signs before the release? Do you go into labor?"

Ruby nodded. "Yes, our bodies prepare in much the same way as a human females would. I have read several books on the subject. The only difference is our labor is quick, lasting somewhere between a half an hour and three hours at most. The actual releases are not nearly as traumatic. Like I said, the egg is soft. It's a private moment. Dragon shifters prefer to be alone. It's an instinctual need. The need to protect our egg while it's vulnerable. I will need to be alone during my release. I might shift, I could hurt you if that happens. Shifting at that crucial time could damage the egg as well." Ruby looked at the human doctor as she spoke. Kai noticed how her cheeks turned red. Becky faced away from him between Ruby's thighs.

"Being alone at a time like that would not be a good idea," Becky said.

"I would hate to hurt you." Ruby repeated, swallowing thickly, her eyes locked with Becky's and then with his.

"Trust me, I'm not as weak as I look." Becky held her gloved hand in the air. Her fingers glistened with gel.

It wasn't something Kai had even thought about. He'd always just assumed he would be there for the birth of his son. His son. Lately he'd envisioned a male because he thought he would end up with a human. A little girl. Maybe. Like Ruby had said, it didn't matter.

"Even a vampire is no match for a dragon shifter. Particularly a female shifter trying to protect her egg. It would be better if I was alone. I will make sure of it."

Becky gasped. Her eyes were wide and her skin pale. He'd never seen her looking this out of sorts. "If anything goes wrong. No, you need to tell us the moment you go into labor."

Ruby shook her head.

"Yes." It came out sounding harsh. "You must. I promise you we'll move to a safe distance if need be. Kai could be there, Eleanor will definitely be present. We need to help you."

Ruby nodded. "As you wish, but you will need to keep a safe distance." She looked down at her belly as she spoke.

Becky's shoulders sagged and she huffed out a breath. "Good. Don't scare me like that. This is not a regular birth…release. You can't be alone. We can talk about it some more."

Ruby nodded, she gave Becky a half smile.

"Okay." Becky lowered the gloved hand. "Let's do this. It might be a little uncomfortable. It might even hurt a little. Are you ready?"

"Yes, I'm ready. I can take the pain. I grew up with three brothers."

"You're lucky." Becky said. "I'm a single child. I used to wish I had siblings."

"It was so much fun." Ruby's eyes sparkled with excitement. "We used to get into so much trouble. I have two older and one younger brother. Not only did I scrape my knees and my elbows but I broke plenty bones along the way as well." She smiled. "I can take the pain."

Becky nodded. Her curls bounced. "Good to know." Her voice was high. "Lucky you guys heal so quickly."

"Yeah…we did such stupid things like jump off of cliffs and change into our dragon form at the last second. It didn't always end well." She pulled a face.

Eleanor made a humming noise low in her throat. "I'm pretty sure bones would've needed to be reset."

"Quite a few. We were such terrors." Ruby smiled. Especially Blaze and I we…" She let the sentence die. "We're mature now. No more adventures." She looked wistful. "I'm ready."

"Breathe in deeply and hold your breath." Becky instructed.

Ruby frowned. One hand clasped her belly while the other gripped the sheet. She was worried, if it wasn't about the pain, then she was worried about the baby. That made two of them.

Becky put her arm forward. He could see that she moved it between Ruby's legs but couldn't see exactly what she was doing. Ruby flinched but if he had blinked, he would have missed it.

Becky withdrew her hand on a sigh. Gel glistened on her fingers. "Your cervix is tight. No sign of ripening."

"What does that mean?" Ruby's hand clutched the sheet tighter.

"Your womb is sealed tight." Eleanor chimed in. "It doesn't mean anything, child. Like Becky said earlier. Some females have a tight womb entrance one day and deliver the next."

Becky nodded. "It is usually a sign that the baby is happy to stay inside for a bit longer. I don't think you will go into labor any time soon."

"That's really bad." Ruby shook her head. Her lip quivered ever so slightly.

Becky removed the glove, ensuring that she pulled it inside out, before tossing it in the trash. "You can cover up." She gestured to Ruby's robe. The shifter pulled the bunched up material down over her thighs. Thank fuck!

Becky sucked in a deep breath. "Bad?" She shook her head. "It might be bad for a dragon shifter but this is a mixed child. We don't have much to go on. Not at all. This could be perfectly normal." Becky shrugged.

"Could be. Should be. Maybe." Ruby moved to sit more upright. She sniffed. Kai could see that she was trying not to cry. "We don't know anything, do we?"

Fuck. The fear rolled off of her. He could scent it. Her eyes were filling with tears and her lip quivered some more. Kai moved towards the bed, he took her hand. "I will stay with you. You're not alone anymore...remember." He knew he sounded like a pussy and that his words would not be much help. He couldn't give her the answers she sought. The ones they both sought, but at least it was something.

Ruby gave him the ghost of a smile. "Thank you."

Kai couldn't make himself let go of her. He should. He really should. He'd said his piece and offered comfort. His fingers only held on tighter to hers.

Becky shook her head, drawing his attention away from where they were joined. "I will discuss the matter with our local veterinarian. Hopefully they have some experience with reptiles. If not I'll have to call around. I know it isn't much to go on but it's at least something. We found with the vampire/wolf shifter mix, there were characteristics from both species present. This was true for the pregnancy, and the birth, as well as in the offspring." She took a breath as she paused. "For example, the pregnancy was longer than what was typical of a wolf pregnancy and much shorter than that of a vampire. The young were much smaller than vampire young, as is typical of a wolf shifter pregnancy."

"Interesting. It gives me hope." Ruby still sounded worried.

"It should. I believe the same will be true for this pregnancy. Another example is that Stephany excreted milk instead of blood for the first three months after the twins were born. Then one day she started producing a mixture of the two." Becky's face lit into a huge grin. "She called me up, sure she was dying. Just for the record…" Becky turned serious. She glanced at Eleanor. "Stephany gave me full permission to discuss this with you. She even offered to come and talk with you if you need some support."

Ruby nodded but didn't say anything. There was a puzzled look on her face.

"So…" Becky huffed. "I am respecting doctor patient privilege." Kai wasn't sure what she was talking about.

Ruby frowned. "What did you mean by excrete milk? Is it the same as humans when they use their mammary glands to feed their young?" She wrinkled up her nose like the idea was weird to her.

Becky nodded. "That's exactly what I mean." She narrowed her eyes at Ruby. "Vampire and wolf shifter females feed their young from their breasts. Is this not the case with dragon shifters?"

Ruby's eyes widened. "No. They are born with teeth. Our babies eat food. We chop it up finely at first, of course."

Becky pulled her gaping mouth closed. "O-of course." She stuttered. "Lactose intolerant. I forgot."

Ruby let go of his hand. "You don't think that…" She looked down at her breasts which were encased in the thin, cotton robe. Then she palmed them using both her hands.

Kai had to bite back a groan. He was going straight to hell. Her mounds were full and so damned soft looking. Kai bit back a groan and tried not to look. Hell was too good for him.

Ruby gave another light squeeze. Kai's dick gave a twitch.

"They have been feeling a bit more sensitive." She frowned. "I'm not sure but they might also be a bit bigger." She gave them a third squeeze.

"They are bigger," he blurted. Kai wished that he could bite off his own tongue. There was no point though since it would just regenerate.

Becky threw him an amused grin. Damnit.

"You think so?" Ruby asked, she looked at him expectantly. She was waiting for an answer.

He rocked on his heels. "Definitely." It came out sounding strangled. "I mean, they were full before but they're...um...fuller now." Why couldn't he keep his mouth closed?

Ruby pushed out a solid breath. "I never thought I would ever feed a child with my mammary glands. I don't know why we even have them since we don't really need them." She shrugged.

Kai could think of a few reasons but he grit his teeth instead of voicing them. Not a single fucking word would pass his lips again during this particular conversation. Certainly not anything concerning her mammary fucking glands.

"You'll get used to it. Have your nipples darkened?" Becky asked.

Oh god! Or her nipples. He was keeping his lips zipped.

"It is another sign your breasts are preparing for milk or blood production. Depending on the species," Becky added.

Both Ruby and Becky looked at him but he decided to check his boots and then the far wall. *Not answering.*

"I think so." Ruby was frowning, big time. "I'm not sure…I haven't paid much attention. They have been bouncing more. They've been in the way more."

*Kill me now. Fuck.*

"Let's take a look," Becky said. "I think it would be good sign if there were changes. It would show us that your child carries vampire traits. It would certainly put my mind at ease about this pregnancy even though I am almost certain, although different from a normal dragon shifter pregnancy, it is perfectly normal for a mixed child." She paused. "Let's undo the tie on your robe and take a look."

"I'm going to step out of the room." He was a colossal pussy but he didn't give a fuck. There was no way…

"I would prefer it if you stayed, that's if Ruby doesn't mind." Becky's gaze held him in place. For a tiny human she was quite something.

"I don't think that Ruby"—He stammered and spluttered— "would be comfortable…"

"I don't mind at all." Ruby shook her head. "I'm not ashamed of my body and besides, you've already seen me naked."

"Exactly." Becky raised her brows. "It is sometimes difficult to pick up subtle changes on your own body. We don't always notice them. You saw Ruby before. You will be able to assess better than anyone else. I'm looking for changes in size…"

"I already told you that they're bigger," he snapped. Kai pinched the bridge of his nose and prayed for calm. "Sorry…that's fine. I'm happy to help out." *Don't act like a dick just because yours can't behave.*

Becky nodded once and helped Ruby with the tie at the back of her neck. Ruby held her hair up. "As I was saying…" Becky gave him a hard stare. "We're looking for definite changes in size as well as any changes to the nipple shape, size and color."

Kai nodded. He could do this. Ruby was the mother of his child. His unborn baby. He wasn't going to react in any way. His body was going to behave itself…for once.

Becky pulled down the garment.

Dear lord in heaven.

Kai hadn't been lying when he'd said her breasts had been full before but they were much fuller now. Her nipples were plumper, darker. His mouth watered and his dick throbbed. He dropped his gaze to her belly. To the beautiful golden tattoos at the top of the curve. "Yeah." His voice was gruff. "Definitely fuller and Ruby's nipples are darker too." Just as pretty. He was sure they would taste magni…no. Not going there.

"That's great." Becky smiled.

"The unborn child must have vampire traits." Eleanor was smiling too. "It's a good sign."

"It still doesn't tell us if I am carrying an egg or not." Ruby leaned back on the bed. She made no attempt to cover herself.

Kai's jeans felt distinctly tight. He felt like the biggest jerk alive.

"I think we need to trust nature to do what needs to be done. It has before and I'm sure that it will again." Becky gave Ruby a reassuring smile. "I will do a bit of research. You are a strong female. A non-human. You'll be okay."

"I'm not worried about myself," Ruby all but whispered. She pulled her lip between her teeth. "My worry is for him."

Becky didn't say anything. It was easy to read between the lines, she didn't want to make any promises she couldn't keep.

"I'd like to feel your belly." Eleanor moved to the side of the bed. "It is our only way of getting a picture of what's going on in the womb. It is something I am used to doing since we can't use human equipment."

Ruby nodded. Thank fuck, she finally pulled her gown over her breasts only to pull it up over her belly.

Kai kept his gaze on Ruby's face. She was looking at Eleanor with such expectation, such hope.

The healer began to palpitate her belly. Using firm but gentle strokes. "Do dragon shifters have water inside the womb surrounding the egg?"

Ruby nodded. "Yes, it surrounds the egg as a protection."

Eleanor made a sound of acknowledgement. "You said the shell is soft?"

Ruby nodded again. "Yes." Her eyes were still firmly on the healer.

"You feel similar to a vampire at about four months of pregnancy. Your belly is more compact but that differs from female to female. I can feel something there but I can't tell whether you are carrying an egg or not." She gave a small shake of the head. "I'm sorry, child. I agree with Becky. This pregnancy will progress as it should. We need to take it day by day. You must inform us of the first signs of labor though. This is even more important with a short labor. You need to stay close to the female." She glanced at Kai.

He nodded. "I will request that our rooms be on the same floor or next to one another. He would draw the line at having her in his space. Maybe in an emergency or if they could have separate rooms in a suite. They still needed to talk. He really needed to try and understand why she had done this. Kai hoped he could understand. He would need to if they were to have any chance of moving forward and finding some sort of even ground as friends. For the good of the child.

"Okay. Come back in three days." Becky smiled at them both. "Like Eleanor said, call immediately if anything changes. It's a waiting game right now."

"I'll change back into my clothes." Ruby glanced at him.

"I'll wait here and carry you back."

Her mouth dropped open. "There is no way you would manage."

"Want to bet?"

"Don't be a hero," Ruby said. "I weigh far too much." She smiled. "You can carry me if it…becomes necessary."

"Get dressed," he growled. "I'm carrying you and that's fucking final." A need to protect rose up in him. Energy surged through him. Adrenaline pumped. Good, he was going to need all the help he could get.

"One more thing." Becky had her eyebrows raised. She looked a little uncomfortable. "One last thing we need to discuss. Sex."

It felt like the floor dropped out from under him. "What about…it?" He couldn't bring himself to even say the word.

"The two of you had it once and might want to have it again."

"Not going to fucking happen." Kai growled and instantly regretted it.

Ruby visibly paled. She put a hand to her chest. A hurt look passed over her face. Had she been expecting for them to become a happy fucking couple? Maybe carrying her wasn't the best idea. It had given her the wrong impression.

"It's not like that between us." He tried to keep his voice even.

Becky folded her arms. "Oh really, because Zane informed me that there is a very good chance of the two of you becoming mates."

He felt his jaw tighten. Everything in him tightened. "It's not happening," he growled.

"There is a very good chance my brother will force us to mate but it will be in title only. We will lead separate lives…I would never expect Kai to…" She turned her beautiful eyes on him and for a second he couldn't breathe.

"We'll think of something." He spoke more softly. "I will talk with Blaze. I'm sure that…"

"He won't listen. He has made up his mind." She made a small noise of frustration. "I'm afraid that when he makes up his mind about something, there's no changing it. Ask me. I know. I won't expect you to be anything other than a father to this child. I am glad you will be in his life. We can try and find a way around this. Maybe."

Despite everything. He believed her. He didn't know how to respond.

"Let's just say hypothetically that you decide to have sex," Becky blurted.

"Why hypothesize something if it's never going to happen?" This whole line of conversation irritated him. He was still attracted to Ruby but there was no way in hell they were having sex. Not a chance.

"Humor me," she growled loudly. Impressive for such a small human. Then she gave a small chuckle. "The thing is…if you were a couple…I would recommend plenty of sex. Sex is known to speed up ripening of the cervix. It could bring on labor."

"It's true." Eleanor nodded. "I have recommended it in the past, unless of course there is a reason why dragon shifters would avoid rutting."

Both Eleanor and Becky turned towards Ruby who was looking at the ground. Her cheeks were a bright red. "Um…" She looked up when she realized the attention was on her. "Sex is fine. Our healers would prescribe the same. They tried to get me to accept a male to my bed to…"

Kai growled loudly. The thought of another male with Ruby was unacceptable. It wasn't jealousy. That was laughable. He was worried about the baby. That was all. He couldn't care if another male touched Ruby.

"Go on…" Becky said.

"They would prescribe sex to bring on labor, only they warned me against…it's silly…" She chewed her lower lip.

"What is?" Both Eleanor and Becky said simultaneously.

"No hard rutting is permitted. It's an old dragon's tale, but it is believed the egg could become scrambled." She was talking quickly and looked nervous. "It's never happened before. That an egg became scrambled because of sex…or any other reason…but…I'll stop talking now."

"Okay…good. Thanks." Becky was trying to hold back a laugh. He could see it. "It would be fine if the two of you decided to have sex. I'm just saying…just in case."

He bit back a couple of choice words.

The little human continued. "Make sure you take it nice and easy…gentle sex is prescribed."

Neither of them said anything.

"Hypothetically of course," Becky added. "Go and get changed." She smiled at Ruby.

# THIRTEEN

His best friend leaned against the door outside his room. Kai noted how her expression changed to one of relief as their eyes locked. The look of relief was fleeting, when Jordy glared at Ruby, daggers appeared in her eyes. As the saying went, if looks could kill…in this instance, Ruby would be, not only dead, but obliterated.

"I'm going to take a flyer and assume that this is her." Jordy folded her arms, and tapped her foot. Her eyes widened as they landed on Ruby's distended belly. "That's not yours is it?" When he didn't answer she made a groaning noise. "Oh my God! It is yours. What the hell, Kai? I wouldn't believe those goddamn rumors but it's true."

"Please can we not do this out here?" Kai noticed how Ruby was clutching her stomach. It irritated him that Jordy was speaking about the female as if she wasn't even there. Judging by Jordy's total shock, it looked as if all of the involved parties were heeding Zane and Brant's request to keep all information quiet. The general population was aware of Ruby's presence, they just didn't know why she was here or even who she was.

He opened the door to his room. "Go in. I'll be back in a few minutes." He gestured to Jordy. She was his best friend ever since they were kids. Even though he was a little pissed off with her right now, he owed her an explanation. He knew her behavior stemmed from her worry over him.

"What about her?" Jordy threw Ruby another filthy look.

"Go into my room or you can leave, you choose," he said between clenched teeth.

"Fine," she huffed. "I can't believe you. How did this even happen?" She muttered the last as the door slammed behind her.

"Was that your female?" Ruby's voice was timid. "I didn't think you were with anyone. I'm sorry if I have caused trouble for you. We really need to talk. I need to explain…"

"They've assigned you a room just three doors down the hallway from me." He ran a hand through his hair and then gestured in the general direction. From the dark smudges under her eyes, he could see Ruby was tired. Beyond tired. "Let me take you there." He started walking and she followed. When they arrived at her door, he turned to face her. "You get settled in, maybe lie down. I'll come by in a couple of hours and we can talk then."

Although she looked disappointed, she nodded. "Alright."

Kai opened the door and gestured for her to go in, in much the same way as he had done at his own door just minutes earlier.

Ruby looked thoughtful, she walked in and turned, taking a hold of the door so that her body was mostly positioned behind it. "Kai." Her voice was timid and had a questioning ring to it.

"Yeah."

"Do you think they were right? Becky and Eleanor…the healers…do you think this baby will be fine? That nature will take it's course, as it should, and that he will be fine?" Those beautiful amethyst eyes were wide in her head. Their entire focus directed at him.

Just yesterday morning, he'd wished for one more chance to meet this female. One opportunity, no matter the cost. And here she was. It was nothing like he hadn't envisioned. He certainly never thought he would be on the cusp of fatherhood. That the child in question would be in jeopardy.

His heart raced, pumping blood through his veins, helping him prepare for battle against an unknown foe. He wished he could tell her everything would be fine. But despite the uncertainty, that everything would be okay. The fact of the matter was, they were two very different species. Maybe too different for this to turn out well. He hoped not.

"You heard Becky." He took a step forward, putting a hand on either side of the doorjamb. "We have to stay positive." He swallowed thickly. "I may not have known about this child yesterday." Kai shook his head and sighed loudly. "One day later and I already love him. I am here for him in every way, which means I'm here for you, as the mother of this child. We will get through this together, regardless of what…"

"Don't say it." She closed her eyes, blinking away the tears. "It's going to be okay. It has to be." It looked like she was trying to convince herself. Maybe she was trying to convince him.

Kai nodded.

"What will happen after he is born? Will I stay here or…?"

"There is plenty of time to talk about it."

She shook her head. "We need to discuss these things sooner rather than later. Despite what Becky said, I know my release is coming soon."

Thank fuck vampires didn't have heart attacks or he would have dropped right there and then. Her release was coming soon. He couldn't wait. At least once the egg was there, they could relax. That was if there even ended up being an egg. There was so much that needed to happen first. "You first need to tell me why you were in that bar. Why you abducted me. Why me?" He held her gaze. "You knew your heat was coming and yet…"

It was her turn to hold up her hand. "We'll talk about it when you come back. I'll tell you everything." He could see how she held back a yawn. "I can't right now. You're right, I need to rest. You need to go and see your female."

Kai nodded. "Yeah." He tried to soften his voice. He didn't correct her about Jordy. "I'll see you later."

"Later." She closed the door.

Kai just stood there for a few minutes, staring at the wood like it might give him the answers he needed. It would have to wait.

When he opened his door, Jordy stood at the window in his living room. She slowly turned around as he entered. Her eyes were red rimmed, like she'd been crying. "I cannot believe you kept this from me. I thought we were friends. Best friends. Dammit. There were some rumors flying around the castle but I refused to listen to them. I didn't believe it. I was so sure that you would've told me if…"

"Calm down."

"Don't tell me to calm down! No wonder you've been acting all weird. It makes sense now. I just wish you had trusted me. A dragon shifter." She was two parts angry and one part upset. "A dragon bloody shifter. What the hell were you thinking? I can't believe you didn't tell anyone. I can't believe you didn't tell me…your best friend."

He ignored the comments about Ruby being a shifter. "I didn't know she was pregnant, I swear." He took a step towards her.

Jordy made a snorting noise. She rolled her eyes. "Yeah right. Like hell you didn't know. It's an impossibility. Her scent would've driven you mad. You wouldn't have been able to keep your hands off of her. You're not some teenager anymore, Kai. Hell, you were with me that one time when…"

"You don't have to remind me. I remember," he growled. "Damn near scarred me for life." Kai had to smile.

Jordy made a sound of frustration but he couldn't help but notice how the edges of her mouth curled upwards. It had been his best friend's first heat. So many years ago. A teenager himself, Kai didn't know what the hell was happening to him. One minute they had been laughing and joking, and the next he couldn't stop sniffing at her. There was a need inside of him. He didn't exactly know what that need was. He told Jordan how wonderful she scented. How he couldn't get enough of it. Next thing he knew, he was pulling her to him hugging her, wanting to touch her. Wanting things he knew were wrong…at least with Jordan they would be. That's when she had thankfully realized what was happening and had hightailed it out of there. She'd never let him forget it either. Teased him for months afterwards.

"You may not have known what was happening when you were a fourteen-year-old, gangly teenage boy but there's no way you could not have known as a grown male. No fucking way." Her hands were on her hips. For whatever reason Jordy often felt the need to mother him at times. He loved and hated it in equal measures.

Had he known that Ruby was in heat? There had been a nagging voice inside him that had made him ask the question at the time. He'd been very quick to accept Ruby's bullshit answer. What if she had told the truth? Would he have been able to walk away from her. To stop himself from having her. Not a fucking chance. The fact remained though, she should never have taken him in the first place, knowing full well she was entering into her heat. It was deliberate and deceitful on her part.

Taking him while she was in heat was the same thing as putting a starving male in front of a delicious blood banquet. Or offering someone dying of thirst a vein full of sweet blood and telling them not to drink. Even if he had known at that point, there would've been no walking away. At least he would've known though. He could've done something sooner. Been involved sooner.

He shrugged. "I was there, she was there. I guess I fooled myself into believing she wasn't in heat. I guess I must have known on some level. Maybe that's why I've been so…like I've been."

"I take it that bitch lied to you about it. She had to have fed you some bullshit story and you fell for it." Jordy's eyes blazed. Her skin was flushed.

"Don't speak about her that way." It pissed him off that Jordy was right but he didn't like the way she called Ruby names.

"She lied to you, Kai. You didn't know she was in heat and now she's pregnant. Next thing you are going to be telling me how she didn't know she was in heat. That this was one big mistake."

He didn't answer.

"I don't know how you can even stand to be in the same room with her," Jordan spat.

"She's the mother of my child. It is what it is."

She shook her head. "You're crazy. You're too sweet, too damn nice. I don't want to have to hear how you've forgiven her."

"I know you care about me and that this has come as a big shock. This is between Ruby and I. I hope you will stand by me and support me. These are my decisions to make…not yours or anyone else's."

Jordan's whole demeanor changed. Her shoulders sagged and she huffed out a big breath. "Of course, yes.

I'm shocked. I'm a little hurt, make that a lot hurt, that you didn't confide in me as well."

"There was nothing to tell." He rubbed the back of his neck. "I didn't know."

"Nothing…really?" She made a sound of irritation. "Do you have feelings for this female? Is that it?" If he didn't know better he would say Jordan was jealous.

Kai shook his head. "This has all come as a big shock. I'm still trying to come to terms with the whole thing."

"You do have feelings for her." Her mouth dropped open. "I can't believe it. I can tell there is more that you are not telling me. You're covering for her somehow. This female lied to you. She rutted you knowing full well she was in heat. I can't believe that some mangy, desperate shifter female did this to you. Why was she even in Sweetwater? Why did she go after you?" She muttered the last.

"Ruby is not mangy."

"She had to have been desperate to leave her own kind."

Yeah, she had been desperate. He didn't know why. He didn't have answers and even if he did, there was no way he was telling Jordy.

"Probably a nothing back home. Can't attract males of her own kind." Jordan rolled her eyes. "Why the hell did you fall for her lies?"

"You don't know." Kai was sure that by now everyone in the castle would have heard, guessed or that someone would have talked despite the kings briefing the guards and all parties involved to keep quiet.

"Know what?"

For just a second, he thought about not telling her. It was crazy to think that this would stay under wraps for too much longer though. Soon everyone would know. "Ruby is a princess."

Jordy burst out laughing. Her laughter quickly died. "You're serious?"

He nodded. "Yes."

"For fuck sakes. You're serious. Why did she go after you in the first place?"

"Thanks, Jordan," he mumbled.

"I don't mean it like that and you know it. What was she doing in Sweetwater at a time like that? A freaking princess. It doesn't make any sense."

He wished he fucking knew. Even if he did know, he wouldn't tell Jordan. It was none of her business. This wasn't something he wanted to share with her.

"Tell me what went down. Maybe I can help you. You can't keep this all inside. I'm your best friend dammit." Jordy looked up at him. "I'm here for you. You need to know that."

"I know. Thank you. It means a lot." It did mean a lot to him but Jordy was wrong about one thing. He didn't plan on keeping it all inside. There was going to be a whole lot of talking going on. It would be a discussion held between himself and Ruby. Although he and Jordan were best friends and although they had always done everything together, this would not be one such occasion.

She threw her arms around him. "I still want to help out, by the way, with that other thing."

"What other thing?" Then he realized what she was talking about and he felt everything in him freeze. The last time he had seen her, she had been naked. He shook his head and gently pushed her away.

"What, you're not actually entertaining the idea of rutting her again, are you?"

*Not a fuck.* "It's none of your business."

Her eyes narrowed on him. "You can't be fucking serious. You cannot possibly have sex, any type of relationship with that lying scheming, conniving—"

"Stop," he growled. "Ruby is the mother of my child." He spoke slowly. "My sex life is none of your business."

"Don't say that." She shook her head, her cheeks had the flushed look again. Jordy was pissed. He knew the look and all the signs.

"You are my dearest friend and I love you very much but who I rut is none of your business. I want you to treat Ruby with respect. Despite everything that's happened, I don't think she's a bad person." He wholeheartedly believed it.

"You're too nice. You're totally going to fall for this bitch. I can see it from a mile away. I'll be here when she dumps your ass or when you find out about the next lie. She's playing you." Jordan gave a humorless chuckle. "You're a total fool if you fall for it. You know where to find me when you come to your senses." She strode from the room.

Shit!

There was a part of him that wanted to go after her. It was nobody's business what had happened during those two days or how they chose to proceed. He wasn't going to fall for Ruby. Not after all that had happened. He was attracted to her. It didn't matter that she carried his child. Hell, maybe he was attracted to her because of it but he wasn't going to act on it. No fucking way.

# FOURTEEN

Kai was still wearing blue jeans when he came by later. He'd changed his shirt. The black one didn't showcase his muscles quite as much as the previous one had. It did make his dark ink stand out more though. He was a good looking male. There was something about him. He was straightforward but played his cards close to his chest.

Ruby felt much better after lying down. Despite her mind being in turmoil, she'd still fallen asleep.

"Did I wake you?" Kai asked as he walked through the front door.

"Yes, but it doesn't matter…" She quickly added when she saw his face. "I won't sleep tonight otherwise, so I'm glad you did."

"Is your accommodation satisfactory?"

"It's fine...thank you." Although quite a bit smaller than what she was used to, the living area, kitchen and bedroom combined were big enough to accommodate a shift but only just.

"I can petition to have you moved into a much larger suite but it would mean being on the other side of the castle. I'd like to be close, you know, just in case..." He really was serious when he said he was there for her...make that, for the baby. She really hoped he would understand, at least to some degree, why she had done what she had done.

"Do you mind?" He gestured to one of the chairs, a wingback in the corner.

"Please." She nodded. "Can I get you something to drink?"

His gaze dropped to her neck. Ruby sucked in a breath. "Oh...um...oh...I'm going to get myself a grape juice."

"That would be good, thank you." Kai sat up right on the couch. Every muscle was corded and tense.

"You vampires drink...juice?" She blurted, feeling like an idiot. "Of course you do otherwise you wouldn't have ordered one. Forget I asked."

He smiled, looking a little more relaxed, for the first time. "Although our beverage of choice is blood." He chuckled. "Hell, if we could have it for breakfast, lunch, dinner as well as for midnight snacks we would but too much of a good thing and all that. No…" He shook his head. "We also eat and drink, like everyone else. Maybe not as much, but we do. Thing is, food would be useless without blood to slow down our metabolism."

"That's interesting. I'm going to have to learn as much as I can about vampires… Especially considering…" She rubbed her belly and widened her eyes. After pouring the drinks, she went back to the living room, handing one glass to Kai.

He nodded his thanks and immediately took a sip before placing the glass on the coffee table in front of him.

Ruby sat down on the seat opposite to Kai. "I need to start by apologizing again. I'll do my best to explain things to you." She put the glass down without having taking a sip. Ruby linked her fingers together across her lap.

Kai locked his jaw, his dark eyes rested firmly on her as he waited for her to continue. All of the tension from earlier was back, only this time it was much worse.

"I told you I'm the last royal female. According to my brother, Blaze, that meant that I was the last hope for the dragon shifters for a true heir. The dragon shifters are divided into four tribes. I am from the Fire tribe. The other three are Water, Air and Earth." She paused and licked her lips.

Kai didn't so much as move a muscle.

"The Fire tribe is the strongest of the four. Although all dragons are capable of breathing fire when they are born, for whatever reason, the Air, Water and Earth dragons lose that ability very soon after. It is why the three of them have banded together against us. Thankfully, there have been no wars for many years, but due to the lack of females it is looking more and more imminent that there will be a war and soon if something is not done about the dire situation."

Kai swallowed hard. He nodded once, urging her to continue.

"My brother and the king of the Air tribe struck up a deal, our tribes would unite. Together, we would be unbeatable. Rulers over the other two. To seal the deal, I was to be given to Thunder."

Kai's eyes darkened up. There was a tic in his jaw.

"I had this stupid fantasy of actually falling in love with the male that I mate one day."

"It's not stupid," he growled.

"No, it was stupid of me. I've read a lot of those romance novels and had envisioned falling instantly in love. Of being this person's soul mate. So close and perfect for one another it would feel like we were made for one another. I couldn't possibly mate with a male I cared nothing for. That I didn't even know for that matter. Blaze did not listen to what I had to say. He wasn't interested. You see, he does not believe in love.

Not like I do…not like I did." She added, her voice quiet. There was no place anymore in her life for love. The only love she had to give was to this unborn child.

"Blaze knew if I carried Thunder's child, that I would not be able to turn away from him. That if I was in my heat, I would not be able to deny him. Blaze promised me that Thunder would take good care of me. I think he truly believed it, or at least wanted to believe it." She laughed humorlessly. "He may have been a descent mate and father. I didn't love him though. Blaze…"

"Your brother is a colossal dickhead." Kai shook his head. "Pretty much selling his own damned sister."

"You're not entirely wrong."

"I'm 100% correct. Fucking asshole!" He raked a hand through his hair.

"Blaze was only doing what he thought was right. As ruler of the four kingdoms, he has a lot on his shoulders. The well-being of my people is in his hands. I just wish he would listen to me. He is so set on following ancient rules and traditions and is not willing to budge." She huffed out a breath, feeling frustration well up inside of her. "If only he would have just agreed to taking a human mate, to allow all of our males to take human mates. He wouldn't hear of it. I had hoped to force his hand." She looked down at her lap, feeling her cheeks heat. "He's so afraid of diluting our royal blood. That his first son and heir will not be a true royal if he mates a human. He also has something against human females."

"So you were being forced to mate with this fucker from the Air tribe. Your brother wouldn't listen to you and your fate was set, so what, you decided to pick up some bastard in Sweetwater? Your whole thinking was that if you were already pregnant, he couldn't force you to mate with this other male? Is that it?" He didn't look too happy about any of this. She couldn't blame him.

Ruby nodded. She licked her lips. "The plan was, to go to Sweetwater and to find an already mated human male. I had done some research on the subject. Even older human males are still fertile. Also, an older, already mated male, would not be interested in any offspring. I could raise the baby myself and—"

"Not feel as guilty about lying and stealing. For me, taking a male's seed, without his permission, is the same as stealing." His eyes blazed. The tic was back in his jaw.

Ruby nodded. "I know." She whispered. There was no denying it. "I knew it was wrong. I didn't feel at the time that I had any alternative options. I was backed into a corner. Desperate. Yes, I always knew the day would come when I would be forced to act. I cursed myself for not preparing more." She made a noise of frustration. "I always hoped it would never actually come to that. I never expected Blaze to actually go through with it. Not so soon after Gram."

Kai frowned.

"My grandmother." Ruby felt tears well. There was nothing she could do about it. "I'm sorry." She took a couple of deep breaths and tried to blink away the tears. "It's these hormones. My grandmother passed away a few months ago…" She felt her lip quiver. Ruby paused for a few seconds. "My gram would not allow Blaze to use me in that way. He waited until after she passed. I never thought he would actually go through with it. I should've been better prepared and I wasn't. I went into that bar out of desperation. I wanted a human male that didn't give a damn. I chose that older male." She knew he would remember.

Ruby pulled in a breath. "One that was mated would've been better. That one." The pig with the onion breath. "I knew the male didn't care, that he wouldn't give a damn about any offspring. I could tell he would be happy just to rut and to move on."

Kai growled. She could tell he was thinking back to the night. That he could remember the male in question.

"I couldn't go through with it. I couldn't…to be with someone like that. I realized, in that moment, that whoever I chose would be the father of my child. I guess I still held onto my fantasy because when I saw you, I…" What was she saying? Seeing Kai that night had not been love at first sight. It was lust at first sight but love?

"You were…are a magnificent specimen. I thought you were a human."

"And what? It wouldn't have mattered if I was a human? You could've done what you did without consequence?"

"Yes…no. This child would've been fully dragon shifter. It would not have been a mix. I know that it was wrong of me. I don't know, my heat was almost on me. Maybe by then I wasn't thinking clearly."

"You were thinking clearly, Ruby. You knew exactly what you are doing"

She chewed on her bottom lip and nodded. "I'm sorry. When I saw you, I knew I wanted you to be the father of my child, that no one else would do. I felt deeply ashamed but I wanted you. In that, I was selfish because I also knew you would care."

Kai cast his gaze to his lap and shook his head. He looked disappointed. Then he squeezed the back of his neck.

"You need to know that I didn't just do it for me. I did what I did for my people as well." She blurted. She needed for him to know everything. Her brother wouldn't like her sharing dragon shifter information but she didn't care. Kai needed to know. He needed to understand. Hopefully he could forgive her. Maybe then she could forgive herself.

"Out of the goodness of your heart." He snorted. His eyes were hard.

"Do you think I wanted this?" Her voice was raised and a little off kilter. "To anger my brother…my king. To possibly start a war between the four kingdoms. Do you think I wanted to throw my life away? Because I can assure you by doing what I did, I gave up on any chance of finding love or a future for myself. No dragon shifter male would take me now. They are desperate but they wouldn't…" She let the sentence die. She needed to compose herself.

Kai kept his eyes on her.

"I knew I would be alienated, looked down upon by everyone. I knew I would be seen as nothing, less than nothing. I had hoped my actions would make my brother see reason, that I could force his hand."

"That you could force him into taking a human mate?" Kai seemed to relax, just a little. "How did that work for you?"

"It didn't. There are only a handful of dragon females across the four kingdoms. Only two of those females are fertile. The rules state that royals should only mate royals. Blaze has decided he will mate a lesser dragon shifter female from another tribe over a human female. He seems to have something against humans. I'm not sure what his plans are exactly, but our species will surely die out long-term."

"I highly doubt it would be sustainable. The guy sounds nuts."

"Like I said, he believes he is upholding our lores. Human matings are strictly forbidden as are mixed species matings..." She shook her head. "Two centuries ago, my egg would've been taken from me and thrown from a cliff."

He moved around in the chair. His face a mask of anger. His muscles roped.

"I couldn't mate Thunder. I had to do what I did to try and get Blaze to take a human. All of the males would've been permitted to take human mates. We have had two illegal matings in the Earth tribe. Males that took humans. It has caused a rift between my brother and their king. The matings were successful. The females become stronger after they are mated and are able to reproduce. The offspring are dragon shifter. There are no signs of any human weaknesses."

She was talking fast. "We could be saved, our male's need not lead lives of solitude. It is unnatural. They fight amongst themselves. My brother doesn't see any of it. He holds onto his old beliefs while a whole species dies. What he doesn't realize is that war is imminent as well. My brother will be overthrown. He might be a brickhead."

"Dickhead." Although his voice was rough, his demeanor had softened.

"Dickhead, brickhead…same thing," she said.

"Not really." He smiled.

"What?" They were in the middle of a serious conversation.

"A dickhead and a brickhead are not the same thing." Then he looked uncomfortable. "It doesn't matter. Carry on with what you were saying."

"I don't want for there to be a war. I don't want Blaze to be overthrown. He would be killed." She wiped away a tear. "He might be a horse's ass but I love him. At the same time, I want my species to live on. I want our males to have families. To have love."

"You thought that by tricking me into making you pregnant that you could change the whole way of life of your people?"

Ruby nodded. "I had to try. I had to put my hopes of finding love aside and focus on what was best for all of the kingdoms. You were never supposed to know."

"It was wrong." His voice was soft.

"I know that. I had no right."

"I have a better understanding of why you did this. Maybe if you'd asked me?" He shrugged.

Ruby had to laugh. "You didn't want to leave the bar with me. I had to kidnap you."

"I wanted to leave with you. I wanted to leave with you very fucking badly." He looked serious.

It was news to her. She thought he didn't find her attractive. Vampire females were so different. They were so lean and athletic. After seeing them, she thought that maybe he didn't like a few curves on a female. Ruby thought that he was a sweet guy who was worried about her but not interested in that way. That he had reacted the way he did because of her heat. Maybe it wasn't just her heat. "So, I should've just blurted that I was looking to get pregnant and that I needed your seed to make that happen? You would've left willingly had I been forthcoming?"

He gave her a half smile. "Maybe not. You could've explained things to me though. Maybe I could've helped in some way."

"Oh…" She dramatized. "So I should have said…Hi, human stranger. I'm a dragon shifter. My brother is the king of my species. In order to gain political influence he has given me to another king in a lesser tribe. I will be expected to release egg after egg until either I die or until I birth a female. Even then, I might still be expected to continue, since not all females are fertile." She gave another hearty laugh, not so shocked to hear it emerged as more of a sob. "I need you to please impregnate me so that I can be spared that fate, so that my future daughters will never be subjected to the same fate…or worse." She whispered. "Please will you help me?" By now she was crying openly. "I would be most grateful."

Kai swallowed hard. She watched as his throat worked.

"Yup…that would've changed your mind." She sniffed. "You would've helped me."

"I would've believed you. I am not a human." His voice was thick with emotion.

"I didn't know that." Ruby shook her head.

"I would've helped you, Ruby. That much I can tell you. I don't know about impregnating you, but…"

Her tears continued to run down her cheeks so she wiped them away with an angry swipe of her hand. "It would've been the only way you could've helped."

"Then I would've agreed," he growled. "I would've gone with you willingly." His eyes bore into hers.

They were both breathing heavily.

"That's so sweet." She cried harder. "These hormones are killing me here."

"I'll be right back." Kai returned with a pile of tissues, which she accepted gratefully.

Ruby blew her nose softly. "I should have told you. I will carry the guilt with me always. I will try and make it up to you…I am truly sorry. I can only hope you believe that."

"I do." He nodded. "I saw it in your eyes that day. After you took me. I knew you were afraid and hiding something. It seemed like you needed help. I forgive you, Ruby."

This wasn't what she had expected to happen. She'd hoped it, but hadn't…oh, then it dawned on her. He was doing it for the good of the child. Their child. He probably felt obligated to forgive her. "You don't have to."

"I don't have to what? Forgive you? I just did."

"No…you didn't."

He made a snorting noise. "Yeah. I'm pretty sure I did. You were desperate. I probably would have done the same. It took some guts. I understand. I will be kicking your brother's ass when he comes back to town." His fists clenched.

She gasped. "You can't. He'll kill you."

Kai frowned. His eyes looked so dark and deadly. "He can't afford a war with his own kind as well as the vampires. I'm going to at least get a punch or two in. He might beat me to death but I won't stay dead. Fucker can forget that. He deserves to bleed, just a little. I will do my best to make sure it happens."

"Don't do it."

"I carried you today didn't I?"

"You looked half dead when we made it out." She smiled, recalling how he struggled to catch his breath. How his brow had glistened with sweat.

"Point being. I made it."

"Leave it alone. I won in the end even if the outcome isn't exactly what I had in mind. I won't let him force you into mating me. I won't let him kill you either so you can tell your female that…"

"She's not my female." There was a rough edge to his voice. He shifted in his chair. "I mean, she's my friend. It's not like that."

"Okay." She couldn't help the feeling of relief, or the smile that slowly blossomed on her face.

"I…" It looked like he was trying to find the words. "I…don't think we can be together after…" His eyes widened. "I'm assuming it's what you might want. I…damn…I'm messing this up." He ran a hand over his face and huffed out a breath through his nose. "I'm here for you and the baby. I understand why you did what you did but I don't think that we…I don't have a female…Jordan isn't my female but we can't…"

"You don't have to explain anything. I would totally understand if she was your female. I get it. It's not like that. You don't need to explain." Disappointment rushed through her but she forced herself to smile. It had been lust…on his part. They didn't know each other.

She kept playing back his words when they had said good-bye…after. When he had told her that their time was special. When he had suggested meeting her again. He hadn't known she was in heat though. He had thought that their coming together was special but it was just the hormones and pheromones talking.

"I hope you're okay with that?" He looked a little pained.

"More than okay. We'll think of a way around my brother." Blaze wasn't about to change his mind. What was she going to do? She had a month to get him to think of something. The last thing she wanted was to force Kai to be with her. She could see herself with this male. She was just trying to recreate the fantasy she'd had for so many years though. Trying to hold onto the dream.

At least they would be friends. Her baby would grow up loved by both parents who liked and respected each other. Ruby could live with that.

# FIFTEEN

*Ten days later...*

Kai leaned up against her doorjamb. "Ready." He could feel his smile was a mile wide. This had become his favorite part of the day.

Ruby nodded her head. "Yup. I really enjoy these walks." Her cheeks reddened. She blushed every time she let slip that she was having a good time with him or if she gave him a complement of some sorts. It was so damn cute. As the mother of his child, he was allowed to think of her in that way.

For the last week, every day, after shift, he would pick her up and they would go for a walk around the gardens. Ruby enjoyed being outdoors. Or at least, she enjoyed being in wide open spaces. He also felt like she enjoyed his company. They were going to be okay...as parents of this baby...they were going to be just fine.

Walking side-by-side, they made their way downstairs, through the lobby and out through the big double doors. Vampires still stopped to stare but it wasn't as bad as what it used to be. At least they waited until he and Ruby were out of earshot before discussing their situation. At least they no longer sniffed at her. It pissed him the fuck off when they did that. A part of him could understand the fascination, she was a species they had never seen before, but come the fuck on. He could see it made her feel uncomfortable. Kai had to work not to growl and snarl at the fuckers. They had no damned respect.

Her belly was a little more rounded. It's didn't look or feel any different than before. At least, Ruby said it didn't feel any different. He hadn't touched her belly again…even though he really wanted to. "How are you feeling today?"

Ruby shrugged. She frowned and looked away but not before he saw the look of concern appear on her face. "I feel good. Perfectly fine." Her hand moved to her belly where she rubbed absently. "I can't believe it's taking this long. I was so sure…"

They had visited with the healers again twice and had gone through the same tests as before with no change. Becky cautioned them to remain optimistic. They had no idea what to expect. The way the pregnancy was progressing could be perfectly normal.

"The…I'm not sure…egg…little one…will come when he or she is good and ready. You're doing great. You look great." He allowed his eyes to move down her frame. Great didn't even come close to describing how she looked. Fucking amazing was better. She wore another pair of leggings. Ruby seemed to enjoy wearing them. They clung to her legs like a second skin. Showcasing lush thighs and one of the sexiest asses he'd ever seen. Her top was gray. It was formfitting, but not quite. The neckline dipped ever so slightly, revealing just a hint of cleavage. It was tight around her belly with a bit of room everywhere else. It stopped short of her drool-worthy ass.

He really shouldn't notice how good she looked. She had a spring in her step and a flush to her cheeks, so how could he not?

"Did you hear me?" She licked her cherry lips, drawing his attention to them. Big fucking mistake.

His cock twitched. "Yes." Just because he didn't want to mate her, didn't mean he wasn't attracted to her. It would complicate things if he…went there. "I mean, no I didn't…I was thinking about something else." *Something I shouldn't be thinking about.*

She laughed. He enjoyed the sound of her voice. He enjoyed her company period.

"I said thank you. You don't look so bad yourself." She gave him the once over in much the same way he had done. "How was your shower?"

His hair was still wet. "Awesome." Would've been better with you in it. *Stop! It!*

He caught her sweet scent and almost groaned. Thankfully they were outside, so it didn't affect him as badly as when they were indoors. Ruby was attracted to him. That, or the pregnancy made her feel aroused. Maybe it was a bit of both.

He had done plenty of reading about pregnancy and had even discussed it with Eleanor in length. One of the things that had come up was that many females became aroused when pregnant. This was at least true for humans and even more so for vampires. Judging by the edge of arousal often attached to her scent, he would say that it was true for dragon shifters as well.

"Did you have a good day at work?" She seemed to genuinely care.

"It was fine." He didn't really want to talk about work so he gave the standard answer.

"Fine." She laughed. "That means you hated every minute of it. Fine is a universal term used across languages, species, races, sexes…you name it…for *not so great*." She pulled a face. "Are you having problems at work?"

"No. Not exactly."

"Oh my word. You know everything about me…well…lots about me and I know nothing about you." Then she looked like she was having a mini panic attack. "I don't mean to pry or anything. You don't have to tell me anything if you…"

He smiled at her. "You're right. I've been assigned to help guard the human females who are a part of *The Program*."

Ruby frowned. Her nose wrinkled just a little. It was adorable.

"That's *The Program* in which human females are paired with vampire males?"

He nodded. They had visited the clinic for Ruby's last two check-ups. The facility had been set up especially for the humans to frequent. This included the humans taking part in *The Program*, as well as the humans mated to vampire males. Becky was in charge.

"Don't you like humans?" She asked. "Are they difficult?"

"They're fine. I don't mind them." His eyes travelled over the expanse of the lake. To an eagle that soared in the distance. Somewhere over the mountains…dragon territory.

She frowned. "Why do you hate your job then?"

"I don't hate my job." It was true, he didn't hate it.

She licked her lips. "Let me phrase it differently. Why don't you like it?"

What was he supposed to say? He didn't want to upset her. By telling the truth he risked doing just that, but if he gave her some bullshit answer or refused to answer then, that would hurt her just as much. He took in a deep breath. "I used to be an Elite Guard. The elites are the best of the best. The mightiest of all the vampire warriors."

"We also have such elite males. Only ours are called the Pinnacles. I understand why that would bother you. Why are you no longer one of these elite? Surely a strong male such as yourself would qualify?" Her eyes were filled with concern.

Despite the awkwardness of the situation, he felt proud she thought him big and strong. It was stupid to feel this way because he knew he was a fierce warrior. He liked that she had noticed though, especially since dragon shifters were so much stronger. They could breathe fire for fuck sakes. "I do qualify, at least, I did." He mumbled. "Thing is, we are not permitted to rut with humans…I ended up being kicked off of the team. What happened was—"

Her face turned red. "You…oh…you don't have to tell me anything…I…" She immediately assumed that he had rutted a human and gotten himself kicked out.

"No, you misunderstand. I was a part of the elite team, as well as *The Program* but we were only permitted to interact with human females within *The Program*. I took part in the previous heat but didn't end up with any of the humans. I was then assigned to transport several of the humans back to Sweetwater. Let's just say that when I got back to the castle..." His hand went to the back of his neck. His muscles always tightened up when he was feeling a little anxious. "It was clear that..."

"You really don't have to explain." She waved one of her arms and stopped walking. "It's none of my business. We're not a couple, we're..."

He couldn't do it. Kai couldn't bring himself to tell Ruby that the so called human, had been her. That she was ultimately the reason he had been thrown from the Elite Team. "It was one of those things that just happened and if I'm honest with myself, I'm angry about it. I have made peace with it though." He looked her in the eye and she nodded. "I don't dislike being a human guard but I'm an elite." He sucked in a deep breath. "I am working on getting back in. I've started going to practices again. There are practices held for vampires that wish to become an elite. They are grueling. Many males drop out within the first few days and many more within the first few weeks. Does it irritate me that I have to start over when I've already proven myself? Yeah, it does but I'll get back in."

"You'll make it." Ruby began walking again. "You seem determined."

"Yeah...I don't know about right now though. I'm struggling a little." Why the fuck had he said anything?

Her brows pulled together. "Why? It won't be easy but if you did it before, surely you could do it again. Are the males trying out with you suddenly bigger or better? Are they stronger?"

"No way." He blurted before he could stop himself. Kai cared about what she thought of him. Whether he liked it or not, he cared.

"I don't understand. Why are you struggling then? If you're strong and fierce for a vampire, and if you have done it before then surely you can do it again? It should be easier for you and not more difficult." She said this matter-of-factly and she wasn't entirely wrong.

"You see..." How did he explain this to her? "Vampires have basic needs. As warriors, we need to have these needs met in order to stay at optimum fitness and strength. I'm not getting everything I need right now. I'm managing to hold my own but I doubt it's enough to secure a place."

"That's crazy." Once again they stopped walking and she turned to face him. "Take what it is that you need then. Our males need balanced diets and plenty of red meat. They also make sure that they get a full nights rest before practice days. I just wish my brother would listen to me because they would be so much stronger if..." Her eyes widened.

He could see by her facial expression she knew exactly what he was talking about when he said needs. "Yeah well, it seems our species do have similarities after all."

"It would seem that way. You shouldn't deny yourself on my account." Ruby looked him straight in the eye, she seemed completely relaxed. Like the thought of him with another female didn't bother her in the least. It was moments like this that he was reminded that he had been nothing more than a seed donor. Yes, she had thought of him as a prime specimen but she may as well have been choosing a prize stallion or a dress to wear.

"Yeah. You're right. I've been taking blood from Jordan. She's still not speaking to me, even though she lets me drink from her. It's a bit of an awkward situation. It would help things if I just took a female. Are you sure it wouldn't be a problem for you? I don't want you be upset or stressed or…"

"Nah…" She huffed out a breath. "I'm sorry to hear about your friend still being upset with you. You need to do what you need to do. It wouldn't bug me at all."

---

It would be terrible.
She would hate it.

Ruby had no right to block him. They weren't together. She could see that being a part of this Elite Team meant a lot to him. The pride that shone in his eyes when he spoke about it was easy to see. His whole face lit up when he talked about going to practice again. It would be wrong if she made him deny himself. Ruby knew that if she asked him not to, he would listen to her. He would agree. Kai cared about their baby. He didn't want her upset.

It took everything in her to remain calm. He smiled at her and she smiled right back. Despite their conversation and the feeling of unease it had brought, the smile came easily. An automatic response. It was quick to falter when she remembered what they had been talking about, so she looked away.

"It's just such a strange situation. We're not together." He made a snorting sound. "We hardly even know each other and yet you are carrying my child. I always thought that I would be mated to the female who carried my young. It does not seem right for me to spend time with another female."

Ruby licked her lips, again she was tempted to tell him not to do it then but she couldn't be selfish about this. Kai had made it clear he didn't want to be with her. She was surprised he was being so...good about the whole thing. "You need to do what you need to do. I'm not going to stop you."

She must have completely misread his facial expression because he actually looked disappointed. Then he kicked some dirt up from under his boot. "Okay then. It's settled."

A yell in the distance drew their attention and they began to walk that way.

Some males were throwing a ball to one another. Sounds of their grunts, yelling and laughter filled the air. As they neared the action, Kai changed places with her, ensuring that he put himself between her and the cavorting males.

"You throw like a pussy." One of the males yelled to the other. He bent down to pick up the ball.

"You couldn't catch if your right nut depended on it." One of the others shouted. He cupped his hands around his mouth as he yelled. The same male turned his stare to Kai. "Hey, bro. Join in. I'm sure your female wouldn't mind sitting down for a few minutes and taking a break. She can watch you in action."

*Your female.*

Hearing the male call her that caused her heart to beat just a little faster.

"Maybe next time." Kai growled back, but she could see by the way that he was watching the game that he really wanted to join in.

"Come on, Kai. You're no damned fun anymore." Another male yelled.

"Shut up, Jenson or I'll be forced to kick your ass." Kai growled.

"Aren't you going to introduce your female to us?" The same male asked.

"No," Kai growled.

"Get over here." The first male yelled as he threw the ball at Jenson who caught it easily.

"Go on." She urged, giving him a nudge with her elbow. "I'll be fine. I wouldn't mind a little break."

"Are you sure?" His brows were raised. "I don't have to."

"Go, have some fun. I'll sit over there. Far out of the way." She smiled, gesturing to a fallen log on the edge of the forest.

He nodded, looking excited. "I won't be long. Here…" He pulled his shirt up over his head. "Take this."

Her mouth became so dry she could only nod in response. She'd seen plenty of well muscled males but for some or other reason, seeing Kai with his shirt off did things to her insides. Sometimes, when in the dragon form, she would close her wings and dip her nose down towards the earth in a freefall. It would feel like her insides were being left behind for a few seconds. There would be a lurching feeling as they returned to her body.

She was experiencing that same lurching feeling right now. Deep down in her belly. Kai gave her a half smile before turning and jogging to where the males were throwing the ball. Even his back was well muscled. His...backside was a thing of beauty. Meaty and full. She thanked the heavens for superhuman eyesight as she watched each cheek tighten with each heavy footfall. She huffed out a breath she hadn't even known she'd been holding.

Ruby found herself riveted to the spot for a few seconds before she finally managed to pull herself together. She quickly turned and made her way to the tree line. She didn't want to miss Kai in action. Ruby took a seat on the log.

Kai had just caught the ball and was tossing it back. They jogged up and down throwing the ball to one another. She didn't really understand how throwing an object from one to the other could be seen as fun. The males laughed. They found it especially funny when one of them dropped the ball or failed to catch it. On these occasions, they would call each other really bad names using human swearwords. This made them laugh even harder.

Then they huddled and split up into two groups. There were three males in each group. She wasn't sure what the rules were but the game had definitely changed. There was plenty of running, kicking, throwing and tackling. They were rough with one another. Her eyes were locked on Kai. On the way his chest heaved as he struggled to catch his breath. A sheen of sweat glistened on his brow. It coated his entire body. Each and every hard muscle was defined. Dragon shifters didn't wear blue jeans. It was a shame.

Kai wore a particularly faded pair today. They rode low on his hips. His muscles roped and stretched beneath his skin, as he tried to avoid being tackled. A really big male slammed his body into Kai. Kai was just as big but the other male was quicker, she could hear how all of the wind was knocked out of him as the two walls of muscle collided. Kai landed flat on his back with the other male on top of him.

She jumped up off of her makeshift seat. Her hand clutched to her chest.

"You can do better than that." The big male growled as he rose to his feet.

Kai stayed on the ground for a few seconds. He made a groaning noise. "How's about a hand, Lazarus?"

The big male chuckled as he helped Kai up. "It's good to see you back at practice." He gave Kai a light tap on the back. "The team misses you." The male paused. "I'd like to see you up your game…you can do better." Then he jogged away.

The male who asked Kai to join called for a break. Kai accepted a bottle of water from the male. Kai downed its contents in one go and handed back the empty bottle.

"Don't be a stranger." Jenson said. "Introduce your female some time."

"Thanks. I needed that." He shouted from over his shoulder as he jogged back towards her. He ignored the comment about introducing her. He also didn't correct the male when he called her his female. As Kai drew closer, her mouth dried right up.

Half naked.

Up close.

His scent was the first thing that hit her. A really masculine smell with a coppery edge. It reminded her of their two days together. Of how good he felt inside her. How perfectly their bodies had fit. Of how her muscles had burned. How she ached from coming so hard.

Her core ached right now. It felt similar to when she had been in heat only without the pain. The need was definitely there. Inspired by the male that stood in front of her with a quizzical expression on his face. "Are you okay?" His nostrils flared.

By all that was scaly, he would be able to scent her need. She'd tried really hard not to allow her attraction to him to show. It was difficult when she ached for him. She tried…taking care of it herself but it wasn't the same. The pregnancy hormones made her over emotional, they also made her seriously aroused and at the most inappropriate times.

Like right now.

Like badly.

His sniffed a second time, his jaw tightened. His whole stance became tense. "Come with me." He took her hand and led her away.

His scent became more musky. He was aroused as well. His shirt was still clenched in her hand.

"Where are we going?" Her voice was shaky.

"Somewhere where we can talk in private." He kept his stare on the path ahead.

"Why do we need to talk?"

He didn't say anything. Her hand burned in his. It didn't really burn but it felt like it was burning up. His skin was against hers. Kai picked up the pace a little.

She swallowed hard. "It's the hormones…it's nothing…just ignore it, it'll go away."

Kai made a humming noise at the back of his throat. "It's nothing to be embarrassed about. I'm a male and you're a female and we've already established that we are compatible."

"I'm not embarrassed and we haven't established anything."

He stopped walking so suddenly that his hand in hers tugged her back. Ruby turned to face him.

He kept her hand in his. Warm. Calloused. Burning a hole in her skin.

"We're compatible." He repeated. "We definitely are."

"I was in heat. Quite frankly I could have had just as much fun if I'd rubbed myself up against a chair leg." Why had she said that? It wasn't true. She doubted that it would have been nearly as explosive with just anyone. An inanimate object...forget it.

His eyes darkened and he leaned in closer. "When I said what we had was special, off the fucking charts...I meant it. It had nothing to do with your heat. There is still an attraction between us." He looked at her expectantly and she realized he wanted her confirmation.

Ruby looked him in the eye. "Yes, there is." She couldn't deny it.

"Your next appointment with the healers is tomorrow?"

It was more of a statement than a question but she answered anyway. Ruby nodded. "Yes."

"Okay then." He paused for a few beats. She could see that he was in thought. "This is one hell of a situation." He pulled his hand across his jaw. She could hear the stubble catch. "We're attracted to each other and compatible. You are carrying my child yet this whole mate thing is not going to happen. We're tied together...for now...at least until he or she is born or released." He gave his head a quick shake like he still couldn't believe this was real.

Then he let her hand go and walked to the opposite side of the small clearing they were standing in. He looked at...she couldn't see anything between all the dense undergrowth and trees. The forest suddenly thickened from here. Kai stared out into the wilderness for a bit longer before nodding his head.

He turned to face her. "Maybe we should rut...each other I mean."

Her mouth fell open in a gape. As in, she was going to catch some flies if she didn't close it soon. Ruby wasn't sure what she had been expecting. Whatever it was, this wasn't it.

"I can scent your need and I'm also in a bit of a bind right now. I need sex and so do you. It's simple really. I could find some female and I know that there are plenty of males." His hands fisted at his side. Kai shook his head, like the idea was abhorrent to him. "Thing is, some dickhead fuck might not give a shit about you or our child. A male could hurt you or scramble my baby or whatever the hell you were saying the other day. I don't want some asshole touching you." He looked really angry. His eyes flashed red and there was a rough edge to his voice.

"Your scent is bound to attract them to you." He continued. It was like he was talking to himself more than to her. "You're really sexy. Vampires are attracted to pregnant females so don't think it would be a deterrent. It wouldn't be." He shook his head, looking angrier by the second. "It would help if my scent was on you...to ward off the others. You could move around more freely." So that was why he had asked her not to go anywhere unattended. Was it because he was afraid she would accept the advances of one of the other vampires? He was trying to keep her safe, to keep their baby safe.

Ruby was still in semi shock. At least she had managed to close her mouth. It fell back open when he said she was sexy but she'd got it closed again. "I am strong and capable. That thing about the scrambling of our egg is an old dragon's tale…not true at all. I don't know why I said anything."

"I don't want to risk it. I don't want you…doing that with other males." He sounded jealous. It was his fear for the baby. She knew that, but still…

"Relax, I'm not going to rut any vampire males." She blurted. It was true, she wasn't. It hadn't even so much as crossed her mind.

His eyes widened and she could see he was preparing to argue with her some more.

"I'm not going to rut any dragon shifters either." She couldn't believe he would even think that. "I'm not looking to meet males. This baby is my first priority. I might be a bit aroused…"

"A bit?" He gave her the ghost of a smile.

"Okay…a lot but it's fine. It's no biggie. I can handle it."

"Well I can't." He growled and his eyes went from a touch red to glowing. A beautiful golden color. By all that was scaly and breathed fire, he was beautiful. Strong, masculine and fierce, yet there was a softness to him as well. Like his full lips and easy smile. His eyes were dark and could be hard but they were fanned by long, thick lashes.

Her gaze dropped to the bulge in his jeans and she gripped her lip between her teeth.

"It's fucking killing me," he growled. "I think we should just rut. It would make things less complicated...for now."

*Yes. Yes. Yes.*

She wanted to shout it. She wanted to throw herself in his arms and demand he take her now. Right this second.

Instead, she shook her head. "I don't know if that's a good idea." She didn't think she could take the idea of him with another female. Not right now. She was just too emotional and she didn't want the stress. Yet, if she rutted him...regularly. It sounded like he wanted this to happen on a day to day basis...for now. Short term. The problem was, that she might fall for him. *Might. Huh!* She would definitely fall for him. Ruby was already half way there and had been since she first caught sight of him that day in the bar.

Kai made a sound that belied his frustration. "Why not? We're on good terms aren't we? We've moved past what happened." By that he meant her lying and deceiving him in the worst possible way. "We're friends?"

They were on two different pages. Make that in different books. He was attracted to her, wanted to have sex with her but on a short term basis. She was attracted to him but saw him as a potential mate…it would only deepen her feelings if they were intimate.

"We're good, but…" She didn't know what to say. *I'm scared I'll fall head over heels in love with you. I'm afraid you'll end up breaking my heart. You might be my soul mate. My love. My everything.* The only way to tell would be to lay herself bare to him. She would need to give him everything and hope he returned the favor. Once her heart was with Kai she could never get it back. It would be his to discard or to cherish. It was a risk.

She must've taken too long to answer because he took a step back. "I'm sorry." He scrubbed a hand over his hair, messing it up some more. "I'm putting pressure on you. It's wrong of me. I thought it was a logical solution. Forget I said anything."

That would mean seeing him with other females. Scenting them on him. It brought a lump to her throat. "It's a good idea. Your…proposal came as a shock. It would solve our dilemma. I think you are right. Let's rut each other…for now."

He smiled. "Are you serious?" Then he frowned for a half a beat before smiling again. "Are you sure because you didn't look like it appealed to you."

"I'm sure." No hesitation. "It's the best possible solution."

"Yeah it is and I really think it could work. There's an added bonus. It might bring on your labor. Remember what Becky said that first appointment?" He stuffed his hands in his pockets and she noticed the bulge was still there.

"When...um...when do we get started?" If she was doing this. Taking the plunge. The leap. The jump. She wanted it to happen right now. No, ten minutes ago. The ache was back. Oh these hormones. Oh this male.

He frowned. "We should double check that it's still okay. We'll ask the healers at tomorrow's appointment."

*Don't show your disappointment. Don't you do it.* "Yes...that's a great idea." Kai was right. They needed to be responsible about this. The baby came first...always.

"What's one more cold shower?" He grinned.

Ruby shrugged. "I'll have to bring *myself* to orgasm again tonight, but hey." She tried to sound flippant.

Kai groaned. "That's too much visual for one male to handle."

"I'm sorry. Dragon shifters tend to be very open about these things. I didn't mean to make you feel uncomfortable,"

"It's not that, although…uncomfortable is the right word." He readjusted himself in his pants and gestured to the shirt in her hand. Ruby handed it to him.

"You can't talk about touching yourself again unless we're naked." The muscles on either side of his neck bulged and his jaw looked tense. "Make that unless you're on my cock or maybe you could show me but only if your mouth is wrapped around…let's drop this line of conversation." He pulled the shirt over his head.

"No more talk of anything to do with sex." Her voice was high pitched. Her insides tightly wound.

Kai shook his head. "Not right now at least. I want you to be open with me. To be honest with me about everything."

She nodded. "I will be."

"Maybe we should go back now," he growled.

"We definitely should." She agreed as he grabbed her hand. They walked in silence. It should have been awkward between them but it wasn't, it was companionable. Once they reached the castle entrance, he released her.

Her mind raced. Her body had decided it was fully onboard with the plan. Having sex with him wasn't the best idea but right now it seemed like the only option she had.

She had noticed how the vampire females looked at Kai. There were plenty of them that were interested in him. He could have his pick. Kai had chosen her. Had he done so to simplify things, because it was the most logical thing to do or was there more to it? Only time would tell. Only, they didn't have much time. Blaze would be back in twenty days. Maybe they would be mated by then, but she knew if things didn't end up working out then she would need to come up with a plan.

# SIXTEEN

It was for the best.

It was perfect.

Why hadn't he thought of it sooner? Like, at least a week ago. It could've solved a ton of frustration on both their parts.

This would take care of his biggest problem. He couldn't help but to grin. Hell, he felt like whistling a tune. His euphoria evaporated when he spotted Jordan outside his door. Damnit! It had been a couple of days since he had seen her. He did need to feed and she would know that. So, here she was. Here for him, like she had always been.

Jordan had offered to rut him every time he took blood from her. When he refused she gave him some more of the silent treatment. She was convinced he was going to fall for Ruby and that she was going to tear his heart out and feed it to him. Those were her exact words. Not his.

Her take on it was that if Ruby had lied to him about something so important, there had to be more. Jordan was convinced it would happen again in the future. It was just a matter of time. Kai wasn't buying it. He understood why Ruby had done what she had done. Without going into any detail, he had explained it to his best friend along with his feelings on the subject, namely, he had forgiven Ruby. He had told Jordan he had moved past it.

Jordan had called him an idiot. A *as-blind-as-a-bat idiot* was how she had put it. It angered Kai that she wouldn't accept his feelings. He'd heard her out and still stood by his original decision. She should respect that.

Kai smiled at her even though she didn't return the favor. She was still his best friend and they would get through this. He knew she was afraid for him. Jordy was worried he would get hurt.

"Hi," he said, as he neared his door.

"How was your walk?" She rolled her eyes to remind him that she thought his daily walks with Ruby were a moronic idea. Her words.

"It was great, thanks." Better than great.

She sniffed at him when he approached. "Did she show you her breasts or something? Sheesh…you really smell."

"Like a bull in musk." He mumbled, choking out a laugh. Was it Jenson, or Stuart…who had called him that after he met Ruby for the first time? He opened his door and gestured for her to go in.

"Nail on the head." Jordan pointed a finger at him. "You stink like a bull in musk. Pathetic."

"Hey, I'm a male." he said. Jordan was particularly chatty this evening. It was a pity she was in such a terrible mood.

She scrutinized him for a few seconds. "Really? You're totally going to start rutting her again aren't you?" Her voice was an angry rush. "I can tell. I'm surprised it hasn't happened already."

Kai had just closed his front door. He held the air in his lungs for a moment before releasing it. Then he turned.

Jordan looked upset. Like ready to cry upset. Her lip quivered. *What the hell!* "Jordy." He narrowed his eyes on her. "What's going on here? Am I missing something?"

"You're thick as two planks on top of two planks, you know that don't you?"

"Okaaaay." He didn't like where this was going.

"I love you, Kai." A tear rolled down her cheek. An honest to god tear. Fuck.

*Don't let this be what I think it is. Please no!* "I love you too, Jordy. You are my dearest friend. By best damned friend. I hope you know that. Ruby doesn't change that. It shouldn't change anything."

There was another lip quiver, followed by another heavy tear. He watched as it rolled down her cheek, along her jaw, it hung onto the end of her chin for a good few seconds before splashing onto her t-shirt. All the while he prayed that he had misread this.

"I don't want to be your friend anymore. I can't be your friend anymore because I love you, Kai." Rushed and angry. "I fucking love you." She finished the sentence on a whisper which turned into a sob.

He'd never seen her like this. A mess. Why hadn't he seen this coming? "Let's sit down."

She shook her head. "This is the part where you tell me it's not like that for you. That you don't feel the same." More tears and more anger. "I've tried to tell you. I tried to get you to notice me. To make you feel jealous but it didn't help. Nothing has helped. I've pretty much thrown myself at you and…crickets."

"When did your feelings change?" He felt shell-shocked. Like a bomb had been dropped on his fucking head.

"I realized it after you came back. I knew that this female had messed with your head. I could see you couldn't stop thinking about her. I was jealous…I still am. You were mine first. I've known you for so damned long. We grew up together, Kai. The thought of losing you to her."

"You wouldn't lose me. I'm still here. I'm still your friend…Jordy…"

"I want more. I want you…" She closed the distance between them and cupped his face with both her hands. "I want there to be an us."

He closed his own hands over hers. "There is an us…just not that kind of us."

She made a noise of frustration and pulled her hands away. "You know what I mean." She sniffed. The tears still fell.

"Please, Jordan. You're right, I don't feel that way about you. I do love you but not like that."

Her eyes widened, they locked with his. "Give me a chance to prove w—"

"No," he growled. Kai didn't need proof of anything. He didn't see her like that. Jordan was the most important person in his life right now. Once his baby was born that would change. His son or daughter would become the most important.

For a very long time it had been just him and Jordan against the world. At least, it had felt like that. She was important to him. He huffed out a breath. "No," he whispered. "We would regret it."

"Don't tell me how I would feel. It's her isn't it? If it weren't for her you would have agreed to us. We wouldn't be fighting. It's killing me, Kai."

Would he have taken her up on her offer? "No, Jordan. You're wrong. I would never have put our friendship in jeopardy. You deserve happiness. There is a male out there for you. Hell, I've punched plenty of males over the years for disrespecting. I think Jenson has an enormous crush on—"

"Don't try and set me up with—"

"I'm not. Not at all." He paused for a moment. There was only one way and that was to be straight with her. "We're friends, Jordy. You're important to me but there will never be more." He kept his voice even. "Ruby and I..." he grabbed the back of his neck and squeezed.

"You're so going there and don't even deny it." She sounded defeated.

"I'm not denying it."

"Bastard," she growled. "You seriously need to have your head examined. She's bad news. You don't have to mate her to be able to be a father to this child."

"I know that."

"Do you?" She shook her head. "I don't think you do. I'm sorry, I can't give you blood anymore. I think we need to...give each other some space."

Kai nodded. "I don't want to lose our friendship but if that's what you really want."

"It's what you want too. I noticed how you called me your friend, just now, instead of your best friend."

"You know what I mean."

Jordan nodded. "Take care of yourself. Don't trust that female…please…just don't. You'll be sorry. Whatever you do don't fall for her, she'll chew you up and spit you out." Jordan left.

Ruby had lied to him but she had her reasons. It was all understandable. He still wished that she had been honest with him, although, again, he understood why she hadn't been. Most males would not have helped her. He wasn't most males.

They were attracted to each other and compatible. It was her brother that was pushing the whole mating thing. That fucker king had Kai's back to the wall. There was no fucking way he was mating Ruby because Blaze held a proverbial gun to his head. Could he fall for Ruby? He wasn't sure. One thing was for sure though, he was not going to be forced into mating her.

Not a fuck.

---

Becky frowned. There was a squelching noise. Ruby grimaced. By the movement of her shoulder, he could see that she had retracted her hand. Becky lifted it and pulled the glove off, but not before he noticed a red smudge on the tip of one of her fingers.

Blood.

The coppery scent hit him. Only a few drops. His mouth watered as he remembered how good she had tasted. He also cringed as he recalled the pain he had felt when he took blood from her. Drinking from Ruby had been sweet torture. Agony and pleasure all rolled into one. He must be completely certifiable because he would drink from her again in a heartbeat. He was seriously hungry right now. His gums ached, his nail beds tingled. His eyes might even have been glowing.

Coppery, sweet, fiery hot. Such a tempting combination. His fangs erupted. Kai grit his teeth and tried to concentrate on what Becky was saying.

"There has been some ripening of the cervix," the human said.

"What does that mean?" Ruby sounded excited but there was also an edge of panic to her voice.

Eleanor was beaming. "It seems your womb has begun opening in preparation for labor."

Ruby gasped, she covered her mouth with both her hands. Her eyes were wide.

"Don't get too excited," Becky cautioned. "In my experience, it can still take weeks before the onset of labor once the cervix starts to ripen."

Ruby dropped her hands to the bed with an audible plop as they hit the mattress.

"It can also take much less time. Normally a couple of days…a week but don't get your hopes up," she quickly added and Ruby smiled.

Kai could feel that he was also grinning. From ear to fucking ear. He moved closer to the bed and gripped Ruby's hand. "It won't be long now. The only questions are, when will it happen and are you going to birth an egg or a baby?" He put his hand on the curve of her belly. Her skin was soft and warm. "Our baby." His voice was filled with awe. His chest swelled with pride.

Her hand covered his. It was much smaller. "Our little one. I can't wait to meet him. Even if he is behind a shell at first."

Kai choked out a laugh. "Do dragons have two birthdays? The day they were…released? And the day they hatched? How does it even work?" He pulled her gown back down.

Ruby laughed. "We only have one birthday…silly. The day we were hatched of course."

Both Eleanor and Becky laughed as well.

Becky threw the glove in the trash. "I think it's probably safe to say, at this point, that you are carrying an egg, otherwise, I'm sure the pregnancy would have lasted longer. There is no way to tell for sure until…the time comes."

"Although it could still take a couple of weeks as Becky pointed out, chances are good you're going to go into labor within the next couple of days." Eleanor looked concerned. "You"—he was looking at Ruby—"need a cell phone. You need to call Kai...to call for help. I know there is a phone in your room but it's not enough."

Kai nodded. "Yeah, that sounds like a good idea. Better yet, maybe I should take some leave from work. I need to be able to be there for you...for him, when the time comes." He looked down at her belly. He hated feeling so helpless. The reality was that there was nothing he could do. Maybe he would be useless for the labor and the release...birth...whatever it ended up being but he sure as hell would make sure he was there.

"Don't be in such a hurry." Becky narrowed her eyes on him. "This could still take weeks. I've known of women whose cervix ripen months before the baby was due. They ended up being three or four centimeters by the time nine months rolled around. They carried perfectly normally, right until the end. It happens. That's the thing with pregnancy...even when we have all the facts, it still doesn't always go according to plan." She paused, looking at each of them in turn. "The thing is, we have no facts when it comes to this particular pregnancy. We have no idea what's going to happen, we can only guess. Although chances are good Ruby will go into labor fairly soon, it might not happen that way. I agree with Eleanor, you need to have a cell phone, Ruby."

Becky picked up a file that was on the desk next to her. "Don't make any drastic changes to your life at this point." She looked pointedly at Kai. "I wouldn't go any extended trips outside of vampire territory but keep working…for now at least. Things could change, we'll have to take it day by day."

Everything the healer had said made sense. There was a driving need to take control of the situation somehow. He wanted to move in with Ruby so that he could be with her. At least then he would be at her side to protect her, help her. It was on the tip of his tongue to suggest it. Instead, he nodded. "You are right. I will make sure my superiors are aware of the situation."

Ruby squeezed his hand. He hadn't realized he was still holding it. "It's going to be okay. I know it is."

Fuck! He hoped she was right. Kai nodded.

Becky wrote something inside the file before closing it and putting it back on her desk. "Fine. I'm happy with your progress."

Eleanor folded her arms. "Yes, things are progressing nicely, child." She smiled warmly at Ruby.

"Great," Becky said. "We'll see you in…three days."

"There was one thing we wanted to ask." Ruby got up off the bed.

How the hell had he forgotten? His whole focus had been on the pregnancy, the labor, all of it...he hadn't even thought about the question he needed to ask.

"Yeah," he blurted. For some reason it didn't feel right letting Ruby ask it. He was the male, it was up to him to make sure the mother of his unborn child was safe. "We were wondering if it would still be okay to have sex?"

Becky pursed her lips. Kai could see that the doctor was trying to hold back a smile. Her eyes said it all.

Eleanor's expression remained completely deadpan. "Rutting would be good for the mother and therefore excellent for the child. I would recommend twice a day. Don't allow yourself to become too tired, child. Although..." She smiled. "Nothing helps one sleep more than a good rutting."

Kai had to hold back a laugh.

"I couldn't have said it better myself." Becky's lips twitched. "Since we don't know exactly what we're dealing with, take it very easy." She looked pointedly at Kai. "Nothing too rough but I'm sure I don't have to tell you that. I know that as a vampire and as the father of this child, your instincts are to protect." She paused, looking thoughtful. "Sperm...seed is known to speed up the ripening of the cervix and to help bring on labor. Although our appointment is in three days, don't hesitate to call if you have any questions or if you experience anything out of the ordinary. For example, spotting…blood in your underwear…" She quickly added. "Or during sex for that matter. Any fluids, even if you appear to wet your pants or the bed. Any pains. Anything unusual, even if it seems stupid. I won't keep you any longer…I'm sure you guys can't wait to get out of here." She grinned and gave him a wink.

Damn, this doctor was too fucking much. She was also right on the money. Kai had to suppress his own smile. "Yeah, go and change. Let's get out of here." Ruby gave him the sweetest damn smile.

Something tightened inside him. He swallowed hard. The things he was about to do to this female…pregnant or not…he would take it slow and easy. There was no way he was going to hurt her or his unborn child but Ruby was going to scream. Loudly and more than once. That was a fucking given.

# SEVENTEEN

Kai put a hand to her back as they turned the final corner that led to her room. There was an urgency to his step that matched her own. They hadn't spoken since leaving the clinic. Not a word. There was no need to speak. The tension between them was thick. Palpable. She could hear his heart beating in his chest. Could hear him breathing. In and out. There was a friction of material against her skin as her elbow touched his arm. Her heart just about beat out of her chest every time his hand touched her back.

Kai was so sure they were compatible. She prayed he was right. Her whole analogy about the chair leg was unfair of her, it was also true to a degree because a female in heat was easy to please. A male under the influence of heat pheromones was just as easy to satisfy. Long story short, the two days they had spent together was an orgasmic haze. It could have been a lie.

Hear hand fumbled on the doorknob. She stifled a giggle as the door finally opened. He was directly behind her as they moved into the room. His chest, flush against her back. His hips, and…oh god…up against her lower back. She could barely breath as he nuzzled into her neck. His breath against her ear. She leaned back for a moment and sighed.

The door slammed behind them as he put his hands on her hips and picked her up. By the way his breathing changed, she could hear it took some effort. Kai stopped at the foot of her bed where he put her down. "Thank fuck we didn't move you to a much larger suite."

As in, he would have struggled to carry her from the door all the way to the bed. She giggled. It sounded nervous. It couldn't be helped. "Good thing," her voice was husky.

"Forget I said anything." He turned her around. "I would carry you for miles, just as long as there was a bed at the end of the journey." Although he was smiling, it was tight. His gaze was heated.

"Good to know."

"I want you." He rubbed his hands up and down her arms. "It's been a long time for me."

She shook her head. "It's been way longer for me so you can…"

His eyes moved to her mouth before moving back up. He gave a small shake of the head.

Wait a minute. Was he saying what she thought he was saying? No way. "I was your last?" She felt the skin of her forehead pull together.

"Yeah. It's been a long fucking time." He cupped her jaw. "It's complicated. I don't want to talk about it right now…I…" He was shaking. It was barely noticeable but there was a definite vibration against her cheek. "I didn't drink from Jordan yesterday. We had a fight. I don't want to talk about that either." He let his hands fall away. "I thought it would be okay but it won't be. I can't rut you feeling as strung out as I do. I…"

"I won't break. I'm strong." She wanted to tell him that she was stronger than him but she couldn't do it. No male liked to hear that. She was a royal dragon shifter, stronger than some of the lesser males in her tribe.

"The baby…" He shook his head. "I need to find blood. I'm not sure where. Vampire females consider it rude if a male drinks from them without…" He shrugged.

Ruby could fill in the blanks. She didn't like the thought of him drinking from someone else. "If we're going to rut, you may as well drink from me, although the last time you did…" She could recall how his whole body had tensed up. He'd made the most horrible noise, like he was being tortured or something and then…

"Don't remind me." He rolled his eyes. "I passed out cold."

"You were out for a while." Ruby smiled. "I'm not sure how true it is but according to our ancestors, our ability to breath fire stems from our blood. Fire dragons have fire in our veins." She cocked her head. "Not literal fire but whatever it is that allows us to have the ability to breathe flames, is in our blood."

"Oh it's true alright." Kai raised his brows. "Your ancestors were right on the money. Your blood was heaven but it was also hot as hell. As in…the deepest, darkest fire pits of hell. It was like my whole body was burning up."

"Okay then…you won't want to experience that again. I understand. Find a female and come back when you are ready." Her heart sank like a rock. She could handle it. It wasn't a big deal. She tried not to dwell on the disappointment. He'd been taking blood from Jordan. She had been okay with that, hadn't she?

"Are you kidding? Didn't you hear the part about your blood being heaven? You might need to wait though"—he smiled—"for me to wake up if I pass out again."

"Good. It's settled." She pulled her top over her head. The clothing was on loan from the vampire queen. Maternity wear. She hadn't been able to bring herself to actually wear the breast coverings. They were stifling.

His jaw tightened but his eyes stayed locked with hers. "Yeah. Looks that way." He moved closer, stopping only when his rock hard abs touched her belly. "I'm glad you're okay with this, I don't want anyone else's blood…right now." He quickly added.

*Right now.*

Don't think about it. *Don't.*

"I don't want anyone else period." The right now went unspoken but she heard it nonetheless. "Sit down on the edge of the bed."

She did as he said.

Kai moved onto his knees. He gripped the elastic at the top of her leggings. "Tilt your hips up."

She did as he said and he slid the garment from her body.

"You're so fucking beautiful." His gaze was still on her face.

She knew she was considered attractive amongst her own species. She was very different from vampire females though. Just as tall and muscular but not nearly as lean. Ruby had thicker thighs and her backside was rounded. Her mammary glands were filled out. More than most of the vampires she had encountered and it was only getting worse.

They were much fuller than before. Fuller than when she had first arrived here. Heavy, cumbersome and in the way. They bounced when she tried walked too fast, or tried to climb more than one step at a time. It was why she had tried the human coverings in the first place. The queen had told her she needed the support. Her breasts were irritating. In the way.

Although, by the way Kai was staring at them, she would swear he liked them. His chest heaved as he breathed harder. His heat filled gaze turned scorching. He swallowed thickly. "So damned beautiful." Using both his hands, he cupped her heavy breasts, squeezing them softly.

He liked them alright.

Maybe she could live with them.

Another soft squeeze. It felt good and when his thumbs raked over her nipples which tightened in response, it felt more than good. Those deft fingers continued to rub back and forth across her turgid flesh and she let her head fall back. A few more strokes and she moaned. Her hips thrust forward.

"I want you," she whispered. Her core was already wet and ready for him. This from a few light touches.

He chuckled. It was a deep, throaty sound. "We need to do this my way." His hands moved to her thighs. "I want to taste you." His gaze was fixed…between her thighs.

"You wish to kiss me between my legs?" Her voice had turned breathy.

"That's one way of putting it. I would love to kiss your sweet pussy." He ran his hands along her thighs, waiting for her to part them.

Panic welled up in her. "No…you don't have to…" It was her normal response. One she had used many times before.

"I want to. I want to suck on your clit just as much as I want to fuck you…maybe more, and that's saying something." His lashes touched his cheeks, his gaze was focused…down there.

Ruby swallowed hard. Could she do this? Could she let him? There was no way she could say no. She wanted him to touch her in this way. She parted her thighs.

Kai bit down on his lower lips for a half a beat. "I'm going to eat you up, sweetness."

He was?

Oh no!

Oh yes!

For fire's sake, she could do this. His focus stayed…well there, with an intensity that scared her. Kai was still completely clothed. He bent down closer. His nostrils flared, his whole stance, tense. His face had a tightness about it. He looked almost angry as his shoulder pushed against her thighs forcing her legs wider.

She sucked in a breath. The groan that left her, as he closed his mouth over her clit sounded raw and drawn out. Kai didn't mess around. He suckled on her a couple of times. Her eyes widened. Her back bowed as his tongue joined the party. Thankfully, although she had a baby bump, it wasn't crazy big or the back-bow might have hurt.

The air felt frozen in her lungs. Her mouth was slack. Her brain raced but couldn't come up with anything coherent, especially since his tongue was flicking back and forth. His mouth suctioned over her clit. It was…so good…so good…oh…oh…it was sooooo good.

A finger breached her opening. One single digit. Another loud, drawn out groan was torn from somewhere deep in her throat followed by a throaty growl. Oh so good went to unreal in a split second. In and out, that finger pumped in time with his tongue flick. The suction was stronger. Her back bowed again.

*No. No.*

This had to stop. It was too much. She was gulping for air, trying to find control. Ruby tried to close her legs but she couldn't. Kai was between them, his shoulders were against the insides of her thighs. She tried to pull back but the hand on her hip, held her in place.

His finger curled inwards. It was a subtle change with astounding results. Her orgasm hit. It hit hard. It rushed through her. Her head fell back as her back bowed yet again. Her eyes went wide and then she squeezed them shut.

There was at first, a guttural moan, then a growl which morphed into a cry. The pleasure that rushed through her had her muscles spasming and her toes curling. There was a ripping noise as her hands fisted the sheets.

When he finally released her, she fell back onto the bed. Her nose twitched…Ruby opened her eyes. "Oh no!" She covered her mouth with her hand. She licked her lips. Her mouth was bone dry.

Kai chuckled. "I take it you enjoyed that and I can safely say that this is a first for me."

"Me too." She shook her head. "It's never happened to me before. Then again, I've never…" She almost told him that he had been the first male to…do that. Ruby shook her head instead.

All she could say was that it was a wonder she hadn't burned down the whole castle. It had been that good.

---

Kai looked up to where Ruby was staring. The ceiling had a charred blackened area right in the middle. He waved his hand, dispersing some of the smoke. "All I can say is, thank fuck you were looking up at the ceiling and not down at me."

When he looked at her, Ruby looked horrified.

He had to laugh. "Hey…" He kept his voice gentle. "I take it as a compliment."

Ruby shook her head. "It's never happened to me…I don't usually…"

He sat down next to her and put an arm around her. "It's not a big deal."

"I could've hurt you. We can't do that again."

"I have advanced healing. I'm not afraid of a few flames. We sure as fuck will be doing that again and soon." Then something she said earlier registered. "No one has ever done that to you before, have they?"

She shook her head. "No. It's probably why I overreacted a little."

What the fuck! Never. "Dragon shifter males are dicks. I'm sorry to have to say it but they're a bunch of assholes. I will be tasting you again very soon and that's final."

She looked like she wanted to say something but didn't.

"Are you feeling okay otherwise? No pains or…I don't know?" He wanted her so damned badly but also needed to be sure that she was fine. That the baby was safe.

Just looking at her made his mouth water. Hearing her cries of ecstasy had driven him almost to distraction. His fangs had erupted before he even went down on her. It was why he couldn't tongue fuck her like he wanted, why he'd had to go easy. In hind sight, maybe it was a good thing. Ruby could've scorched the whole room. He held back a grin. He'd hoped for a scream and got one. That and flames. The roof was a fucking mess.

Ruby smiled. "I'm fine." She gripped the bottom of his shirt and he lifted his arms so she could pull it over his head.

Her eyes turned greedy as they swept across his chest. He liked that she found him attractive. Especially since he found her to be the sexiest female he had ever laid eyes on. He wanted her lush thighs around him. He wanted to fuck her, to make her come all over again, but not yet. He stayed her hand as it moved to the button on his jeans. "I need to drink first." His voice was rough with need. His dick was so damn hard it throbbed. His balls. What balls? They were pulled up so tight you wouldn't think he had any.

"You don't need clothes to drink. You can take my blood and then I want you inside me."

Kai had to smile. "If I'm still awake." He didn't want to pass out again. He was excited and nervous. "Let's do this." He nodded once, looking down at his pants. She yanked his jeans so hard that the button popped off, hitting the far wall with a ping. This was a female after his heart.

She giggled. A sound he'd come to love and in such a short time. He toed his boots off and his pants followed suit. Then he moved away from her. "Sit on my lap."

She shook her head. "I'm too heavy."

"Bullshit." *Maybe a little.* "Okay. Sit on the edge of the bed and I'll sit behind you. I'd prefer to drink from your neck. I wouldn't want to hurt you or him." He gave her stomach a light stroke, feeling something inside him clench and it had nothing to do with his desire for her.

"I told you I won't damage easily but let's be safe rather than sorry."

He nodded. Kai swallowed thickly as he moved in behind her. His legs around her. His erect cock against her back. He circled his arms around her and gave her a hug before splaying his hands on her belly. His baby. It was still surreal.

Ruby put her hands over his and leaned back into him. Shit! This felt too much like a moment. It felt intimate…it felt good. It also scared him a little. What if Jordan had been right? He couldn't allow himself to fall for this female. Not yet. He still felt the need to tread carefully.

Kai nuzzled her neck. Her scent was so damned intoxicating. One noseful and he was practically salivating. Ruby gripped her long mane of hair and pulled it over one shoulder so that he would have all the access he needed.

Her neck was slender. The pulse at the base of her throat was strong. He could scent her blood as it pulsed through her veins. Rich, sweet...so tempting. The smokiness was there, just as delicious but also misleading. The scent didn't convey the burn.

Ruby was breathing quickly.

"Don't be afraid." He would never hurt her. Not a fuck.

"I'm not, I remember liking it...very much. I want you to drink..." She swallowed and he watched her throat work. A thing of beauty. "I promise," she whispered.

It was the only push he needed. If this female liked it when he bit her before then he was going to do it again. Any hesitation left him. He said a silent prayer. This was going to hurt.

Kai put his lips to her pulse, feeling it beneath her skin. Then he opened his mouth and sank his fangs into her. Not too deep. She made a noise of ecstasy. His dick twitched against her. Then he pulled in a mouthful of blood and swallowed it down. It was his turn to moan. Such an exquisite taste. He sucked again and she cried out, arching into him. It was only on the third sip that the pain hit. Searing, burning. The agony so intense he growled. He fought against the white hot flames licked at him. The agony didn't matter. He wanted more anyway.

*More.* It was pain and pleasure in equal measures. Heaven and hell all rolled into one. Addictive.

Ruby moaned, she rubbed up against his dick. Mother fucker! A zing of intense pleasure rushed through him at the contact. He swallowed another warm mouthful and sucked again. Even in his drowning haze, he heard Ruby moan louder. Heard her pants. She was jerking against his cock. Rubbing. The pain, the bliss. Fuck. A rush of ecstasy pierced him and he groaned so hard he released her neck. It was quick but fierce. It left him shaky. Black faded in and out around his vision. He kept his arms around her like an anchor. He had to fight not to pass out.

Kai shook his head, trying to clear it. His whole body throbbed. Endorphins made him feel sleepy. There was still an edge of pain present. His nerve endings felt like they had been rubbed raw. Not a fuck!

"Please tell me I'm asleep and having a nightmare." His voice was barely recognizable. He sounded drugged.

Ruby gave him a contented sigh. "Not a chance. That was so good." Her voice was thick. "At least you didn't pass out." He could hear she was smiling.

"There was more pleasure this time…with the pain." It came out sounding stronger.

Ruby laughed softly. She vibrated against him. "It was wonderful. You can drink from me anytime."

Kai laughed. "I'm glad you enjoyed it and I'm really fucking embarrassed." He tried not to move. He felt so uncomfortable, Kai was sure she would feel it as well. "Let me get a towel. I'll just be a second."

She bit down on her lip, which twitched. Ruby found this whole thing hilarious. Fuck! He grabbed a towel and wet half of it with warm water. Kai cleaned himself off, tossing the material in the basket. He grabbed a fresh one and wet that as well. Instead of handing it to Ruby, he moved to where he had been sitting at her back and cleaned her up too. Fucking embarrassing. "It's never happened to me before." He cringed inwardly.

"If it makes you feel any better, I may also have had an orgasm at the same time as you." She shrugged. "I'm sure that makes it okay."

"It doesn't make me feel better and it's not okay." He folded his arms. "You can come fifty times but I should only come when I allow myself to. That's how it works. It's how it's always worked for me in the past, but not with you, Ruby." He kissed her neck. "I lose control with you."

"That's good, right?"

*No way. Not if I fall for you. I need to be sure first.* "Yes and no."

"Don't be cryptic." She turned and gave him a little push. He allowed himself to fall onto his back. Ruby straddled him. "I think it's good." She was positioned over his dick.

Everything in him tightened and his mouth felt dry.

She took his cock into her hand. Kai suppressed a hiss. She looked him straight in the eye as she pushed herself onto him. Her eyes closed and her mouth turned slack. That mouth. Those lips. "Fucking good." He groaned. He was talking about how good she looked on his cock. Stretched around him. Completely seated inside of her.

She was breathing deeply. For endless seconds she just sat there, content just to be filled or maybe adjusting to him. Kai wasn't complaining. Being inside her warmth. Feeling her squeezing the fuck out of him, felt so good. He gripped her hips lightly with his hands.

On a soft moan, she pulled back before easing forward. She rocked slowly. Kai had to grit his teeth. She felt so damned good. Then she leaned forward, placing her hands on his chest. She lifted and dropped. Her eyes on his. Ruby's forehead was lined. She moaned in time to her movements. She was breathing deeply. Her breasts swayed. He was damned if she wasn't even more beautiful in this moment. Her hair a wild tangle down her back, her lips parted and wet.

He helped her as best he could but she weighed a ton. It was that, or he wasn't strong enough. He sure as fuck hoped it was the first reason, although, he suspected it was a bit of both. Kai might be one of the strongest males on vampire territory but he was no match for the dragon shifters. He was still going to teach her dirtbag, asshole of a brother a lesson. He felt like looking up all the dickhead males that had been in her life - the ones that hadn't treated her right - and giving them a piece of his mind. He might not survive but it would be worth it.

He groaned as she picked up the tempo, working harder in the process. She was breathing hard. He drove his hips upwards to meet her. Trying to help her as much as he could.

As good as she felt, as sexy as she was. Hips pumping. Her bottom lip between her teeth. "Let me." He growled. His voice gravelly.

Ruby stopped moving. "What's wrong?" Her eyes were wide.

"Nothing." He sat up. "You're just working too damned hard. You shouldn't be exerting yourself…not now." His gaze dropped to her distended belly.

"I'm not some delicate flower." She smiled.

"Yes, you are." He kissed her softly on the forehead. "Let me take over, turn around."

Still frowning, she moved to all fours. "Like this?"

Kai groaned. "You have one hell of an ass." He palmed both her cheeks.

Then he shook his head. "On your side."

She did as he said and Kai moved in behind her. He gripped her hips and pulled her against him. There was a sense of urgency, of possession reflected in his touch but there was also a softness. It was a powerful combination. It made her feel weak and desperate for more.

He was so hard up against her. "Bend your knees." His voice was commanding. She did as he said.

Ruby pushed her ass out, trying to give him all the access he needed. He was sweet for being so concerned. It had been unnecessary but this was nice too.

"Just like that." His voice was deep and against the shell of her ear. Then the tip of his cock was at her entrance. He pushed into her, just a little. A few seconds later, he seated himself inside with one easy thrust.

All the air left her lungs on a hard moan. Ruby had orgasmed twice already but not with him inside her. This was what she needed, what she had been craving. His hard cock, deep inside her. "Oh god," she whimpered. It had felt good when she was on top but this felt better. Kai began to move, he rut her with hard, careful strokes.

His breath was ragged. "You feel so good," he groaned. "Fuck. I can't believe we didn't do this sooner."

She closed her eyes, knowing the answer. It was more than just sex to her. Even though he was all warrior, he was also sweet and kind. Her belly was supported. Her breasts didn't shake as much. It was more comfortable. He thrust into her. Slowly, carefully but with definite purpose. Fully seating himself with each push, his hips came up flush against her backside.

Kai grunted softly, he trembled. His movements became more frantic. Ruby could feel how hard he was working not to let go. She was so close…right on the edge.

He slid a hand around her hip and gave her clit a pinch. At least, it felt like a pinch. He gripped the bundle of nerves between his fingers and squeezed. It didn't hurt. Not even a little.

Ruby groaned. It turned into a loud growl as every muscle in her body pulled tight before relaxing. The sensation started at her clit, it moved to her core and then flooded her whole body. Kai muttered something that sounded like *thank fuck* before jerking against her. He continued to thrust while making the sweetest grunting noises. She whimpered as her body gave a last shudder, his movements slowed, his arms banded around her. "Are you okay?"

Ruby nodded. "More than okay." She was totally out of breath. She couldn't stop smiling.

"I hope I didn't scramble our egg." He chuckled and kissed her softly on the shoulder.

She chuckled right back. "No…I think we're good." He had been so careful with her. Almost too careful.

He stopped moving but stayed seated inside her. He wasn't as hard but still very much there.

"Are there any dragon tales about cracking or denting the egg?" Although he used a joking tone, she could hear something more in his voice.

She turned her head slightly. "Are you serious?"

He sort of smiled. "Humor me…I worry." Kai pulled out of her. He really was concerned.

She couldn't help the laugh that escaped.

"My concern for our unborn child is funny to you?" He smiled. "Are you sure you feel okay? Any pains? No strange fluids…down there."

"I think your concern is sweet but really unfounded. You won't crack or dent the egg. Yes, there are some strange fluids but they're perfectly normal after sex."

"You know what I mean." He huffed out a breath. Kai moved, propping himself up on his elbow.

Ruby turned to face him. Kai touched her belly. "I went as easy as I could, but"—he grit his teeth— "you can take all of me so I couldn't hold back I…" Kai frowned. He was really serious. "I wasn't rough but I gave you all I have, which…" He looked really nervous. He was seriously worried. Ridiculously so.

She grabbed his hand and squeezed. "Is perfectly fine." She finished the sentence for him. "I'm fine and so is the baby. I feel great. Please don't worry."

He frowned. "Maybe we should go to the healers. Becky can check you out. It would make me feel better."

"No." She shook her head. "We're not going to the clinic. I'm fine…" She put a hand on her belly. "The baby is fine. You would really hurt me if you went that far into me to where you could reach him…" She could feel her cheeks heat. "Besides…dragon shifter males are…they're pretty big. I'm good." She waved a hand, trying to look blasé about it.

His whole facial expression changed. He went from serious to serious with just a hint of humor. "Okay…are you trying to tell me that I don't measure up to dragon shifter males?" There was definitely a hint of humor there but he clenched his jaw. A sign of anger…maybe. She wasn't sure how to read this.

"Um…all I'm saying is I have, possibly…nevermind…let's just say that I know for a fact that the baby is going to be fine."

"Oh really now?" He sat up and folded his arms. "And you know this for a fact because you've been with males with bigger dicks than me? That's really nice, Ruby, you could hurt a male's fragile ego by talking like that." He laughed. "Fucking awesome. Just awesome. Quite frankly I'm hurt." He laughed again.

He didn't look hurt. Kai looked like he found it hilarious. She knew that male's cared about stupid things like the size of their members. Maybe he was trying to act like he was okay with it when he wasn't. She didn't know him well enough to tell. "It's not about size. Trust me, it's really not. You're plenty big enough…I swear."

It's not that he wasn't big, it's just he wasn't as big. The thing was, he could run circles around the guys she'd rutted. All of them. He was hands down the best lover she had ever had. She touched his arm. "It's not a thing for me."

Kai groaned. "Right, so dragon shifter males are stronger than me and my dick doesn't compare either. That's really great." He lay back down and put his arms around her. She buried her face into his chest, not sure what to say. "Good thing I'm a confident, well-rounded male. I don't have a problem with it."

"You're sure? Because you really shouldn't." Her voice was muffled. "It's not important. It's really not."

"Shhhh…" He placed a feather light kiss on the top of her head. "It's not important." He played with the strands of her hair. She hoped he meant it because she had never felt more safe, more relaxed, more content than what she did in this moment.

She couldn't help but to smile. How could she not fall for Kai? It was impossible. Just as quickly as the smile arrived, it faltered. This was a dangerous slope she was navigating. One that might see her seriously hurt. Ruby had no choice but to keep moving forward.

# EIGHTEEN

*Two weeks later...*

Time had gone by quickly but it had also dragged. Spending time with Kai was wonderful. They still walked around the castle grounds every day. They made love every evening, as soon as they got back from their walk.

It was the same every time. Their walk back was filled with anticipation. Tension crackled between them. They practically jogged down the hall to her room. Okay, maybe they just walked really fast. Her belly had grown. Between its rounded, curve and her in-the-way mammary glands, jogging had become impossible. Kai carried her to the bed every time. He insisted. He also insisted on kissing her between her legs...often. Thankfully there had been no more flames. Smoke may or may not have poured from her nostrils but there had been no more actual fire. Despite her growing belly, sex between them, only got better. He drank from her every second or third day. He orgasmed hard every time but then again, so did she.

They ate meals together, he even tucked her in and kissed her good night before returning to his own room. It didn't feel like just rutting. Two people taking what they needed from each other. It felt like more. Although he kissed her between her legs, on her cheeks, her forehead. Kai kissed her everywhere…only, he'd never actually kissed on the lips, or stayed the night. He definitely drew the line. It felt like they were a couple only…not. There had been one or two occasions where she wanted to bring it up with him. To ask him where this was headed but it didn't feel right just yet. She was afraid that laying everything all out there too soon might end up scaring him off. She didn't want this to end just yet.

Her belly had expanded. She was big, for a dragon shifter at least, she was big. Not ridiculously so but big enough to warrant concern. Even Becky and the vampire healer, Eleanor, had looked worried at her last visit, which had been just yesterday.

Her womb continued to ripen and had even began to open. According to the human healer, she was already one centimeter…whatever that meant. The time dragged because with each passing day, she worried more for the baby that grew inside of her.

There was still no movement. She had not wanted to tell Kai, for fear of alarming him, but she had felt heat inside of her. Once yesterday, and again this morning. Not hot enough to hurt her, but certainly warm enough that she could feel its glow.

She walked to the window and peered out over the vast lands. There were acres upon acres of grass. The ground was flat. This led to thick forests. Way across the far side of the fields, groups of males trained. Kai was amongst them. If she looked hard enough, she could make out his form. Hand-to-hand combat. He was skilled and strong. The male he had been fighting lay sprawled on the ground. She was sure he would make the team again. It meant so much to him. She turned away.

What would the future hold for them?

Another concern was Blaze. Her brother would be back in a week. He would expect for them to be mated. She needed to tell Kai. As far as he was concerned, Blaze had accepted the terms that Zane had set out. The main one was that they would first wait for the baby to hatch and only if he was alive and well, would Kai be expected to mate with Ruby. The last thing she wanted was a forced mating…even with Kai. Ruby had wanted to tell him but something held her back. If she was honest with herself, she was hoping they would get together on their own. Not just pretend together but for real together.

Kai didn't know her brother. Blaze would not budge. He would not hesitate to kill Kai. The problem was, she knew that Kai could be stubborn as well. He was also angry with Blaze after hearing how he tried to give her to the Air king. He had already said he was going to take Blaze on. If her brother arrived on vampire territory and they weren't mated and then on top of that, Kai provoked him, Blaze would kill him. The thought of Kai's broken, bleeding body caused a sob to leave her.

She would tell Kai as soon as he came back from training. There had to be a way around this. Only, she could think of none. Blaze would be angry. If Kai provoked him, he would lose control. Kai didn't stand a chance. She sniffed and realized she was crying.

The first real pain hit. It was sharp and piercing. Her belly tightened. Her hands automatically clutched her rounded stomach. What was…the pain intensified…he was coming. How could she have been so stupid? Her lower back had been paining her all day. At first it was a constant dull ache then it morphed into a sharper pain which had come and gone. Ruby had assumed the pain would start in her belly, just like she was feeling now but she had been wrong.

She breathed through her mouth. Short pants to help ease the pain. Thankfully, it didn't last long. Within a few minutes, it happened again. She was definitely in labor.

She couldn't stay here. This room was too cramped the walls felt like they were closing in. The urge to shift rose up in her, scales rubbed beneath her skin. Ruby closed her eyes and tried to blank her mind. A feeling of calm settled over her.

She needed to get away, to be alone. Ruby had planned this. She opened the closet and removed the backpack which she slung onto her back. Fear and excitement coursed through her. She moved quickly to the door, but another pain hit, sharper this time. She leaned against the wall, breathing hard, fighting for control. It would be better once she was outside in the open. She instinctively knew that the need to shift would diminish and maybe even go away altogether. Once the pain subsided, she turned back. Her cellphone was on the coffee table. She had practiced using it. Kai's number and that of both the healers was programmed into the contacts list. Hopefully she wouldn't need to use it.

Ruby went and fetched the phone, just in case. It wasn't long before the next pain ripped through her, more severe this time. It was happening quickly. As soon as it passed, she put the note on the table where he would spot it easily and then left the room

Ruby prayed she would make it outside before the next one hit. Praying even harder she would get through this and that her baby would be okay. He had to be.

There was no other option. Either she would birth this egg or she would die trying.

---

Kai looked down at his fist. *What the fuck?*

"What the hell was that?" Lazarus roared. The Elite Leader, as well as several other males, rushed forward. Lazarus crouched over Jenson's lifeless form.

Kai swallowed thickly, his legs finally decided to work and he too jogged to where the small group had formed. *What the hell had he done?* "Is he okay?" He shouted. "Is he at least alive?" He snarled, feeling panicked.

Jenson's nose was crooked. Both of his eyes were swollen shut. The male moaned and Lazarus sighed loudly. "Thank fuck," his leader growled.

"Trying to kill me?" Jenson croaked. The male tried to grin but it ended up looking like more of a grimace. "What the fuck are you on anyway?"

Kai looked back down at his fist. He could feel he was gaping but couldn't seem to close his mouth. The feeling of power coursed through his veins. It crackled and sizzled inside of him.

Lazarus grinned. "I've never seen anything like it. Never." The smile left almost as soon as it had arrived. "I would prefer it if you didn't use that level of force during training. Save it for battle…although, God willing, it doesn't come to that."

Kai nodded. He didn't know what the fuck to say. They had started up by running laps, push-ups, sit-ups followed by lunges. The normal stuff. He and Jenson had messed around at first. Tapping each other rather than actually hitting. Then they had started sparring, just like everyone else. He'd hardly touched the male. It should've been a light punch. A nothing punch. Enough to sting, maybe. It should not have sent the male flying. He had heard the crunch as his fist struck. Bone and cartilage had crushed beneath his fist. One fucking punch and look at Jenson's face? Broken and bleeding. The male had flown at least twenty feet, right through the air and Kai hadn't even tried. What if he'd put a bit of muscle behind the punch? His friend probably wouldn't be alive right now.

He looked back down at his fist. Kai knew there was something to Ruby's blood. It fueled and invigorated. He had known he was becoming stronger. He found it easier and easier to carry her. Although her blood still burned him. It had gone from barely tolerable yet enjoyable, to all out fucking heaven. He was becoming accustomed to the burn. More than that, he'd begun to crave it.

Kai knew there was power in her blood, he hadn't realized just how much power though.

"Let's call it a day." Lazarus bellowed, making sure everyone could hear him. "Can you walk?" He looked down at Jenson.

The male nodded. "My face might be fucked but my legs are working just fine." He moved into a sitting position. Kai could see he was trying not to do anything that would cause his face anymore pain. He rolled his shoulders and arched his back. "Yup…I'm good," he added.

"Fine." Lazarus nodded his head. "You can get yourself to medical then."

"I'll take him." Kai felt terrible. He had done this. This newfound strength had come so quickly. So unexpectedly. Fucking hell! Jenson looked like shit. It looked like he could only see out of one eye. And then only through a tiny slit. His skin was puffy and an angry red although it was mottled with hints of purple. The healing process had begun already.

"I need to have a word with you." The Elite Leader turned to look at him. He was frowning…big time. Fuck. How the hell did he explain this?

"I'm fine." Jenson said, giving a wave of his hand like what had just happened was nothing.

Kai put out his hand and helped the male to his feet. Jenson clenched his teeth and sweat beaded on his forehead.

"You're not fine," Lazarus growled.

Jenson carefully touched his face. He winced as his fingers touched his nose. He cursed. "You did a really good job of it." In one quick move, he straightened his nose on a loud roar. He looked down, putting his fingers to his temples. Blood dripped, from his newly re-broken nose, onto the ground for a few seconds. Jenson was breathing hard. Then he made a groaning noise and looked back up. His eyes were watering badly. "All done. I'll go and shower now. In a couple of hours, I'll be as good as new." He choked out a laugh. "Remind me not to spar with you ever a-fucking-gain." He chuckled as he walked away, not far behind the rest of the males.

Kai folded his arms and turned to face Lazarus.

"What was that? That was not fucking normal." He shook his head. There was a ghost of a smile. Though the male mostly looked shocked.

Kai felt just as shocked. "I'm not sure." Dragon blood was potent.

Lazarus looked at him pointedly. The male knew he was full of shit.

He had to give Lazarus something. Kai was sure the male already knew. "I'm…seeing a female." *Seeing*. Fucking, seeing. He wasn't sure how to put it. What was happening between him and Ruby? It was more than just seeing. It was more than just fucking. However, he wasn't exactly sure what it was yet, or where it was going. All he knew was that he didn't want others in his business, certainly not where Ruby and the baby were concerned.

Lazarus didn't say anything.

"She's a dragon shifter. She's pregnant with my child. I have been taking blood from her and, let's just say dragon shifters are much stronger then vampires. She's a royal of the species, her blood is potent."

Lazarus nodded. "I take it you didn't know that you would change in this way. You probably looked more shocked than the rest of us combined. You're going to have to be very careful."

No shit. The male was stating the obvious. As his leader, it still needed to be said, so Kai understood. He gave a nod. "I might need to train on my own for a while…maybe avoid any hand-to-hand combat."

"Thank fuck this wasn't a sword fight. You may have cut poor Jenson clean in half." He choked out a laugh.

It wasn't funny but Kai couldn't help but to smile. It had been a close call…too close.

"Go and shower like the others." He gave Kai a tap on the back. "Good luck with the female you are…seeing." He smirked, his brows raised. "Thank you for confiding in me. I was already aware of this. Congratulations on the pregnancy. I will need to discuss this development with Brant and Zane."

Kai nodded. He turned and jogged towards the gym. "The two of you look good together." Lazarus yelled at his retreating back. Kai rolled his eyes but he also smiled. It was true, they did look good together.

Some of the males were already toweling off, while others were dressing. There were still a couple of showers running. Jenson was underneath one of them. His head was bowed, the cascading water rushed over his shoulders and back, which was bruised.

Fuck.

He felt like such a dick. Kai quickly undressed and turned the faucets on in the shower next to Jenson. The room was large, with faucets all along the one side of the wall. There were no separate stalls.

He turned the heat up, feeling some of the tension drain from him as the warmth hit his body. Steam rose up but dissipated quickly within the open, airy space.

"How are you feeling? I'm so fucking sorry." He glanced over at Jenson who was focused on his…Kai felt himself frown. The male might only be able to see out of one eye for the moment, but that one eye was definitely focused on his…not a fuck. "Um…Jenson." The male didn't react. "Are you seriously looking at my cock?"

That finally managed to rouse him from whatever it was that he was doing.

"You do realize that your cock is much bigger than it used to be, don't you?" He still stared…at Kai's dick. As in, all out stared.

Kai had the unnatural urge to cover himself or to turn away. He grit his teeth for a few beats instead.

When the male looked up, he was smiling.

"Okay." Kai held up his hands. "I'm getting worried here. Why the fuck are you checking out my dick? Make it good cause you know what my fists can do." He spoke under his breath.

Jenson chuckled. Then he made a pained noise, his smile quickly turning to a wince. He groaned and then chuckled again, this time in a much more reserved fashion. "We shower together all the fucking time. I don't look at your dick…not like that." He lowered his voice. "It's just"—he shrugged— "it's very out there…a monster dick if you will."

"What the fuck?" Kai growled. "You didn't just say that."

"You have a big dick and I noticed…so fucking sue me." The male had the good grace to look sheepish. His gaze was on the far wall. He squirted some shower gel into his hand. "It's much bigger than it was now though…monster dick turned Godzilla." He chuckled at his own joke. He began to wash himself. "If extra strength and a bigger dick are a direct result of being with a dragon shifter, I want one. Are there any single shifter females in dragonville? If any of them are as hot as your female, excuse the pun, I'm game."

Jenson glanced at Kai. His face looked even worse, the bruising was so purple it looked almost black. His nose was so swollen he was talking funny. "So, are you going to hook me up or what?"

Kai shook his head and laughed. "I thought you liked Jordan." It hurt to say her name. True to her word, Jordy had been ignoring him flat out. She deleted his messages and refused to take his calls. He had stopped trying after a few days. If space was what she wanted, he would honor her wishes.

"She won't give me the time of day but I will keep trying. I'm a tenacious fuck. Jordy is the one for me…unless of course you can hook me up with a dragon." By the way Jenson laughed, he could tell the male was joking.

"You had better not hurt that female. Jordy is more sensitive than she looks."

"Hurt her?…I need to at least be in the same room with her for more than two minutes in order to be able to do that." He turned serious. "I wouldn't though, you know that. What's going on between the two of you?"

The male had carried a torch for his best friend for as long as he had known him. "It's complicated."

Thankfully, Jenson left it at that.

Kai pressed down on the dispenser, shower gel squeezed into his hand. He rubbed his fingers together before lathering himself up. Fuck! His dick was bigger. It was longer and thicker. Motherfuck, what was happening to him? What else was going to change? Next thing he knew he'd sprout scales, or grow wings. He sure as fuck hoped not.

Moving quickly, Kai rinsed himself off. He couldn't wait to see Ruby. To hold her hand, to talk to her, to touch her. The more he pictured her sweet smile, her warm gaze, the more anxious he was to be with her. He couldn't fucking wait.

# NINETEEN

It hurt.

Pain tore through her and she growled.

Her belly tightened. She grit her teeth for a moment before panting hard. The breathing helped. This one lasted longer. She felt the urge to go into a crouching position. It was too soon. She needed to wait until there was an urge to push. If she moved onto her haunches too soon, she would tire herself out.

Ruby could hear the wind blowing through the trees. There was the quiet rustling of the leaves. Despite the agony, she felt at peace. Dark had almost completely descended. She'd been in labor for almost three hours. A long time. Too long. She tried not to panic. Tried to hold onto the sense of calm.

The pain subsided and she allowed her head to fall back onto the tree. The respite would not last long. This egg was coming. She only hoped it was an egg. What would she do if a baby emerged? What if her child was unwell? What if there was a problem with her egg? Maybe she should call for help.

"No," she growled out loud. Her teeth erupted and smoke curled from her nostrils. No one was allowed close. Her egg would be here soon. Everything would be fine. She would release her egg and it would be perfectly oval. It would also be soft and vulnerable. She would kill anyone who came near it. Claws broke through her nailbeds. She wished Kai could be here. He could hold her hand. Talk her through this. Her teeth ripped through her gums. It wasn't safe for any of them though. She had to do this alone. If anyone approached, she would shift, she would kill and her egg would fall to the ground. It would break.

"No," she growled. The sound no longer human. *You are alone*, she reminded herself. *Breathe. Calm.*

Kai would be angry. Hopefully he would understand. Please let him understand. She groaned as another pain overtook her.

---

At first he'd been disappointed at discovering her note. The late afternoons and evenings had become their time. Ruby had received an invite from the queen. Tanya had invited her to high tea. Whatever the fuck that was.

Kai liked that the two of them had spent some time together. It was important that she make some friends and have some other interests besides him. Tanya had a young son. It was also a mixed birth since Tanya was a human. Although nowhere near the same, the queen and Ruby still had enough in common to warrant a budding friendship.

Highfuckingtea.

He doubted high tea went on this long. The sun had set. It was getting late. Ruby wouldn't stay away this long. Would she? He'd gone from sitting on the couch, to pacing the room. Was he acting like a jealous male? It was possible. Ruby wasn't even his female yet.

*Yet.*

He was beginning to think of her as his. The fact-of-the-matter was that she wasn't his female. He had no right to be jealous or demanding. Ruby was carrying his child though. Surely that gave him some rights. Something wasn't sitting right with him. Ruby would probably laugh at him for being worried over nothing. This probably was nothing but he'd be fucked if he sat around any longer in order to find out.

Kai was at the royal wing of the castle in minutes. He leapt up the stairs like a male possessed.

The guards at either side of the door did a double take as he banged on the door.

"Stop that," one of them warned.

"You are not permitted to disturb the royal family." The other male chimed in.

"It's the prince's sleep time." The first guard added.

"I'm looking for my female." He knocked again, louder this time.

"Do that again and I will remove your hand at the wrist." The same guard harbored a deep frown. He looked like he wouldn't hesitate to follow through.

"My female is in there. I need to see her…now." Maybe yesterday, Kai would have been hesitant to take on two royal guards but today that was a whole other matter. He didn't want to hurt these males though. Just thinking of how Jenson had looked after a light tap, made him think twice about any violence. "Look." He sighed. "My female left a note to say she was visiting with the queen."

"There is no one visiting the queen at this time," the other male said. "Your female is definitely not here."

Kai felt himself frown. "What?" That didn't make sense. Maybe they had missed each other on his way here. No fucking way.

Just then, the door opened and Brant was there. He was wearing his suit pants but without a shirt. He frowned, his eyes were dark. "This had better be good."

It was evenly delivered but Kai wasn't fooled. The male was not impressed.

"Is my...Ruby here? She said she was visiting with the queen. It's getting late and I'm worried."

Brant shook his head. "I've been here all evening and I haven't seen her. Wait a minute." There was the sound of a child's laughter as he closed the door, disappearing behind it.

Brant returned seconds later. "Tanya hasn't seen your female." He cocked his head. "Is everything okay?" He pulled a phone from his pants pocket. There was more laughter from behind Brant, as well as the sound of little footfalls. "I'll call for a team to look for her. I'm glad you came to me."

"Oh fuck!" Kai slapped a hand on his forehead and pulled it over his face. "I'm such an idiot. She said she was meeting Jordan. I got that completely mixed up. I know Tanya and Ruby have spent some time together and I..." He let the sentence die. "I'm sorry for disturbing you." His heart was damn near beating out of his chest.

Brant narrowed his eyes on him. "Are you sure that—" There was a loud bang followed by an even louder wail.

"Oh no...oh..." Tanya sounded worried.

Brant turned back. He cursed.

"Oh, Sammy." Tanya said. "It'll be healed in a second." She cooed. The crying only became louder. Kai could scent the coppery tang of blood. By the way Brant's nostrils flared he could tell the male could scent it as well.

"I'm sorry I disturbed you." Kai pointed behind him. "I'll head to Jordy's place."

"Let me know if she's not there. If anything happens to her…" He shook his head. "We'll be toast…burned fucking toast."

"I fucked up. She's fine. Ruby is with Jordy." He kept it simple. Although he was dying inside, he forced himself to remain completely calm.

Brant nodded once before shutting the door in his face.

Kai turned and raced back downstairs. He didn't stop until he was at the door to Ruby's room. He got down on his hands and knees and put his nose to the floor. He didn't give two fucks how it might look to anyone who happened to come down the hallway. Ruby had been in and out of this room many times. He needed her most recent scent marker.

*Got it.*

Once he had the faint tendril, he latched onto it. It was slow going because every so often there was an overlapping scent. It didn't help that there were so many other smells around as well. Things became infinitely worse once he got outside. There was a light breeze blowing and a crispness to the air. It was difficult to hold onto her scent. He kept on having to go back because he was sure he was following an old trail. Had she gone for a walk on her own? Had something happened to her? Where the fuck was she?

Kai turned a three-sixty circle so that he could look around himself. There were acres upon acres of wilderness surrounding them.

"Where are you?" He growled. His stomach was wound so tight it felt knotted. He was tempted to run. To scream her name. It would be a futile exercise because she could be anywhere. Panic boiled just below the surface.

Kai retraced his steps and got down on his knees, his nose on the ground. Why the fuck couldn't he have been born a wolf shifter?

Wolf shifter.

*Fuck. Yes.* He pulled out his phone. Kai scrolled through his contacts list and pushed Becky's name.

"Is everything okay?" She sounded worried. "It's Ruby isn't it?"

"She's gone," Kai growled.

"What do you mean gone?" Her voice a panicked edge.

"Gone as in when I went to go and collect her earlier, she wasn't home. There was a note saying she'd gone to Tanya's for tea. Only, she never went to Tanya's.

I don't know where the fuck she is." He scrubbed a hand over his face. "I'm worried."

"I was afraid this would happen. Ruby was adamant she wanted to be alone. I think she's gone into labor and is trying to do this herself."

"I think so too." His voice was thick with emotion.

"Where do you think she would go? Shit! This is really bad." Becky sighed. "I need to call Brant and Zane. We need to assemble a team. We need to find her ASAP."

"Wait," he growled. "Ruby is out there alone somewhere. I looked through her room and she took her cell phone. She can call us if she needs us…"

"Are you telling me we should just leave her?" Becky practically yelled the question at him.

"No. That's not what I'm saying. I don't think we should send a team of males out there though. She's alone, frightened…" His voice hitched and he had to pause a few seconds in order to get himself under control. "She's very strong, Becky. If a bunch of males do end up finding her, they might not survive it. Ruby didn't want us there so she won't want a group of strangers walking in on her either. I have a plan."

He could hear Becky breathing on the other end of the line. A few long seconds went by and then she sighed. "You're probably right. What are we going to do then?"

"Please tell me that your mate is on vampire territory." He squeezed his eyes closed.

"Who Ross? Yeah, he's sitting right next to me."

"No, the other one. Your wolf." Kai squeezed the back of his neck.

"Rushe?" Becky sounded confused.

"I tried to follow her scent trail. I'm pretty sure she's somewhere outdoors. I think I may have been able to track her if she'd stayed within the castle. The wind is making it difficult for me to hold onto her scent. I need your wolf to help me find her." Kai had seen the male often. Becky was mated to Ross, one of the elite, and to Rushe, a wolf shifter. A more unorthodox couple did not exist.

Unless he mated Ruby. Maybe they would take the honors. Anger burned in him, followed by fear. He couldn't believe she was actually trying to exclude him from the birth. It wasn't completely unexpected though. Every time any of them discussed it, she would shut down and just nod. He should've known this was coming. That was, if she was even in labor.

She had to be.

Everything in him told him that she was. Fucking hell! He clenched his fist and grit his teeth, fighting his instincts to run. To go all out. To do something.

"Yeah." Becky gave a breathy reply, after a long wait. "He's here but I'm coming with. Don't even try and exclude me."

"I don't think it's a good idea…"

"Tough luck! I'm coming." Her voice was stern. It had a don't-even-think-about-arguing edge to it.

"Fine," he growled. "But you'll need to stay back…both of you will." He told them where he was and ended the call.

It only took five minutes for them to arrive. All three of them. A human, a wolf and a vampire. May as well have been an hour. Kai was pretty much crawling out of his skin by the time they got there.

"About fucking time," he growled. "No offense but what are you doing here?" He looked pointedly at Ross. He didn't have a problem with the male but four was fast becoming a crowd. "You know that my female doesn't want anybody to be with her. That's why she snuck off like this."

Ross grit his teeth. He narrowed his eyes at Kai. "I'm here to protect my female. Where Becky goes, I go." He hooked an arm around her, his hand splayed on her belly.

The other male, the wolf, grinned. "Having a bit of trouble with your nose?" He rolled his eyes. "You vampires and your terrible sense of smell." He glanced at Ross who instantly relaxed somewhat.

"Don't hit me," the wolf growled. He took a step towards Kai, right into his personal space and sniffed at him.

What the fuck?

"I just need to get a handle on your female's scent. Give me a few seconds. Thanks for showering and making this difficult for me." The wolf, Rushe, sniffed some more. The male was impressive in size and stature. This time he took a few steps to the left and then back to the right.

The male pointed. "She went that way."

Kai swallowed hard. He was pointing towards the forest. They began to walk, he had to work hard to make himself stay behind the wolf. The male stopped every so often, to sniff the air or at the ground.

They moved quickly and quietly. Ross kept his arm around Becky. He carried a black bag. Kai recognized it as her healer bag.

Once they reached the tree line, Kai had a good idea where Ruby was. If he was right, they would reach her within a minute or two. They had walked plenty over the last two weeks, always taking a different route. They had only ever entered the forest once. That day. She had to be in that clearing.

He called for a halt, by tapping the wolf on the back and putting his hand up. "Think I know where she is," he whispered. "I want you guys to stay here…please." He added when he saw Becky's face. "I have my phone and if I'm right, she's very close. If I shout loud enough, you'll be able to hear me."

Becky didn't look too happy. She shook her head. Her eyes were wide. Then she looked him in the eye. "I don't like it," she whispered. "But I'll wait here. Text me, call me or something once you find her. If I don't hear from you, I'm going to walk towards you."

Rushe growled. It was a deep, gravelly noise. It sounded just like a fierce wolf. He had nothing on the dragon shifters though. On his female.

Ruby.

The sense of urgency returned with a vengeance. He needed to get to Ruby and it needed to happen right now. "I will." He kept his gaze on Becky for another two seconds before turning and making for the clearing. Once inside the confines of the trees, he could scent her better. It was fresh. She was here.

Within a half a minute, he could hear her. Her low growl's, her heavy pants, her sobs and cries. He had to force himself to slow down, to approach her slowly.

"Ruby, I'm here." He announced, making sure she was aware of his presence, even before he got a visual of her.

"No!" A loud wail. "Stay away." Her voice was deep and gravelly. He could tell that she was fighting a shift.

"I'm here for you. I want to come closer, sweetheart. I want to see you."

"No." A sob. "Just give me five more minutes. Please." The agonized plea tore at him. She sounded so lost and afraid. He had to make himself stay where he was instead of running to her like he wanted.

"You are not doing this alone. Let me hold your hand." He moved in closer. She was there, in the clearing. She wore a T-shirt and was bare from the waist down. Ruby was on her haunches.

She was sweating. Her hair clung to her forehead. Her cheeks were flushed red. Her bottom lip was chafed. She clutched her T-shirt. Her gaze moved from him to between her legs, back to him.

"Don't come any closer." She was pushing. A deep, gravelly, growling sound emerged from her throat. It was deep and drawn out. He tried to inch closer but her eyes locked with his, holding him in place. "No." It came out sounding like a breathy plea. "Please don't. I'll hurt you." She moaned. "My egg is coming...I can feel it."

Kai removed his cell phone. He sent a quick text off to Becky, telling her that he had found Ruby and that she seemed to be doing okay. He hoped.

"Please," he begged. "You can't hurt me...you won't hurt me. I'm the father of this baby. Ruby, I would never hurt you or him...I promise you."

She was openly sobbing. Tears ran down her cheeks. She shook her head. "No. Stay there. Don't come any closer." Her eyes glowed. They were vertical slits. More dragon than human. Kai didn't give a fuck. His female needed him and he was going to hold her hand. He was going to be there for her dammit. Even if it fucking killed him. Literally.

Kai moved closer.

"No," a low growl. "It doesn't matter that you are the father. Males of our species are never present during the birth. We do this alone."

"That's fucked up, Ruby. Take deep breaths. I'm coming to you." He took a single step. "I won't let you do this alone."

He could hear the air moving in and out of her lungs. Could hear her sobs and cries. Kai could also see that there were claws on the ends of her fingers, that her teeth were sharp and dagger-like. Lord help him. Despite his extra strength, she would probably tear him to pieces if she shifted now. It didn't matter.

He moved slowly. Ruby looked down. She was breathing hard and began to push again. Kai crouched down next to her. "I'm here, sweetheart, I'm here." He touched a single finger to her arm and she visibly jumped.

A snarl was torn from her. Her teeth were more vicious up close.

"Easy." He rubbed a hand down her back. "You're safe."

Within seconds, she went from fierce to timid. Sobs wracked her. Her shoulders shook. "I'm so scared. I can feel my egg but it won't come out."

Kai swallowed hard. "Maybe we should call Becky."

She snarled a word that sounded like a no. Ruby sucked in a couple of deep breaths and shook her head. "No healers. They will cut him from me, he will die, do you understand me?"

Kai nodded. "I'm here." He grabbed her hand, her nails were like razors. "You can do this."

Her body tensed, her face contorted in pain, signaling the arrival of the next contraction.

"Get ready to push." He had fuck all idea what he was talking about. Sure he'd read a few books and had spoken in length with the healers but he wasn't qualified for this.

Ruby nodded. She clutched his hand tighter. Her nails bit into him. She groaned and panted and then pushed hard. After taking a few breaths, she pushed some more. At long last, the contraction seemed to dissipate because she slumped back, leaning against a tree.

This went on for what felt like the longest time but was in reality only ten or twelve minutes. His phone vibrated inside his pocket but he ignored it. Becky needed to be patient. He would call her if he really needed to.

"I want to take a look…" he paused. "Is that okay?"

Ruby was out of breath. She nodded, too tired to talk. This couldn't go on for much longer. She was exhausted. "I can do this," she whispered.

"I know you can." Kai crouched down so that he could see…down there. He could see Ruby gearing up for another contraction. Her belly pulled tight. She began pushing. She cried out with the sheer effort it took. That's when he saw it, a glimpse of…something. A flash, a hint. Something!

"I see it!" He yelled. "I see it, sweetheart. You're doing great." Instead of answering, she pushed some more. This time, he saw more of it. "Oh my fuck…" He laughed. "It's coming." More than just a flash…it was a solid, shiny surface. "It's our egg."

Although she was panting noisily and looked completely spent, she smiled. By the end of the contraction, she slumped against the tree and even fell to one knee. The egg was coming, but at this rate Ruby would be too tired to push it out.

"You need to lie down," he said, but she shook her head. "What if you were to sit or maybe if you were to go onto all fours or something?"

Ruby shook her head even harder. "No, has to be like this." She tried to rise back onto her haunches but she was too unstable. Her legs shook, her muscles too fatigued at this point to hold her. She finally made it up, but only just.

"I have an idea." He said as her belly began to tighten up again. "I'm going to come in behind you. I'll hold you up."

Her face was contorted in pain and yet she choked out a laugh. "Too heavy," she growled. Kai could see the pain was becoming worse, as her contraction took hold.

"No, you're not." He growled right back and slid in behind her. Kai put his hands underneath her, holding her somewhere between where her ass ended and her thighs started. *Light as a fucking feather.*

Ruby pushed. She pushed some more and then she pushed again. Sweat coated her entire body. It made her T-shirt stick to her back. The muscles in her neck were taut. She grabbed his thighs and squeezed. He could feel the blood drip as her claws tore into him. Kai held steady. Ruby screamed towards the end of the contraction.

It took a few seconds for her to catch her breath. "It's coming." There was an excited edge to her voice. "I can feel it." He could feel her shift her weight away from him, so that he wouldn't have to hold her up.

Fuck that. "I've got you, sweetheart." He squeezed her thighs and she allowed her full weight to fall back on him with a sigh.

It didn't last long. Ruby tensed. She groaned.

Kai wished he could do more. He held her tight and whispered words of encouragement. Then she began to push just as before, only this time instead of a scream, she gave a triumphant yell followed by a fierce growl. There was a whole lot of smoke and even the flicker of a single flame.

"Don't move." It came as a warning. "Don't even breathe." She probably didn't know it, but she still clutched his legs in a tight grip. It was the longest minute of his life.

He could hear her heart rate slow down, her breathing ease. Some of the tension drained from her body.

"It's here. Our egg is here," Ruby announced.

He figured, but didn't want to assume. Joy coursed through him. Keeping one arm underneath her, so he could support her, he banded the other arm around her and nuzzled into her neck. "I'm so proud of you. You did it." He kissed her brow.

She turned slightly so that she could look him in the eye. "Thank you for being here. You helped me more than you will ever know."

"Anytime, Ruby." He kissed her on the cheek. "Can we move yet, I'd like to see it…him…our egg."

"Yes, but very slowly and carefully. The egg is still soft and fragile. Don't try and touch it. I might accidentally take your arm off and I'm not joking."

Kai smiled, even though he knew she meant every word. He slipped out from behind her and moved away a little. He kept the movement slow and deliberate. He could see Ruby watching him out of the corner of his eye. His focus was on the beautiful golden egg that lay between her legs. It was bigger than any egg he had ever seen but at the same time it looked too small to hold a baby. "Oh wow! It's beautiful."

Ruby's stare moved to the egg. "A royal." She sounded shocked. "I didn't expect he would be a royal. I'd hoped but I never imagined."

Kai's pocket vibrated again for about the 20th time. "I need to take this. Is that okay? Becky is concerned about you."

Ruby nodded.

Kai answered. He had to hold the phone away from his ear for a few beats, that's how loud Becky's scream was. He finally got her to calm down enough to have a conversation and explain to her what happened. It took some convincing to get her to believe that both Ruby and the egg were perfectly fine. He also asked her to give them some more time while the egg hardened. It was a miracle. It felt surreal…his baby was growing inside the golden egg. Their little one.

Kai ended the call. "How are you feeling?"

"I'm fine. Just a bit tired but I'm good otherwise."

Kai let out a breath he had been holding. "What did you mean by royal? How can you tell that he is a royal?"

"The egg is golden which means he will also have golden markings. That is significant because it will show he is a royal." She paused. "Lesser dragons are born from silver eggs and have silver markings. It is one of the reasons why Blaze was so against mixing our blood. The lores state that it will dilute our royal bloodline. He is afraid we will lose our golden color. No royal dragon has ever mixed their blood. This is a good sign, Kai. It shows we should retain our royal heritage even if we mate with humans or other non-humans."

"I'm just fucking thrilled everything's okay. I mean, the egg, is it…he normal?" He felt himself frown.

She gave him the most radiant smile. It made something inside his chest clench. "Yes, our egg is perfect in every way."

Thank fuck. He reached out and cupped her jaw, his thumb stroked her cheek. Everything was going to be okay. It was. For the first time since this whole thing started, he really believed it

# TWENTY

*Four days later…*

Everything she owned fit into one suitcase. Kai closed the door behind them and put the suitcase down.

The first thing Ruby did was to go down the hall. She opened the first door. The bedroom was large and airy, it housed a huge four-poster bed and was beautifully decorated. The main bedroom. She swallowed hard, her bedroom. It seemed Kai would be staying where he was for the time being. It was something that needed to discuss but right now, she had to tell him about Blaze.

The last few days had been a whirlwind. The healers had insisted on examining her…more than once. Her egg had been examined as well. Ruby had allowed the small, human healer to have the honors. There was no way such a puny female could possibly damage her egg. It had still been difficult for her to sit by and watch the healer touch her egg. There had been a whole string of visitors as well as this move to a suite.

They were all excuses, she had been putting it off but she couldn't put it off any longer.

She held her egg carefully, cradling it to her chest with both her hands. It was silly because it's shell had become almost indestructible. Only severe heat would crack it. She went back down the hall, Kai was directly behind her. She opened the next door.

"Whoever heard of a fire proof nursery?" Kai chuckled. It had taken a couple of days to prepare this room.

"Fireproof or not, let's hope that the room survives the hatching. It will be a good test to see if it can hold up to the first year of the baby's life."

There was somewhat of a makeshift nest on the floor in the center of the room. The area was devoid of all furniture. Only once the egg hatched would they furnish the room with fire retardant…everything. Ruby placed the egg carefully in the center of the nest.

"There is a heat sensor underneath," Kai said. "Give me your arm."

Confused, she did as he said. Kai took a watch out of his pocket and put it on her. He showed her his arm. He had a larger version of the one she was wearing. "If the heat sensors pick up heat above a certain level an alarm will go off and that way we'll know if he's coming." He wrapped his arms around her and breathed her in.

She smiled, her stomach in knots. "That's great." Ruby paused. "There's something that we need to talk about." She turned around to face him.

"It looks serious." He frowned. "What's up?"

Ruby sighed. "It's Blaze."

Kai's eyes darkened up. "What about him?"

Ruby licked her lips. "He's going to be here in three days and if we're not mated..." She shook her head. "He's going to..."

"Going to what...?" He made a noise of frustration and looked out the window for a few beats. "I thought he had agreed to waiting until the baby came. Agreed to giving us some breathing room."

Ruby shook her head. "He gave us a month...and a month is up in three days."

"Why didn't you say something sooner?" He jammed his hands into his pockets.

She shrugged. "A month, two months...five. What does it matter? He's going to expect the same outcome no matter the time frame. Even if I manage to talk some sense into him when he gets here, he will still expect it to happen at some point. For the record, I don't think he will be willing to wait any longer. I think your life is in jeopardy." She blinked back the tears.

Kai looked mad. His jaw was locked. His muscles tensed. "I'm not going to be bullied by the likes of Blaze. He can't tell us what to do."

"Yes he can and he will kill you."

"So what are you saying, that we should just mate?" He looked like the idea was abhorrent to him.

Ruby sniffed and widened her eyes for a second, trying hard to keep her emotions in check. She couldn't blame it on the hormones anymore. This was all her.

"Ruby." His voice softened and he took a step towards her. "I don't want to mate you just because some asshole says I have to."

"The asshole you are referring to is my brother and he is only doing this out of some…ill conceived notion that it is in my best interest or something."

"He can't keep telling you what to do. You are a mature female, capable of making your own decisions. This whole thing could have been avoided if he'd stayed out of your business in the first place."

*This whole thing could've been avoided.* It stung to hear him say it. Almost like he was wishing their baby away. She knew it wasn't the case but it still hurt. She took in a deep breath and held it inside before slowly releasing it.

"I'm not mating you because your brother says I have to. You shouldn't have to mate me for that reason either. We shouldn't have to do anything. This is bullshit." Kai shook his head. His voice was raised.

"I'll talk to him." She bit down on her lower lip. "I'll buy us some time."

"I don't want time. I want him to back the fuck off." Kai narrowed his eyes. He paused, his dark gaze still on her. "We might have something here, Ruby. We get along, we're compatible." He shrugged. "I don't want to have this hanging over us. I want to be sure that whatever we do, that it's for the right reason and not because your brother held a shotgun to my head. Don't you want that security someday? To know I mated you because I really wanted to and not because I was forced? I know that I want it. I don't want to think that you mated me because you had no other choice."

She hated the idea of him mating her for that reason. Hated it. The thing was, Ruby was sure she wanted Kai. She was so sure, that hearing him speak right now killed her. Hearing him say he wasn't sure about his feelings for her, hurt her in ways she never thought possible.

If she mated Kai, she would never regret it or question it. Her decision would have nothing to do with Blaze and everything to do with how she felt about this male. It just so happened that he was the father of her child but that was coincidental. He wasn't sure and yet she had fallen hard. The pain inside rekindled with a vengeance.

Ruby sniffed. "I don't want this to happen under duress. I understand your feelings." *Even if I don't share them.* "I would hate it if you regretted it. I don't want that for us, Kai."

He grabbed her hand and squeezed. "I don't either. I want things to progress at their natural pace. I like where we are right now…I fucking love where we are. Blaze needs to back off."

"I'm scared for you." Ruby buried her face in his chest and he put his arms around her. "I don't want you to get hurt."

"I'm stronger than I was…much stronger. Your brother might be surprised." She could hear that he was smiling.

Ruby pulled back so she could stare into his eyes. "I don't want the two of you to fight." Her eyes filled with tears. "I can't stand by and watch him hurt you. I won't."

"Have some faith, sweetness." He cupped her jaw with both his hands. They were big and warm. A real male's hands, she could feel the calluses from handling a sword. "I'm loving us right now. I'm so proud of you." His jaw tightened for a second. "I wish we knew how long we have to wait before our baby hatches…" He frowned. "Not something I ever thought I would say."

She had to smile back. "If he follows a dragon shifter timeline then five or six weeks, but I have a feeling it will be a bit longer. My pregnancy was longer." She shrugged. "We will have to wait and see."

"I thought I would relax once the egg came but I still worry. I think once he hatches...maybe then." He pushed his hand into her hair. "At least I don't have to worry about you anymore." He gave her a half smile.

"I'm perfectly fine."

"Yeah, you sure are." He leaned in, his eyes on her. Then his gaze dropped to her mouth for a second before locking back with hers. What in reality felt like the longest time, was probably only a couple of seconds. Kai moved slowly. So irritatingly slowly. He stopped mere millimeters from her mouth. She could feel his breath caressing her lips.

Please.

For a second, she was sure she'd said it out loud. She wanted Kai to kiss her so badly. Most dragon shifters didn't kiss. Only because they'd had so little experience with females. When they went on their stag runs it was so that they could rut. Kissing didn't feature.

Kai had wanted to kiss her before and she'd turned him down. He hadn't tried again...until now. *Maybe*.

Please.

The hand in her hair clasped her around her neck and Kai pushed his lips against hers. His kiss was soft, yet firm. His breath was a little unsteady. Hers was all over the place, it matched her beating heart. Kai pulled away after a second or two. *No*.

More.

He kissed her again. *Yes.* Softer this time, his mouth a little more slanted. There was the briefest catch of his tongue. Oh. She'd read about kissing. Dreamed about kissing. He pulled away again and she almost screamed in frustration. A small growl escaped.

More.

More.

Kai pushed himself more firmly against her. His hands closed more firmly around her. When his lips touched hers this time there was a sense of urgency attached. His mouth opened and his tongue breached her mouth. Their tongues collided and they both groaned, the sound intermingled, becoming one. Their bodies meshed together, their breathing synced. Loud, ragged, fast-paced. Then her back was up against the wall. There was a ripping noise. Her legs were around his waist and his cock was inside of her. Ruby groaned. *Yes.*

Kai broke the kiss and stopped moving. His eyes widened. "Oh shit. Is this okay? Are you okay?" He was buried deep inside her. "I wasn't thinking. I'm such a fucking Neanderthal."

Ruby nodded. "It's fine. Perfectly fine." A breathy, moan. "But only if you keep moving."

Kai smiled. His features were tight and his eyes glazed. "I missed you so damned much."

"I'm perfectly fine. I want you."

Kai squeezed his eyes shut. "Thank fuck." He pushed back into her. Kai had her pinned against the wall. There was nowhere for her to go. Nothing she could do. He held her thighs and thrust into her. Kai didn't go easy like he had when she was pregnant. Ruby threw her head back, her mouth was slack. She made animalistic noises. "This okay?" He growled, easing off just a little.

"Yes," she ground out. "More." His hips came up flush against her. His cock was angled just right. They hadn't rutted since before she had released her egg. She was ready to come.

Kai took back her mouth in a frantic kiss that had her toes curling and her nails digging into his back. There was a tightening inside.

When he sank his fangs into her and growled, all hell broke loose inside her. She came so hard that her muscles hurt from spasming. Her back hurt from bowing. Her jaw hurt from gritting her teeth. Her clit hurt from throbbing. Ecstasy tore through her.

Kai roared. He jerked against her, his thrusts still strong and true. He buried his face into her neck. He was breathing so hard. They were both shaking.

Kai's whole body seemed to vibrate. She was in his arms and had been for some time. "Put me down." She finally whispered, when he stopped moving.

He shook his head. "You're right where I want you, sweetness." His breathing evened out and the shaking slowed down.

"I'm too heavy."

"You're not. Not anymore. Your blood has changed me...I'm stronger."

Ruby smiled. "I had noticed. There are a couple of things that have changed." She giggled.

"Oh yeah?" He kissed her, pulling away with a smile on his face.

"What, you thought I wouldn't notice?" She smiled again. "If it makes you feel any better, you measure up now." She had to laugh. Males and their competitiveness.

Kai chuckled. "Hold on to me."

She did as he said.

Kai began to walk. There was no straining or grunting. "I told you, I'm a confidant male. It didn't bug me...not at all."

Sure.

Ruby could feel the extra swag in his step.

"I felt like biting you just now." She said, hearing the uncertainty in her voice.

"You did?" There was an edge of excitement in his voice.

Ruby nodded. "It lasted for a second or two. My mouth felt dry and my teeth ached, wanting to erupt. I wanted to bite you and to…" She felt her stomach roll. "Drink from you."

"You should try it."

He carried her the whole way to the bedroom and gently lay her on the bed. "I might hurt you."

"Not a fuck. I'm stronger, Ruby." He covered her with his body. "I can hold my own against your brother."

"No…"

He kissed her softly. "Yes, I'm going to make love to you now." Another kiss. Kai circled the tip of his finger around her clit and she groaned.

Oh god. How did she make Kai understand that he didn't stand a chance against Blaze? If Blaze stayed in his human form there was a slight chance but in his dragon form…forget about it. If Blaze wanted to kill Kai, then Kai would die.

Ruby swallowed thickly. Kai slid down her body, she moaned when his tongue breached her channel. She cried out when he licked at her clit. She groaned when he sucked on her clit.

Her stomach remained tightly wound. Even after he made her come with his mouth, even after he made slow, sweet love to her. Even as he lay sleeping peacefully, his leg over her thigh and his arms locked around her.

She had to come up with some kind of plan. Kai had saved her once, it was her turn to repay the favor. He had no idea what Blaze was capable of.

# TWENTY-ONE

The moon looked like it was hung low in the sky. Big and bright. A wolf shifter's wet dream. There were very few stars visible. Like most vampires, Kai preferred the new moon. The very dark nights. Especially when they were cloudless and the stars were out in their millions. He needed to take Ruby stargazing during the next full moon. They could have a midnight picnic and make love. There were many things he planned on doing with this female. First, he needed to survive this confrontation.

He clutched Ruby's hand tighter. "It's going to be okay." He spoke with a conviction he didn't quite feel. The dragon shifters were a bunch of fuckers. At least the royal males were. Unfortunately, they were strong motherfuckers. He didn't give a fuck. Blaze had treated his own sister like a commodity. Like a stock or bond he could trade. It was bullshit. The male was still trying to run her life…their life. Kai wasn't having any of it.

When he and Ruby mated, it would be on their own terms. It was going to happen and soon. Before the birth of his son, if he had anything to say about it, but not because this asshole said so. He hadn't lied to Ruby when he had told her he didn't want either of them to feel like they had been forced. If he was honest with himself, it was also because he didn't want to give the fucker the satisfaction. His days of ordering his sister around like she was a pet dog were over. Kai prayed he survived the coming meeting.

He could hear her heart beating. He could feel how she clutched the living shit out of his hand. "Hey." He pulled her into his arms and stopped walking. "It'll be fine."

Ruby shook her head. "Let's just agree to mating one another. I don't care…I can't see you hurt."

"No. We need to stand up to him. He's not going to kill the father of his own sister's baby." He was counting on it.

"I wouldn't be so sure. He's ruthless. You're taking a huge gamble." Her eyes were red rimmed from lack of sleep.

Kai had stayed with her the last few nights. It felt so right. There was a part of him that was tempted to give in and to just agree to mate Ruby, but he needed to stand up against this bastard. He might be one of the dragon shifter kings. The most powerful dragon shifter king, but that didn't give him the right to dictate another person's life. Certainly not if that other person happened to be the female that Kai loved and wanted to spend the rest of his life with.

"I've got this." He kissed her and she clutched his hand tightly.

"I hope so." She whispered as he pulled away.

"So little faith." He nipped her lower lip.

Ruby pulled in a big breath. She nodded once. "Let's do this."

The dragons had arrived half an hour ago. Three of them this time. Blaze had insisted they meet outdoors. In the open area behind the castle. Was it because he didn't want to ruin the castle carpets and wallpaper with blood stains? It was most likely because they found the castle to be cramped.

By the noise, he could hear a large group had gathered. There amongst the crowd were Zane and Brant, as well as, about twenty royal guard.

"I thought we had decided to wait until the...hatching." Zane folded his arms.

"You decided that. I never agreed. I gave Ruby a month to mate..." The shifter's cool gaze landed on Ruby. "There you are, dear sister." The male ignored Kai, which pissed him the fuck off. "I just heard some disturbing news." He finally had the good grace to glance Kai's way. "I hear the two of you are not mated."

"It is a situation that can quickly be rectified," Brant said.

Kai squeezed Ruby's hand. "No, we are not going to mate just because you say we have to." There was a growly edge to his voice. It couldn't be helped. "Ruby and I will mate when we are good and ready to do so, and not a second sooner. That is, if both of us…and I mean both of us, decide it is what we want."

"Like hell," Blaze snarled. "I thought I made myself very clear." He continued, although his voice was once again calm, his eyes glowed ever so slightly. They were slits and no longer looked human. "You lay with my sister, you got her with child and therefore you must mate her. Against my best wishes, I gave you time to come to terms with it. My patience has now run out."

"Please, Blaze." Ruby stepped forward. "Don't do this. Leave us alone."

"Let's talk about this," Zane said.

"There is nothing to discuss." Blaze glanced at Zane before looking back at Kai.

"Please." Ruby tried again.

It angered Kai that his female had to beg her brother for the basic right of deciding her own future. It was utter bullshit.

Kai moved in next to Ruby, he put his arm around her. "There are too many people here to be able to say the things that I would like to say to you." He paused.

"Don't," Ruby pleaded. Her lip quivered.

"I have to speak up about this, Ruby." He gave her, what he hoped was a reassuring nod. Then he looked at Blaze. "Your sister is not some bargaining chip. She is not an item you can sell or swap."

Ruby sucked in a breath.

"You don't know what you're talking about." Blaze narrowed his eyes.

"I know how you wanted to use her for your own gain and it's not right. There's got to be some moral conscience inside you."

"Moral conscience?" He made a sound of disgust. "My moral conscience has got nothing to do with it. I would never do anything for my own gain. Everything I do is for the good of my people. I expected the same of Ruby, but I was mistaken." Blaze spoke calmly.

"Ruby cares more about your people than you think. If you actually listened to her, you would know that."

"I've listened plenty." There was an irritated edge to his voice.

Kai could see that the male was full of crap. A driver type personality, he only heard what he wanted to hear. He was a my-way or no-way-at-all kind of guy. The male may have stood silently while Ruby spoke but he never actually listened, never heard what it was she was saying.

"I don't have to give you any explanations." He sneered, looking down on Kai like he was a piece of filth. "I wouldn't expect you to understand, but I believe in traditions and in my lores." He slapped his chest as he spoke. "Things like respect and honor are important to us. You need to honor Ruby. You need to respect me as her brother and leader. You need to mate my sister or die. It's simple and I'm done talking."

"You speak of honor and respect." Kai kept his eyes locked with that of the male's. "It is you that needs to honor and respect your sister. Respect her enough to listen to what she has to say and to what she wants for her own future. You need to honor her wishes." Blaze moved with a speed that startled him.

One second he was fifteen feet away and the next he had Kai's throat in a vice-like grip. "Decide now, vampire, are you going to mate with my sister or am I going to finish you?"

"No!" Ruby screamed. "Don't." The word was drawn out and agonized.

It was clear that the male expected no retaliation. The arrogant idiot was greatly mistaken. Kai kneed the fucker in his groin using every ounce of strength he possessed. The male made a grunting noise and released his grip on Kai's throat.

Kai punched him full on in the face and Blaze staggered backwards. He heard the satisfying crunch of bone. "That's for Ruby." He managed to grunt. To his satisfaction blood blossomed immediately. Blaze looked shocked. His victory was short lived. The shock morphed into white hot anger. Blaze roared. It was a terrifying noise accompanied by the cracking of bone as he shifted. What a pussy. The male couldn't even fight him in a one on one basis.

He was fucked. It was an unfair fight. At least he took solace in the fact that he'd gotten two hits in. It wasn't over yet, if he had anything to say about it he was going to get in the third. Maybe even a fourth.

On a loud snarl, Blaze came at him.

Kai snarled right back, his claws erupted, as did his fangs. He was momentarily taken aback when smoke plumed from his mouth and nostrils. It made his eyes water. *What the fuck?*

Blaze must have seen it too, because he faltered in his approach.

Kai had been so focused on the other male he hadn't heard or seen Ruby shift as well. He recognized her sleek, beautiful dragon as she appeared at his side. Gone was the soft sweet female from before. Gone was the calm beast. Her eyes were filled with rage, she tore out chunks of earth with her talons as she reared up. She growled a warning at her brother.

Just as the male was bigger than his sister in human form, he too was much larger than her in dragon form. Blaze snarled back. His eyes were still focused on Kai. Blaze took a step towards him.

Ruby jumped in front of Kai, blocking Blaze as he tried to advance. She growled a second time, sounding even more menacing. Ruby pounced on her brother, going at him with fang and claw. They looked like rabid dogs at each other's throats. Kai could see it was a lot of fanfare with very little actual contact being made.

Blaze gave her a mighty shove. For just a second it looked like she was going to be hurtled backwards but with a gentle flap of her wings she halted in midair.

It gave Blaze enough time to shift. "I'm not here to fight you. Or to argue."

Thank fuck. There was nothing Kai could have done to help.

Blaze looked up at Ruby who was still in dragon form. "All I ask is that the male"—he pointed a finger at Kai— "do what's right."

Ruby returned to the ground. She pulled her wings in and shifted. It was quick and looked easy. Her skin was pale against the moonlight. Kai pulled off his shirt and tugged it over her head. She glanced his way and gave him a sad smile. Her eyes filled with tears, she blinked them away before turning back to face her brother. "For once, Blaze, I would like you to listen. It was all me. I orchestrated this whole thing. You know this. Kai is not to blame and he should definitely not be forced into doing something he does not want to do. It would be wrong."

Kai took a step forward, he sucked in a deep breath wanting to set the record straight. "Ruby, I—"

Ruby blustered on. "Kai is right, you never once asked me how I feel about this. Well, if it means anything to you, I don't love this male. Yes, he is the father of my baby. I do wish for him to be involved in the child's life. I like Kai very much and have come to see him as a friend. There is nothing more between us and it's as simple as that. Don't force me to accept a male I do not want. I choose a life of solitude. I will raise my child and that is all I need."

Blaze rolled his eyes. "You and your ideals of love. You get along, you are friends, so what is the problem?" He sighed. "Suit yourself. I don't have time for this. As much as I would like to kill this male, I can see it would greatly offend you. Although I care nothing for him," he gestured in Kai's direction. "Enough with the back and forth. I have more important things to concern myself with. If you don't want the male then I will not force him to mate you."

"You can't kill him either," Ruby growled. On any other day, he would have loved the way she was standing up to her bastard of a brother. He would have loved the growl in her voice and the way her hands had curled into fists.

Right now his heart was pretty much breaking though. She didn't love him or want him. That couldn't be true. Could it?

Blaze pinch the bridge of his nose. "I won't kill him. I'm glad to hear that the egg is...healthy."

"Would you like to see it...him...your nephew?" There was a timid edge to her voice.

Blaze shook his head.

Ruby's lip quivered but she stood tall. "He might not be a pure dragon shifter but he is still family. He is still a royal."

Blaze didn't say anything. Such an asshole.

Ruby shook her head, she turned and ran. Although Kai called after her, she didn't turn back.

"You're one helluva dickhead." He growled when she was out of earshot.

"Don't push your luck, vampire. My sister is not here to protect you this time," he spat.

"No, but we are," Zane growled. Even Brant folded his arms across his chest and looked at the dragon shifter with narrowed eyes.

"You and your team of puny warriors? Hardly." He gave a shake of the head. "I said I won't kill the male and I meant it. I would, however, like to have a word with him."

Zane narrowed his eyes.

"I won't hurt him, kill him or maim him. I gave my word to my sister and I am a male of honor."

"It's fine." Kai said, feeling defeated. "I'll be fine," he added. He didn't feel a threat from the male. Not anymore.

"What do you need to discuss with this…" It was a large male that spoke. Kai had never seen him before. The asshole clearly thought himself superior, he looked down his nose at Kai. "Vampire?"

"None of your business, Coal. The two of you can head home." Blaze pointed to the sky. "I will be five minutes behind you."

Kai could see that the male was not happy with the answer. He kept his dark, piercing eyes on Blaze for a few moments longer before shifting and taking to the sky. Inferno was right behind him.

"You have made Ruby upset." Blaze turned those eerie green eyes on him. The male did not look happy.

"Me? What the fuck are you talking about?"

Blaze got right in his face. "She has feelings for you, you idiot vampire. She fought me…her brother…me…her king…for you. She went against me in front of everyone. Here I was, thinking this whole time that you didn't want her. I can see I was wrong." He chuckled while moving away. "You feel the same way about her, don't you?"

Kai didn't respond. It was none of his goddamned business.

"Go after her." Blaze's voice was commanding. "Take her as your mate so that we can all breathe a little easier."

"What are you talking about? I thought you said we didn't have to mate and yet here you are dictating again."

Blaze snorted. "Not at all," he growled. "It couldn't be further from the truth. I'm not commanding anything. I'm simply stating the obvious."

Then it dawned on him. "The only reason you commanded that I mate your sister in the first place was because you thought you were doing her a favor. You thought that you were helping her by forcing me into doing what you thought she wanted. That's so fucked up." He ran a hand through his hair. "In a sick twisted way, I can see you did it because you care for Ruby. You really shouldn't meddle in her life like that though. Don't you get that?"

"I do care," he growled. "She is my only sister." By the way his eyes burned with emotion, Kai could see he meant it.

"But you care more for your precious kingdom."

"The kingdom must always come first." He paused. "I spoke with all three kings and carefully selected her mate. I truly believed she would've been happy with Thunder. That he would have taken good care of her."

Blaze looked thoughtful for a moment. His features tightened. The male looked...sad. "It was not to be. Please take good care of her and the child."

"When will you return?"

Blaze shrugged. "Our future is in jeopardy. Threats of war between the kingdoms looms. It looks as if the other kings have formed an alliance. They wish for us to mate with humans."

"And you?"

"I will take one of the fertile dragon females by force if I have to. It looks as if their ruler has gone against my wishes to mate with one of them. It is a difficult and tense situation. It is safer for Ruby here."

"Maybe taking human mates is the answer. It is what the wolf shifters are doing. It is what we are being forced to do. Only, it's working out better than we ever imagined. Human females are highly desirable...you should give it a try."

"Human females are overrated. They are not trustworthy and are without honor." Kai got the distinct impression that the male spoke from experience. Blaze growled. "I refuse to dilute our blood." He shook his head. "I can't believe the other kings are so quick to go against our old ways."

"Our egg is golden," Kai blurted. The male needed to know. It was something that would mean a lot to an arrogant male like Blaze.

"What?" He shouted. "It can't be."

"It's true. The egg is golden despite my genetics being strong. My vampire traits will also feature in the child. It would not be the case with a human mate. Your offspring would be royal."

He looked thoughtful for a moment. Then he shook his head. "We don't know that for sure. Besides, it would go against all of our traditions and beliefs. It would not be right. Take care of Ruby." Blaze shifted and leapt into the air, disappearing quickly into the night sky.

Kai didn't know what to make of it. The male was an arrogant asshole. There was no doubt of that but he wasn't the uncaring bastard Kai had thought he was. It was clear that Blaze loved his sister in his own way. That he loved his people. Times changed, situations changed. It was important to be flexible and change with them. Keeping his head up his ass was not going to solve the current crisis the dragon shifters were facing.

Kai breathed deeply. He had his own situation that needed facing up to.

# TWENTY-TWO

There was a knock at the door. "Ruby, sweetheart, open up." Kai knocked again.

She was crying. Ruby hated crying. *Hated it.* "Go away." It came out sounding like a sob which irritated her. She was a strong female. A capable female. Crying never solved anything. The problem was that she couldn't seem to stop doing it. Kai was probably here to tell her that even though they weren't together, that he would still be there for the child.

There was another knock at the door. "I'm not going away so you might as well open for me." Kai sounded determined and like he meant it.

Ruby went into the bathroom and blew her nose. Then she splashed some water onto her face. The reflection that stared back at her in the mirror looked awful. Her hair was a mess. Shifting would do that to a female. Her eyes were red rimmed and puffy. Her nose was red as well. Her face was blotchy. She made these hiccup noises. In short, it couldn't get too much worse. "Come back later!" She yelled.

"I'm not leaving." He knocked again.

Maybe he was there to tell her that they could carry on with their arrangement despite there being no chance of a future together. If that was the case, then he could go to hell.

"You're just as bad as my brother." She ground out as she opened the door. "I asked to be left alone. I want a couple of hours to myself, but no."

Kai smiled. It was a timid, half smile that almost broke her into little pieces. "Yes, it's too much to ask. We need to talk and it can't wait. Can I come in?"

"If I say no you'll come in anyway." She kept her eyes on his.

"Let me say something really quickly and then you can kick me out if you want to." He actually looked afraid that she would say no. "Please."

Ruby nodded. "Fine." She stood to the side. "Come in." She wouldn't hesitate to kick him out if he wasn't careful.

Kai kissed her on the top of the head as he passed by. It was a small gesture that could easily be interpreted as something other than what it was. It was the type of kiss that friends used to show affection. How brothers kissed their sisters. It was nothing to get excited about.

"What did you want to say?" She folded her arms and looked him deep in the eyes. She would stay strong even if it killed her.

"Ruby." He took ahold of her hands. "You are the mother of my egg…my unhatched child." He frowned but there was humor there. It quickly evaporated. "You're beautiful and courageous. I love our walks. I love your smile, your laugh. I love how good your body feels against mine. How good it feels to be inside you. Fuck…what I'm trying to say…" Kai looked nervous. "Is that I love everything about you."

"Stop." She pulled her hands free. "Don't say another word." It wasn't what she expected. Not at all but it didn't mean she wanted to hear it.

He frowned and ran a hand through his hair, grabbing onto the back of his neck.

"You don't have to say all of this. You can be a part of our child's life. I'll stay here, although, I would like to take him to meet my people, to see where I come from…it would be his heritage too. My brother won't bother us. I can see he isn't interested in this child." She was proud of herself. Although it hurt inside, she managed to keep from showing it. No tears, no quivering lip or shaky voice. She could fall apart once he left.

"You think I just said all of that because of our child. You're right I'm going to be a part of his life because we're going to be a family. The three of us are—"

She huffed out a breath. "Didn't you hear a thing I said? I meant every word. I don't love you. I don't want you as a mate so you can stop this." He was such a sweet male. Ruby believed he really did care about her. In his mind he was doing the right thing though. This wasn't about love. She screwed up, she should've gone with that mated male from the bar. There would've been no come back that way. She had been selfish in choosing a male like Kai. A male with honor.

"Ruby. Dammit! Listen to me please." He reached for her.

She stepped away. "No! You were right. I don't want to have that constant worry that you're doing this for the wrong reason. I don't want you to wake up one day and realize I'm not what you what. You might start to hate me."

"It would never happen because I lo—"

"Wait!" She yelled. *Don't say it.* She felt like putting her hands over her ears. If he said those three words…really said them. She would never be able to walk away. "I lied to you. I used you. You can't truly ever forgive me for that." Next week, next year, he would realize it and she would be completely invested. Kai wouldn't just break her heart, he would obliterate it. She could still walk away now. She could. Ruby would, at least, try.

"I did forgive you, sweetheart, and I would do it again. I understand why you did it. I just wish you would have told me back then."

She shook her head. "No, it's not okay at all. I lied to you about the birth. I planned on releasing the egg on my own. I packed a bag, I left the note. I lied then too."

Kai gave her the ghost of a smile. "I know. You did it to protect us. You were trying to protect me. You did it because you care, not because you're a lying brickhead."

"There's no such thing as a brickhead." She tried not to smile.

"There is now…you're one." Kai took her hands back and squeezed. "You need to listen to me…"

"I lied about Blaze…I didn't tell you about the one month timeframe. I couldn't…I was hoping that…" She pursed her lips. What the hell was she doing? She almost told him she had hoped he would mate her before the month was up. That he would agree to being with her out of his own accord. It hadn't happened.

"I lied to you as well," he growled.

*What?*

"I lied about several things. I didn't tell you why Jordan was, has been, avoiding me…" He looked down at their clasped hands before looking back into her eyes. She loved his eyes. So dark and expressive.

"She's in love with you and only realized it when I came into the picture." Ruby chewed on her lower lip.

Kai looked gob smacked. He nodded. "Yeah…I don't think she really loves me but…How did you know?"

"Oh, she does." Ruby smiled at him. Males were clueless. "I saw it written all over her face when I saw you guys together on that first day. It's why she hates my guts and why I assumed you were together in the first place."

"She doesn't hate your…" He pulled a face. "Maybe a little, but it's not personal. She hates me too. I hope she can get past it. I miss our friendship." Kai shook his head and smiled. His expression turned serious and he huffed out a breath. "I was scared initially. Jordan made me believe you were hiding things, that you were going to break my heart eventually, but now I know that I was wrong to listen to her."

"I was hiding things." She said without much conviction.

"No, you weren't. Not really. I was keeping you at arm's length so I can't blame you for not fully trusting me." He was right about that. Ruby hadn't thought about it like that.

"There's something I kept from you. Something really important." He didn't say anything for a while.

"That day you abducted me…you didn't really abduct me."

"Um…I'm pretty sure I did." She laughed softly. "If it wasn't you then who was that male I spent two days with because he sure looked like you. I picked up your SUV and carried you to the middle of nowhere…I abducted you."

Kai smiled but it was tight. He looked worried. "No. You didn't. I was at the back of the convoy. My team mates Stuart and Jenson were in front of me. I let them move ahead and, after a brief conversation, I called for radio silence."

She swallowed thickly.

Kai moved in just that little bit closer to her. "I was planning to turn my SUV around. I was about to go back to the bar."

She felt her mouth drop open. Ruby breathed out. It was a little ragged.

"Yup. I couldn't leave you in that bar. I could not bear the thought. I tried to do the right thing…which was to hightail it the fuck out of there, but I couldn't. I kept seeing your eyes…your sad smile. You had my stomach in knots right from the moment I laid eyes on you." He let go of her hand and moved to the other side of the room. His gaze was on the far wall. His hand was wrapped around the base of his neck.

Her heart was pounding in her chest.

Kai turned. His eyes narrowed on hers. "Seeing you for the first time was like being hit by a ton of freaking bricks. I could barely breathe, could barely think. Your scent..."

"It was my heat." She felt herself blush.

"No it wasn't. It killed me to leave you there and I planned on going back. My decision had nothing to do with sex. I had convinced myself that I was going to take you home and leave right away. That there was no need to tell my team because it wouldn't take long. I would not have been able to do that. My initial intentions were good, they were honorable. I need you to know that."

Ruby nodded. *It didn't change things though.* "I abducted you but—"

"You didn't abduct me. Well you did but you didn't. I was on my way back to you anyway."

He still didn't get it. Pheromones during the heat could make a male do strange things. "It was my scent, my heat—"

"Bullshit." His eyes blazed. His muscles tensed. "You weren't in heat yet...not fully. I could still think clearly. You were no longer in heat when I left to come back home. I didn't want to walk away from you then either. I didn't think I had a choice. You wouldn't even let me kiss you. I couldn't think straight when I returned to vampire territory. I was stripped from *The Program*, lost my place in the Elite Team. I was totally fucked up but not because I..."

*Oh god.* "It was my fault. I was…the human you had sex with? I'm the reason you were kicked out."

Kai nodded. "Yes and no. I was on my way back to you. Things may have played out differently, but I still would've stayed with you, Ruby. It wasn't your fault. My kings believed that I had been with a human female and I didn't correct them. I was so fucked up because I wanted to be with you. I wanted to see you. It had nothing to do with losing my place. I wracked my brain trying to think of ways to find you. If you had been a human I would've gone to you. I was happy when I found out you were here on vampire territory. I knew there would be a shit storm but I didn't care…as long as I got to see you again."

"Then you found out about my pregnancy."

His face clouded for a moment. "I'm not going to lie, I was pissed off at you, but I get it. I understand. I hope you get it too because what I'm ultimately trying to say is that I knew from the moment I saw you, Ruby."

He was breathing hard. Kai closed the distance between them. He cupped her jaw in both his hands. "I knew that you were mine. My soul mate…my everything. I tried to talk myself out of it. I've tried to talk myself out of it a dozen times since, but it's a fact. It can't be erased. I love you. I want you to be my mate." He smiled. "I can only hope you feel the same way because you have my heart already. It's yours. It has been for a long time. I won't walk away again unless you make me and even then—"

"Stop talking," She growled. Her voice thick with emotion.

"If you push me away." He put his forehead to hers. "Please don't do it because you think it would be best for me or because—"

"Who's being a brickhead now? I'm trying to tell you that I love you but you won't give me the chance. Please keep quiet for a half—"

Kai didn't give her a chance to finish. He kissed her. It wasn't a friendly kiss. Or a brotherly one. It was hot…fiery, scorching hot. There may even have been flames exchanged. It was desperate. It was beautiful. Their two souls kindled somewhere in the middle. It was everything she had ever hoped and dreamed for. Kai was everything and she was everything to him right back.

He pulled away for a second. "We *are* going to mate." His voice was commanding.

"Are you telling me what to do?" Her eyes were on his lips. *More. Right now.*

Kai shook his head. "Yes…only this once, after this, you can make all the decisions."

"Deal."

"Deal," he growled, against her lips.

She was going to make him stick to it.

He nuzzled into her neck. "We also have to agree to never be brickheads again."

Ruby had to laugh. "Okay…I can live with that."

"We make really good eggs." He growled as he kissed her softly on the nose.

"Beautiful eggs." She nipped at his lips.

"Do you want to practice making more?" He bobbed his eyebrows up and down.

"Definitely." She yelped as Kai picked her up and tossed her over his shoulder like she weighed nothing. Ruby's smile couldn't get wider if she tried. She gave his perfect ass a slap. "Get us to the bedroom and be quick about it."

"Yes, boss." Kai laughed.

# TWENTY-THREE

*Nine and a half weeks later...*

There was another knock on the door.

"Please excuse me, my lady." Kai dipped his head in the queen's direction as he rose to his feet.

Tanya nodded. "No problem. I'm quite comfortable." She closed her arms more firmly around the swaddled baby in her arms. His baby. Only five days old. Pride swelled inside him.

He glanced at his mate. Ruby gave him the sweetest smile and for a moment he could hardly breathe. He was the luckiest male on the whole damned planet. Another knock sounded, it was harder this time.

"I'm coming." He yelled...softly. It was amazing how even noisy things could be done quietly when there was a sleeping baby in the suite

"At long last." It was the human doctor, Becky. "How is my favorite patient?" Her gaze was already somewhere over his shoulder. The healer smiled. "I hope you don't mind me being here. I heard Tanya was visiting so—"

"Hey you skanky cow." The queen smiled broadly.

"I don't give a damn if you're the queen. It doesn't mean you get special privileges, you've had her long enough…" Becky held her hands out. "Hand over my little sugar plum."

Skanky cow? What the? Kai gave Ruby a shrug when she looked at him with wide eyes. Kai ignored the strange human banter. It didn't make sense. The two females seemed completely at ease with one another.

"Forget it." Tanya raised her brows. "You can have little Tinder in a while…I only just got here."

His baby daughter began to squirm.

"It is her feeding time." Ruby blushed. "You'd better give her to me before she starts crying. We've already lost a couch and a side table."

Tanya handed the little one to Ruby. His daughter. So small. So perfect. There had been zero warning. One minute their watches were silent and then the next, the alarm screamed. They got to the room four minutes later to find little Tinder…fast asleep on a pile of shell. The room was scorched. The ceiling, the floor as well as all the walls were black. The window was shattered. The egg was blown to bits. Their little daughter had arrived to this world with flourish.

Ruby took the squirming, fussing baby. She pulled down her top and the little one latched on right away, making eager suckling noises.

"I'm holding her when she's done." Becky put her hands on her hips before turning to face Ruby. "How is the nursing going? How many times does she wake up at night?" The little human looked…worried.

"Is something wrong?" He kept his gaze on her. "Should we be worried?"

Becky looked down at the floor. She was blushing. The feisty human was blushing. What the?

"Yeah and since when do you want to hold a baby this much?" Tanya asked. "What's going on with you? Are you…"

"I'm pregnant," Becky blurted. "I'm pregnant and nervous as hell. I don't relish the idea of…"

Tanya squealed and threw her arms around Becky. "How far along are you? I thought I scented pregnancy on you the other day but I assumed it was from all the pregnant females you are treating. Do you know if…well…if it's a vamp or a wolf baby?" Tanya squealed again. "This is so exciting."

Becky's eyes were wide. "I'm crapping myself. I'm already three months and not showing at all so I think it is a vamp baby. Why did he do this to me?" She looked up at the ceiling and gestured upwards. "You could've given me a smaller baby to push out first, God. I should've planned this better. I have no idea how to be a mom. No idea what to do." She swallowed thickly.

"You'll be a great mom. You're honest, and caring and tenacious." Ruby said as she adjusted Tinder into a better position.

"I pushed out a vampire kid." Tanya shrugged. "I'm not going to lie to you. It hurt like a bitch."

Becky put a hand over her face. "Not helping right now. As much as I'm freaking out." She put a hand to her belly. "I want this baby. I would be devastated if anything…"

"Don't think like that." Tanya wagged a finger.

"You need to stay positive. Remember?" Ruby raised her brows.

"Don't use my own advice on me. I know all the things that can go wrong. Oh god!" She huffed out a breath. "Maybe once he is born…I'll relax a bit then. I just need to get through the pregnancy."

"No, you won't." Kai laughed. "You will worry about your baby until the day you die. Even when, to everyone else, he isn't a baby anymore, he will still be your baby and you will still worry about him. It doesn't get better. That's something I've come to realize." He kept his gaze on the precious girl in his mate's arms.

"What have I done to myself?" Becky sat down and leaned back. "I must be nuts. I am nuts. Why did I agree to this?"

Ruby laughed. "Here..." She handed little Tinder to Becky. "Please, can you burp her for me."

Becky looked down at the tiny baby in her hands. "Hello, little one." She cooed. "You are a cutie." When she looked up, she was smiling. "I can do this. I can."

"Yeah you can. I'm so excited for you." The queen gushed. "How do Ross and Rushe feel about it? They must be so excited."

Becky tapped Tinder lightly on the back while supporting her neck. "Well, they—"

There was a knock at the door.

"I'll get it," Kai said.

"They're both thrilled." Becky said, her gaze still on his beautiful daughter. Her eyes were open. They were a bright, vivid green. Just like her uncle and her grandmother after whom she had been named.

Another knock. More timid this time.

"On my way." Kai said as he opened the door.

Unexpected.

"Um...hi!" Jordy waved her hand. "I hope I'm not interrupting." Her cheeks were bright red.

Jenson was standing next to her. "Congratulations. A female child. Wow." Jenson gave him a tap on the side of the arm. "I hear that her flame throwing capabilities are astounding."

He would have heard from Lazarus who was there yesterday when his daughter burned the couch. Ruby was in the bathroom when Tinder had woken up demanding food and the couch had been ruined as a direct result. Kai almost laughed as he recalled how big Lazarus' eyes had been. The male had quickly ushered his female out. It wasn't lost on Kai how he had put his own big frame in front of his mate.

Kai shrugged. "She is half dragon shifter so it is to be expected. Would you like to come in?"

Jenson went inside but Jordan stayed at the door, her eyes on the carpet at her feet. It took about ten seconds for her to meet his gaze. Jordy cleared her throat. "I'm sorry. I'm such an idiot. I guess, I was really afraid of losing you. I never had to share you before. I…" She paused and licked her lips. "You were right about everything…we would've regretted it. I only wish I had realized that sooner. I'm so sorry…I'm the worst friend in the world. I hope you can forgive me."

"Of course, yes." He held his arms open and Jordy grabbed ahold of him and hugged him right back. Their relationship wasn't going to be the same as it was but Jordan was his friend. The history they shared would never change no matter what.

"And?" he asked.

"And what?" Her voice was muffled. "Anything new?" Kai used his eyes to signal behind him.

Jordy's gaze moved over his shoulder and instantly softened. Her lashes dropped and her stare morphed into something that told him everything he needed to know.

Kai made a sound in his throat. "So the two of you finally got it together? It's about damn time." When he glanced at Jenson, the male had a smile plastered on his face that was, at least, a mile wide.

Kai chuckled. Ruby smiled as she caught sight of their guests. "I'm so glad you both came."

Jordy nodded and the two females exchanged a look. "Thanks for the invite," Jordan said.

Fuck! Kai felt his heart melt and his love for his female grew even more. Ruby knew what his friendship to Jordan had meant.

"You are welcome any time. I feel like I almost know you. Kai has spoken of you often," Ruby said. "It's good to see you again, Jenson" she quickly added.

"I really hope this baby takes more after its mother than its ugly mug father. Tinder..." Jenson frowned. "Is she named after the internet dat—"

"Our daughter is named after her great grandmother," Kai growled.

"Yeah, my gram would have loved this little angel." Ruby looked down lovingly at their little one, who was still nestled in Becky's arms. "I need to take her before she falls asleep. She needs a diaper change and then I have to finish her feeding." Ruby gave her other breast a squeeze. The one that Tinder hadn't fed from yet.

Kai turned to Jenson. "You need to leave." It came out as a growl. No male was going to see his female naked. Not if he had anything to say about it. It didn't matter that she didn't have any qualms about it. It didn't matter that she was a shifter and shifters ended up naked in public from time to time. The need to pull out other males' eyeballs, namely Jenson's, still rode him hard.

"Honey," Ruby used her please-be-reasonable voice on him. "I can use a blanket to cover up."

Jordy looked highly amused. Jenson looked worried…no he looked afraid. Good! The male had better be afraid. "No," he snarled. Then he sucked in a deep breath. He needed to try and control these base instincts. "Fine…but if you so much as look in my female's direction I swear to fucking god…"

"I'm too busy looking at my own female." Jenson shook his head. He pulled Jordy onto his lap.

Becky pulled a face. "Are they all this bad?" She glanced at Tanya. "What am I saying? Of course they're all this bad."

The queen rolled her eyes. "Worse. You should've seen Brant and Zane…oh my gosh."

"So this is what I have to look forward to?"

"It's quite sweet, actually." Ruby said, as she took Tinder from Becky. "I don't mind."

He fucking loved this female.

"I hope you guys don't mind but once I put Tinder down, I think I might take a nap as well. I'm bushed."

"Are you up half the night?" Becky held a hand to her chest. "Is that why you're so tired?"

"She slept really badly those first few nights. We could hardly think clearly but last night wasn't too bad. She only woke up once, but…" Ruby's eyes widened. "I'm still really tired. Must be accumulated sleep deprivation or something."

"Oh yeah." Kai fake yawned.

"I hope he's a good sleeper," Becky rubbed her belly.

"I'm sure he will be." Ruby smiled. "Um…Kai also looks really tired so if you guys don't mind too much…"

Becky laughed. "Oh my god…the little one is here, she's kept you really busy the last few days, but let me guess, things have settled and you're both ready to get back into the saddle?" She gestured to Ruby. "You can't wait to have at each other. Afternoon nap?…Yeah right."

Jenson choked out a laugh. "Come on, Jords. Let's get out of here."

Ruby blushed so hard he thought he might see smoke at any moment. Her stunning amethyst eyes met his and her blush deepened. "Out," he growled. "You heard my female." He couldn't wait to be alone with her.

Their little girl would be fast asleep very soon. The things he was about to do to this female. His female. His mate. It didn't matter that they were oil and water. Ying and yang. All that mattered was that they belonged together. They were soul mates.

# From the Author

Thank-you for reading *A MATE FOR KAI*!

If you would like to be kept updated on new releases please sign up to my Latest Release Newsletter to ensure that you don't miss out http://mad.ly/signups/96708/join. I promise not to spam you or divulge your email address to a third party. I offer sneak peeks of future instalments before release day exclusive to my mailing list.

If you enjoyed this book please review it so that others can find it. Even if just a line or two, every review is greatly appreciated.

I also love to hear from my readers so please feel free to drop me a line mailto:charlene.hartnady@gmail.com

Find me on Facebook - https://www.facebook.com/authorhartnady

Charlene lives on an acre of land in the country with her gorgeous husband, three sons, and an array of pets including a ball python. In her spare time you can usually find her typing frantically on the computer completely lost in worlds of her own making. She believes that it is the small things that truly matter like that feeling you get when you start a new book or a particularly beautiful sunset.

# Also By

**The Chosen Series**
Chosen by the Vampire Kings
Stolen by the Alpha Wolf
Unlikely Mates
Awakened by the Vampire Prince
Mated to the Vampire Kings
Wolf Whisperer

**The Program Series**
A Mate for York
A Mate for Gideon
A Mate for Lazarus
A Mate for Griffin
A Mate for Lance
A Mate for Kai

**Demon Chaser Series**
Omega
Alpha
Hybrid
Skin
Books 1-3 now available in a boxed set!

Printed by Amazon Italia Logistica S.r.l.
Torrazza Piemonte (TO), Italy